COMING HOME TO STARR'S FALL

KATE HEWITT

Boldwood

First published in Great Britain in 2024 by Boldwood Books Ltd.

Copyright © Kate Hewitt, 2024

Cover Design by Head Design

Cover Imagery: Shutterstock and iStock

The moral right of Kate Hewitt to be identified as the author of this work has been asserted in accordance with the Copyright, Designs and Patents Act 1988.

Every effort has been made to obtain the necessary permissions with reference to copyright material, both illustrative and quoted. We apologise for any omissions in this respect and will be pleased to make the appropriate acknowledgements in any future edition.

A CIP catalogue record for this book is available from the British Library.

Paperback ISBN 978-1-83603-242-7

Large Print ISBN 978-1-83603-241-0

Hardback ISBN 978-1-83603-240-3

Ebook ISBN 978-1-83603-243-4

Kindle ISBN 978-1-83603-244-1

Audio CD ISBN 978-1-83603-235-9

MP3 CD ISBN 978-1-83603-236-6

Digital audio download ISBN 978-1-83603-237-3

Boldwood Books Ltd
23 Bowerdean Street
London SW6 3TN
www.boldwoodbooks.com

Dedicated to my first Connecticut friend, Dawn. Thank you for being such a good friend to me during my New England years!

1

Laurie Ellis had learned to be an optimist. It was a matter of sheer will rather than some kind of quirk of her personality; there had, unfortunately, been many times in her life when optimism had seemed, well, *optimistic*, if not downright foolish. Stupid, even.

This was one of those times.

Above, the sky was a bright, deep blue of early September, the air summer-warm yet with that hint of crispness that fall always brought. The leaves of the glorious maples and majestic white oaks lining Highway 44 were touched with crimson and the sunlight was like syrup, pouring over the pastoral New England scene and bathing it in liquid gold.

Really, it was a perfect day. At least, it had *started out* as a perfect day, when Laurie had loaded up the rental van with all her worldly possessions—which admittedly did not amount to very much—and drove, haltingly because she wasn't a hugely confident driver, from Trenton, New Jersey, all the way to this bucolic corner of northwestern Connecticut. For the whole three hours of the trip she'd been humming along to the radio, her dearest friend and lovable mongrel Max perched on the bench seat next to her, his ears pricked in anticipation as well as a little anxiety, because Max had never been the most confident of creatures. She'd made sure to give him a reassuring pat every so often, and when they'd turned off Interstate 95, leaving the gasoline fumes and rumbling eighteen-wheelers thankfully behind, she'd rolled down the windows a little bit so he could sniff the sweet country air, his plumed tail wagging hopefully.

Really, it had all been *wonderful*. Her heart had been both full and light, and she'd felt nothing but hope and determined optimism, like a scouring of her soul. Finally, she was leaving it all behind—the depressing top half of a duplex, a measly three rooms, where she'd lived alone for the last four years. The dispiriting, dead-end job in marketing she'd been so thrilled to get when she'd been twenty-one and newly graduated with an associate degree in marketing had started to feel more than a little defeating and dull three and a half years on. The lonely little life she'd chosen to be content with, even as she couldn't help but feel there *had* to be more to it than this—another chapter, or even a whole exciting book, just waiting for her. She simply hadn't turned the page yet.

Today she finally *had*, and it had felt amazing, until just outside of Wassaic she'd started to hear a clunking noise coming from somewhere in the nether regions of the van.

"Do you hear that, Max?" she'd asked, glancing at her little dog. She'd got Max from the SPCA four years ago, when he'd been little more than a puppy, skeletally thin and cowering from everyone, his wiry brown fur patchy and sparse. Life hadn't treated him kindly, and Laurie understood all too well how a few well-placed kicks could knock you flat on your back and leave you struggling to stand up again, ever. It had taken a lot of patience and love and rawhide chews for Max to begin to trust, and then to love, her. Now they were an inseparable pair. She couldn't have started this adventure without him.

"No?" she'd prompted as she gave the little dog, who was eyeing her with his usual bright-eyed seriousness, his little ears perked, a nod. "Me neither. I don't hear that clunking sound at *all*."

That, Laurie supposed, was when her optimism had descended, as it unfortunately sometimes did, into plain stupidity. The clunking had continued and become louder, and then it had been accompanied by a burning smell that couldn't signify anything good. Laurie had determinedly ignored it all, knowing she had no choice but to keep driving, because there was nowhere to stop, and her cellphone had no signal. And, she'd told herself, she was so very close to her destination of the picturesque little town of Starr's Fall, Connecticut. Surely the rental van could rattle and wheeze for just fifteen minutes more, inching down the Main Street and then conveniently conking out right in front of her new home.

That would have been perfectly acceptable, but it was not to be. Seven miles outside of Starr's Fall, according to her GPS that was thankfully still working despite a less than stellar phone signal, the van gave a last gasp and then an alarming death rattle, before it rolled to a defeated stop. Laurie had had, at least, the foresight to jerk the wheel so the van came to its inglorious end on the shoulder of the road, away from traffic. Still, this was not good. This was not good at all.

She sat in the driver's seat and stared up at the bright blue sky, trying to recover her optimism. Also trying to figure out what to do, because she still had no phone signal and she couldn't see anything, anywhere, besides trees and sky and warm, golden sunlight.

Max, sensing that things were not as they should be, clambered into her lap and put his paws up on the window. Laurie stroked his wiry fur and marshaled her thoughts.

Seven miles was too far to walk, but at least it was a beautiful day, and she was in a beautiful place. She could lock up the van and walk down the road until her phone got a signal or she came to a house and could ask to make a phone call. Then she could find a garage to call, get the van towed, take a taxi into Starr's Fall...

Briefly, Laurie closed her eyes. It wasn't impossible, she told herself, but it still felt hard, several laborious steps she really didn't want to have to take at this particular moment in time, when she wanted things to be, if not easy, then *easier*. Easier than they had been for most of her life, not that she was about to throw herself a pity party.

But today was meant to be her new start, the first chapter of the book of her life she was longing to write. Having adventures. Making friends. Maybe, if she was brave enough, even learning about her own history. It was all meant to happen *here*, in Starr's Fall, except she wasn't even there yet, and this did not feel like the kind of prologue she wanted to have to the book of her life. Far from it.

"Never mind, Max," Laurie said aloud as she sank her fingers into the dog's fur to give him a good scratch, which he loved, squirming with pleasure as she got behind his ears. *Never mind* had become something of a motto for Laurie, whenever things went wrong, which had happened with somewhat depressing regularity, or at least often enough for it to become a motto. *Never mind, I'll make new friends. Never mind, I'll just work harder. Never mind, I'll find somewhere else to live. Never mind, I can work extra hours. Never mind, at least I've got a job and a roof over my head, if not much else.*

"Never mind," she said again, and the words sounded hollow in the silence of the sunny afternoon, with no one but Max to hear them. Taking a deep breath, Laurie reached for Max's leash, clipped it on and then scooped him up and stepped outside onto the shoulder of the road.

She noticed the stillness first. Back in Trenton, there were all the noises of the city, all the time—rumbling buses, police sirens, people shouting in the street, disgruntled neighbors, clanking plumbing. She'd become used to it, to the point she'd mostly been able to tune it all out.

But here there was nothing but quiet, this stillness that seemed to vibrate in the air and penetrate her bones, her very soul. It was both peaceful and the tiniest bit frightening; she felt almost as if she were the last person in the whole world, parachuted into an empty and unfamiliar landscape. The road stretched endless in each direction, the pavement baking under the warm sun, and on either side of it there was nothing but towering trees. High above her, the wind whispered through their branches, their soft soughing the only thing she could hear.

Laurie set Max down on the ground, and he immediately wiggled his way between her ankles, his head tucked firmly between them, which was his favorite place to be, especially when he was feeling nervous.

"I guess we'll start walking," Laurie said aloud, and, after sliding her phone into the back pocket of her jeans, she locked up the van and started down the side of the road, Max trotting so close to her heels she had to be careful not to trip over him.

The gravel crunched under her worn sneakers and the sun, that had been so lovely and warm while driving, now started to feel uncomfortably hot. Sweat prickled between her shoulder blades and trickled down the nape of her neck. Laurie pulled off her sweatshirt and tied it around her waist, then retied her hair—a completely unremarkable light brown, as far as she was concerned, and with a weird wave right in the middle she'd never found a way to straighten—into a tighter ponytail. Then she kept walking, past the trees lining the road, casting welcome shade, and then along a stretch of gentle meadow where the sun beat down even harder, and she couldn't see so much as a barn in the distance.

For five whole minutes, not a single car passed her. She glanced behind her and saw the rental van had disappeared into the haze. Up above was nothing but more road, trees, and sky. She was thirsty now as well as hot, and wished she'd thought to bring her water bottle with her.

"This is starting to feel like the Sahara," she remarked wryly. She was used to talking out loud to Max, as he was pretty much her only companion, but it felt a little strange in the utter emptiness of her current surroundings. Max, seeming to sense her uncertainty, pushed his head between her ankles once more. With a good-natured sigh, Laurie reached down and fondled his ears. "Sorry about this, Max."

She'd just begun to straighten when she heard a vehicle in the distance. Laurie put one hand to her eyes to shade them as she squinted into the sunlight. A rusty red pickup truck with an open bed was coming down the road at an alarming pace, fast enough that Laurie decided to scoop up Max before she took a large step back, near to the ditch running steeply along the side of the road. The truck didn't even slow as it passed her, sending up a fine spray of gravel, and Laurie had a brief glimpse of a solid-looking woman with a head of salt-and-pepper curls at the wheel before she zipped past.

"I should have flagged her down," Laurie realized out loud, although the woman had been driving so fast, she doubted she would have even noticed. The truck had gone about fifty yards or so beyond her, when, with a sudden squeal of brakes and another spray of gravel, it stopped and then swung around quickly, driving back toward Laurie.

Laurie hugged Max to her chest as the truck slowed to stop right in front of her. The woman rolled down the window and peered out; her face was brown and weathered, her eyes a deeper brown, her hair wild and curly. She looked to be around forty.

"That your van pulled up on the side about a quarter mile back?" she asked in a brisk, no-nonsense way that was both matter of fact and, Laurie at least hoped, friendly.

"Yes, it is," Laurie replied in the manner of a confession. The woman was squinting at her, her head thrust out the window, her hair springing from her head in a silvery halo of curls. "I broke down."

"You know there's nothing much between here and Starr's Fall? Seven miles of nothing. That's pretty far to walk, I'd say."

"Yes, I suppose it is," Laurie admitted humbly. "I was hoping to come across a house or something. I'm new to the area. I'm—I'm moving to Starr's Fall, actually."

"Moving to Starr's Fall!" This was an exclamation of deep surprise, even disbelief. Clearly not many people moved to Starr's Fall, tucked up in this northwestern corner of nowhere, too far from Boston or New York to attract the urbanites, or even the suburbanites. Hartford, the capital city of Connecticut, was an hour and a half away, down country roads, too far for commuting.

The woman heaved a large sigh that seemed to come from the depths of her solidly built being. "You'd best get in, I guess," she said, and she leaned over to open the passenger door of the pickup truck, which, with a rusty-sounding squeak, swung out wide.

Still clutching Max, Laurie walked around to the other side of the truck and clambered up inside. She had a second's pause of wondering whether to trust this woman, and a brief vision of being kidnapped and taken to some backwoods cabin where she'd be blindfolded and tied up danced through her mind before she dismissed it. She'd be foolish not to trust her, because she was right, seven miles was a long way to walk. In any case, her optimism, having flagged fairly significantly when the van had broken down, was now flickering back to life.

Things, Laurie decided, were looking up.

"So, moving to Starr's Fall," the woman mused, giving Laurie—and Max—a considering glance as Laurie closed the door and the woman made a jolting three-point turn in the middle of the road before speeding back toward Starr's Fall. The truck smelled strongly of old apples, musty and sweet, and looking behind her, Laurie realized the bed was filled to the brim with burlap sacks of them.

"I'm Annie Lyman, by the way," the woman said. "I run Lyman Farms, down Route 44. We grow apples and pumpkins this time of year. Do you know it?"

Laurie shook her head. "I'm sorry, I don't know much around here. Not yet, anyway."

"Where are you from?"

"New Jersey." In response, Annie wrinkled her nose, which made Laurie smile ruefully. That was most people's reaction when she said she was from New Jersey, nice a place as parts of it were. "But I had family here, a long time ago," she ventured, feeling brave enough to admit that, as well as a little bit reckless. She'd trusted very few people with this information—in fact, only one. Nadine, her as-good-as foster mother from days of old, who had died nine months ago. Laurie had grieved the idea of her more than the reality; she and Nadine had more or less lost touch years ago, after she had aged out of the system. But it turned out that Nadine hadn't forgotten her, which was partly why she was in Starr's Fall at all. "The Lysanders," she told Annie. "Do you know them?" If she'd been attempting to sound casual, Laurie knew she'd failed; she'd heard a tremor in her voice, as well as an eagerness. What if Annie knew them? Knew them *well*, even?

"The Lysanders..." Annie frowned in thought, her gaze on the road as they bumped along, trees blurring past. "Can't say I do, and I thought I knew everyone around here."

A flicker of disappointment whispered through Laurie, but she pushed it away with determination. It was early days, after all, and *someone* in Starr's Fall had to know the Lysander family, surely, if she worked up the courage to ask again. She wasn't sure she would. She'd come to Starr's Fall for a new start, not to dig deep into the past. *Mostly*.

"Well, like I said," she replied with a philosophical shrug, "it was a long time ago."

Annie's frown deepened, carving lines into her weathered face, tanned a chestnut brown from a life clearly lived outdoors. "Still," she said thoughtfully, "I grew up here, and so did my father, and his father, and his father before him. The Lymans came here in 1790, one of the town's oldest families, although we're nothing on the actual Starrs, who founded the place. Henrietta Starr still lives here, not that you'd know it. No one sees her around anymore."

Laurie, who had basically no family history to work with, could only marvel at such long lineage. "Wow," was the only response that seemed appropriate.

"I'll ask my mother," Annie stated definitively. "Lysander... She knows everyone, or she used to, anyway." She jerked the wheel of the truck to turn right down a narrower road; with one hand cradling Max, Laurie couldn't keep from flinging the other out to the door handle to steady herself.

The trees that had been lining Route 44 now became denser, a thick forest of evergreen along with the maples and oaks, so it felt as if they were going right into the woods, with hills rising steeply above. The last and only time Laurie had been to Starr's Fall had been in May, on a wet and windy day when the rain had come down in gusting sheets. She'd barely been able to take anything in and had sprinted from car to storefront with her coat pulled over her head. She'd been hoping to have more of an explore of the place she'd firmly decided to call home, but the weather hadn't made it possible, and in any case, she was here now. She was looking forward to seeing the town—and her very own home—on a day like today, sunlit and mellow.

"So what's brought you to Starr's Fall?" Annie asked bluntly. "Because, I'll be honest with you, there's not much going on here, much as I love the place."

"Well, there will soon be a little more," Laurie replied with a determined smile. "I'm opening a pet store and bakery on the Main Street."

"A pet..." Annie swiveled her head to gaze at Laurie directly, her jaw dropping as the truck started to drift toward the center of the road. "Wait, did you buy the little place right across from Reilly's Books?"

Laurie couldn't remember a Reilly's Books, but it *had* been raining a lot. "I... think so? It's number forty-six, halfway down the street, white brick with a bow window and an apartment above. I'm only renting, though, although I might have an option to buy later."

"That's the one. I thought I saw a sign saying it had been rented out." Annie jerked the wheel back to even out the truck, and Laurie found herself clinging to the door handle once more. A ride with Annie Lyman was clearly an exciting, if not downright dangerous, experience.

Annie frowned. "A pet... what did you say?"

"A pet store and bakery," Laurie replied firmly.

When she'd applied for the business loan, the perplexed bank manager had not been immediately convinced. "Pet... *bakery*? I've never even heard of such a thing."

"I saw them in New York," Laurie had assured him. "They're getting very popular. You know how people are with their pets."

She'd shown him spreadsheets of statistics and sales projections that she'd labored over for hours, but whether such fanciful notions would be popular here, in the backwoods of Connecticut, remained to be seen, although Laurie had done at least some homework. She knew that this part of Connecticut had a lot of dog owners and also that the nearest pet store was over twenty miles away. She'd researched how people wanted an in-person experience when it came to shopping for their pets, rather than online anonymity. It had been enough to convince the bank manager but this still might, Laurie had forced herself to acknowledge, be another instance of optimism straying into serious stupidity. However, she was still determined to take a risk... and follow her dream. For once.

"All right, so humor me," Annie declared, propping one elbow on the driver's open window. "A pet bakery. What is that, exactly? Cookies for cats? Donuts for dogs?"

She sounded so genuinely perplexed that Laurie couldn't keep from laughing. "Well, I guess, in a way," she replied, "but not *actual* donuts and cookies. More like pet treats... baked dog biscuits, and flavored chews, and things like that. All healthy, of course, and good for animals." She'd already tried out several recipes on Max —sweet potato pumpkin chews, peanut butter and banana hearts. He'd gobbled them all up. "The store part will have all the pet accessories," she told Annie. "Bowls, leashes, dog and cat toys, that kind of thing. No actual pets, though," she hurried to state. "I don't think it's very humane, to keep pets in cages in a store, and to be honest, I'm not sure I could manage that much responsibility."

"We've never had a pet store in Starr's Fall," Annie mused, "that

I can remember, although we certainly have plenty of dogs! And cats too, to be fair." She grimaced as she continued. "Not that we've got much anymore in town, to be honest. Amazon and all the online shopping have forced so many people to close. At least half the stores on Main Street are empty, which is such a shame."

"It is," Laurie agreed. She remembered seeing several empty or shuttered storefronts from her trip back in May, beneath the sheets of rain. "But I'm hoping to change it, at least a little." Despite Starr's Fall's lack of retail, Laurie believed it *could* be a place where people came to shop, eat, enjoy life. At least, it could become that, with a little effort. Laurie had chosen to come to Starr's Fall for a lot of reasons, but one big one was that she'd felt sorry for it, its Main Street looking so forgotten. She understood how that felt.

"And who is this guy?" Annie asked with a nod toward Max, who was sitting on Laurie's lap, his head pressed close to her body as he surveyed Annie warily.

"Max." Laurie rested her hand on top of his head. "He's got a little bit of everything in him."

"Looks like it, too," Annie replied with a laugh. "I've got a black lab, George, at home. He's the seventh one we've had, and they've all been named George. My grandfather named the first one after a neighbor he didn't like."

Laurie smiled. "That sounds like a story."

"It is," Annie told her. "You'll have to come out to the farm for dinner one night and I'll tell you the rest of it. Do you know anyone here?"

The question, so bluntly asked, made Laurie wilt inside a little bit, even though she appreciated the unexpected invitation. "No," she admitted as cheerfully as she could manage, deciding she would be as blunt as Annie. "Not a soul."

"Then you'll definitely have to come," Annie replied. "I'll introduce you to a few people, too. How about Thursday? Assuming your van is fixed by then."

"Actually," Laurie confessed, "it's only a rental. I don't have a car. I thought I might buy one eventually, but I wanted to see how I managed without one at first."

"No car!" Annie marveled. "You're a real city person, aren't you? Well, I can always pick you up. Seven?"

"That would be great, thanks so much." Laurie could hardly believe she had already made plans with a potential friend, and she hadn't even arrived in Starr's Fall yet. Stuff like that never happened to her, no matter how optimistic she tried to be. Back in Trenton, she'd made a few friends through work, but the extent of the relationships was coffee in the kitchenette, the very occasional drink out. She'd made a few other friends as well, through various community links, but no one she could depend on. No one who would miss her.

Maybe, Laurie decided, Starr's Fall had a little bit of magic, of optimism, in it, after all. Either that or Annie Lyman really was a serial killer.

It certainly felt magical as Annie drove down the Main Street, past the white wooden sign that announced:

Welcome to Starr's Fall, incorporated 1731, population 2,200.

Old-fashioned-looking stores in a variety of gracious brick and more homely wooden clapboard lined either side of the street, behind wide sidewalks of deep red brick and interspersed with wrought-iron benches and square wooden planters bursting with the bright oranges and reds of fall chrysanthemums. At the far end of the street, a verdant town green rolled out in front of the historic Congregational church, its tall white spire pointing heavenward and piercing the bright blue sky.

Despite all this, it was impossible not to notice the boarded-up storefronts, just as Annie had mentioned. Starr's Fall was a quaint little town, but it definitely could use some TLC, or really, just some more people doing business there.

Annie pulled up to number forty-six and turned off the truck. "Here we are. You've got the key, I hope?"

"Yes." Laurie patted her pocket. She'd kept the key on her since she'd been sent it last week, from the realtor in Hartford. It had felt like a talisman of sorts, an anchor to the life she wanted to have, was going to make.

"You'll need to tow the truck, I guess?" Annie wondered aloud. "Mike at the garage on the other side of town can do it. Do you want me to give him a call?"

"Oh... if you wouldn't mind..." Laurie wasn't used to having people offer to do things for her. It made her feel both humbled and guilty. "Thank you," she said as Annie whipped out a cellphone with a screen so cracked Laurie wondered how it was still functioning. As Annie made the call, she opened the door and slipped out of the truck, still clutching Max to her.

She was here. She was finally here, and it seemed almost too good to be true. Laurie stood in front of her store, marveling at the building before her. The white paint was flaking off the door and the glass of the bow window was dirty and smeared, but it was hers, the whole thing—two rooms downstairs for the store, plus a tiny office and a half bathroom, and upstairs a living room overlooking the street, with the kitchen in the back, and two bedrooms and a bathroom on the floor above. She could hardly wait to explore it all, to begin the adventure she felt she'd been waiting for her whole life.

Finally, *finally*, she was about to turn the page.

From the truck, Annie called out to her. "Mike's going to fix it for you. I told him where the van is, and he'll tow it straight here. Two hundred bucks for the job. Is that okay?"

Laurie swallowed hard. Hopefully the rental company would reimburse her, but for now she needed her stuff. "Sure, thanks," she called. "And thanks for the lift—"

"Not a problem." Annie waved her thanks aside. "I've got to get going with these apples. Joe is waiting for me at the cider press. See you Thursday!" And then, with a rev of the engine and a belch of smoke from the exhaust pipe, she was off, rattling down Main Street at a good clip, leaving Laurie and Max by themselves.

2

Laurie put Max down, keeping hold of his leash, as she fished in her pocket for the key, which was pleasingly old-fashioned, made of brass with a curlicued end, like something out of *Harry Potter*, and perfect for the little store. The building, the realtor told her, was over a hundred years old, and had first been a milliner's shop and later a stationery store, both of which Laurie thought were charming.

Now she inserted the key into the lock, breathing out a small sigh of relief as it turned smoothly, and the door opened with a puff of dusty air. She set Max down and stepped inside.

Admittedly, it wasn't much to look at—a small front room and an even smaller back room, with an office tacked on and a set of narrow stairs crammed into a hallway on the side. At the moment, the only furniture was a dented metal filing cabinet the last tenant had left behind who knew how many years ago. A few yellowed leaflets lay on the floor, having been pushed through the tarnished brass letterbox. Laurie stooped to pick one up—it was an advertisement for the town's annual Fall Harvest Festival, from four years ago. The realtor had told her this place had been empty for a while.

"Starr's Fall is just a little too far off the beaten path," she'd said with a wry grimace and a discreet glance at her wristwatch. "If it was on a major road, like Litchfield..." Her tone conveyed all the wondrous financial possibilities for a storefront in such a promising location.

Litchfield, Laurie knew, was half an hour to the south and seemed like a bustling community, with a full array of boutiques, upmarket delis, and independent shops. On a good day, she'd read online, you might glimpse Meryl Streep or Michael J. Fox, both local residents, browsing the stalls of the town's popular farmers' market. Starr's Fall, as far as Laurie knew, didn't have one... or much of anything else.

But that was okay, Laurie told herself, because now it had a pet store and bakery! This was the beginning of something wonderful —for her *and* for Starr's Fall. Closing the door behind her, Laurie unclipped Max's leash to let him have a good sniff around the dirty floor and deep into dusty corners. Sunlight streamed through the dirt-smeared front window, highlighting all the grime. With his nose covered in dust, he let out a terrific sneeze, which made her laugh.

"We'll have to get this place cleaned up," she told him, and then, with her heart feeling the way it had this morning, both full and light, she went to explore.

In the first room there was a high, old-fashioned counter of weathered mahogany—original, the realtor had said—running along the back wall. Laurie could already picture the wonderfully antique cash register she would get to go on top. She'd already looked on eBay and they weren't too expensive. A door in the back right corner opened into the back room that would become her stockroom, and then an even smaller space that would have to make do for her office. It was all a little crowded, but Laurie thought it was still manageable. A back door from the stockroom led to a little courtyard and tiny rectangle of grass—or right now, weeds—in the back, just enough space for Max to do his business when he needed to.

After checking Max was all right—still happily sniffing around —Laurie headed upstairs. The narrow staircase running alongside the store went up to a door that led to what would be her home.

Her *home*. Laurie still found the whole concept miraculous, even magical. She'd never actually *had* a home, except for the depressing apartment she'd been living in for the last three and a half years, and that didn't count. It had been semi-furnished, with brown shag carpeting and a tiny bathroom in avocado green. Laurie hadn't been allowed to paint or put anything on the walls; even the dishes hadn't been hers.

Before that, she'd been living in a halfway house for foster kids who had aged out of the system, and before that, a home for kids *in* the system. That had probably been the closest thing to a home she'd ever had, but it had still fallen far short of what she'd always dreamed of. When you had to carry your belongings in a black garbage bag, and your only remotely private space was your bed in a room you shared with four others, with kids cycling in and out as they were placed with foster or adoptive parents... well, it didn't feel very *homey*. But without her years there, and getting to know the home's supervisor, Nadine, Laurie would have never been able to come here. All things, Laurie told herself, worked together for good. It was another one of her life mottoes.

She unlocked the apartment door and stepped into the little hallway. Coat hooks lined the wall, and two steps was all it took to come into the tiny living room, with its gabled window overlooking Main Street, and the cutest little fireplace, the brick painted white, complete with mantel and colorful tile surround. In the back was the kitchen, just as quaint. Admittedly, the units were ancient, the battered stove and refrigerator clearly on their last gasp, but it was *hers.* This place, Laurie reflected, could be a falling-down wreck—and it was already pretty close—and she'd still love it, simply because it was hers. At least for the twelve-month lease she'd signed, which was more than enough.

She headed up the next flight of narrow stairs to the two bedrooms—the bigger one in front, also with a fireplace, and the smaller one at the back, ostensibly for guests, although Laurie didn't actually know anyone who might visit. It *might* seem a little bit depressing to get to the grand old age of nearly twenty-five and to realize you hadn't made many friends, at least not the kind that kept in touch and texted you to make sure you were okay, but Laurie's optimism was out in full force now. She was going to make those kinds of friends, here in Starr's Fall. She thought of Annie and wondered if maybe she already had.

She peeked into the bathroom with its ancient enamel units and floor of white diamond-shaped tiles, and then headed back out to the main bedroom to survey the town. The street was quiet save for a few pedestrians—a woman pushing one of those fancy strollers that could transform into a highchair or a crib; a man decked out in bright blue Lycra going for a run. A gentle breeze was sending a few leaves drifting lazily down like scarlet and yellow confetti, and as Laurie propped an elbow on the windowsill, she closed her eyes to enjoy the feel of warm sunshine on her face.

Then she heard Max bark. Not his usual bark, friendly and inquisitive, but a high-pitched, alarmed yap that was, Laurie knew, his cry for help. Her eyes flew open. She turned from the window, about to race downstairs. What if Max had cornered a rat or gotten his paw stuck in a mousetrap leftover from the previous occupants? How could she have left him? Laurie flung open the door to the stairs only to stop in her tracks as Max barked again.

The sound, she realized, was coming from *outside*.

"What on earth..." she muttered as she ran down the stairs and out the front door of the store, which had been, she saw with deepening alarm, ajar. She'd thought she'd closed it, but either the wind or Max's curious nose had nudged it open again. Or maybe he'd wiggled his way through the cat flap she now saw at its bottom. In any case, he'd, most uncharacteristically, made a run for it.

As Laurie stepped outside, she saw that the street looked just as sleepily peaceful, except for Max directly across from her new home. He was in front of the store opposite hers, positively cowering against the doorway. In front of him was the most enormous Persian cat, white and fluffy and majestic.

"Oh, *Max*," Laurie cried in equal parts exasperation and relief. "It's just a cat." Admittedly, an enormous cat, twice as big as poor Max. No wonder he was scared. Plus, Laurie couldn't help but notice, the cat had that regal bearing of so many Persians, staring disdainfully down its snub nose at Max, who looked tiny and terrified.

Before she could rescue him, however, the door to the storefront he was cringing in front of was thrown open, making Max cower all the more.

Laurie, half-crouched to reach for Max, had the looming sense of a man without actually being able to see his face. It didn't help that the sun was slanting directly down on him, casting the doorway in shadow, backlit by glorious light so he seemed, fancifully, like half-god, half-monster.

Then he took a step toward her, and she realized he was just a quite ordinary man.

"What," he snapped, "is your dog doing, harassing my cat?"

"Harassing your cat?" Laurie repeated in disbelief, before, thanks to her infernal optimism, she started to laugh. *Surely* he couldn't be serious? Except it seemed he was.

He stood in front of the store, his hands planted on lean hips, dark eyes narrowed to near slits. He looked, Laurie thought, a little bit like a grownup Harry Potter, with wire-rimmed glasses and a mop of dark, rumpled hair. He was lanky yet muscular, dressed in a *very* old t-shirt and faded jeans... and he was scowling. A lot.

"Sorry, is this meant to be funny?" he asked in an arctic tone.

Laurie took her time scooping a trembling Max up into her arms as she tried to organize her thoughts as well as compose her expression. "Not funny," she said at last, as she straightened and risked looking him full in the face. He was still scowling, but even so, she couldn't help but notice how handsome he was. Dark, glinting eyes, high cheekbones, and a sensuous, mobile mouth. Just like the heroes of the romance novels she sometimes read... except for the scowl, and over a *cat*. The heroes of those novels might *brood*, but definitely not over a Persian cat.

"It's just..." Laurie tried to explain, but unfortunately, she couldn't think how to end that particular sentence. This was, she was fast realizing, not funny. At all, apparently, judging by this man's perma-scowl. Not the best welcome to Starr's Fall, then, Annie aside.

A sudden, uncharacteristic irritation spiked through her. What was *wrong* with this guy, anyway? The Persian cat had clearly been in control of the situation, as most cats inevitably were, and the creature was, as of this moment, licking its paws with studied indifference. Meanwhile, Max was trembling in her arms. Now, Laurie realized, she was the one who was scowling—along with Mr. So-Not-a-Hero.

"If anything," she said, unsure whether to pitch her tone accusatory or laughingly wry and managing neither, "your cat was the one who was harassing my dog. He must be twice his size."

The man's eyebrows rose in incredulity, as if he couldn't believe her sheer affrontery in suggesting such a thing. But it was true, wasn't it? The cat looked to have suffered no harm, while wimpy little Max was still cowering.

"Why wasn't your dog on a leash?" he demanded. "You know it's actually the law, in public spaces?"

"He was inside my store," Laurie replied, trying not to sound irritable and defensive but feeling both. "He got out without me realizing. I'm *sorry,*" she flung at him, knowing she didn't sound sorry at all. "It won't happen again."

She turned to head back across the street, now trembling nearly as much as Max. Why did some people have to be so *rude*? Of course, she was used to it. She'd been dealing with rude people —and much worse—all her life. You didn't go through fourteen years in the foster system without encountering a lot of pretty darn unpleasant people, along, thankfully, with some really kindhearted ones, but somehow here, in what was meant to be her beautiful beginning in Starr's Fall, it felt worse. People here were meant to be *friendly*. Annie Lyman had been, Laurie reminded herself, but the man across the street was clearly in a category all his own.

He didn't speak as she headed back to her door, although she felt his gaze on her, like two red-hot holes burning into her back. She just knew if she turned around, she'd see him glowering at her, but she resisted the temptation. Then she heard the door of his own place open as she set Max down and reached for her key. She was expecting Max to do his usual thrust of his head between her ankles, but to her surprise—and horror—her little dog didn't. Instead, he shot back across the street and, Laurie saw as she whirled around, desperate to call him back, right through the closing door, into the man's store. Reilly's Antiquarian Books, Laurie read on the old-fashioned sign swinging from an iron hook above. And Max was in there, no doubt creating all kinds of havoc... and proving the man right, darn him.

"*Max!*" Laurie shouted and then, suppressing the urge to swear, ran back across the street. She tapped timidly on the door before she pushed it open and entered the store, blinking in the gloom.

Books were everywhere—shelved untidily, stacked in tottering piles, overflowing from tables, armchairs, and windowsills. And the *dust*—it coated every surface, a fine gray patina. The place smelled of leather, old paper, and dust. Lots of dust. More dust, perhaps, than Laurie's own empty store had. And running through all the dust and books and papers was... Max. Chasing the cat, who no longer looked majestic but frankly terrified, bounding on its velvet paws while Max barked furiously from behind it. *Oh, help.*

"Max," Laurie called desperately. "*Max!*"

Her little dog, normally so docile, paid absolutely no attention as he continued to race around, barking wildly. Laurie risked a glance at the man, who was standing by a desk cluttered with papers and books, his arms folded, his dark eyebrows drawn together. Although he was still scowling, he looked, she decided, almost smug. Point proven, she supposed, and in spades. And there didn't seem to be much she could do about it.

"I'm sorry about this," she told him stiltedly. "Max has never behaved this way before..."

"No?" He arched one dark eyebrow, clearly skeptical.

Laurie felt herself flush. "No, he really hasn't," she replied a little more sharply. "Honestly. Although he hasn't actually come into contact with many cats before..." Especially big, fluffy Persian ones. Such a designer purebred would be a rare thing in her part of Trenton. The cat, surprisingly graceful despite its size, leapt onto a pile of books stacked on the floor, out of Max's reach, and sat there for a moment on top, staring down at her little dog.

Laurie breathed a very quiet sigh of relief. At least the cat was out of harm's way, if harm meant Max. Max had skidded to a stop at the bottom of the pile of books, and as Laurie reached down to scoop him up to safety, he raised himself on his hind legs, putting his paws on the pile of books, and started barking again.

"*Max*," Laurie exclaimed in exasperation, just as the cat, with a yowl, leapt from the pile of books onto the top of a shelf. Laurie, now lunging to grab a wriggling Max, watched it all happen as if in slow motion. Max, pushing with his paws on the bottom of the pile. The cat leaping from the top. The pile itself starting to list to one side like the Leaning Tower of Pisa, book style. Laurie realized what was going to happen a split second before it did. With Max tucked under one arm, she leapt forward, one hand flung out to keep the stack of books from falling, but it was too late. With a great cloud of dust, the pile of books collapsed, sending, with a tremendous thud, books and papers flying everywhere.

Her optimistic day had just very much taken a turn for the worse.

3

Joshua Reilly stared at the mess of books, some of which were, semi-arguably, somewhat rare and valuable. The ridiculous cat was perched high above, and the crazy little dog was still barking furiously. He felt his temples pulse with a headache. Today was not a good day. But he'd had a lot of not-good days in the last three years since he'd returned to Starr's Fall, so maybe he shouldn't be surprised. He raked a hand through his unruly hair and spared a glance at the stranger who had stormed into his bookstore.

Her blue-green eyes were wide with horror, and she was clutching the dog—Max—to her like a life preserver. Wisps of light brown had escaped her ponytail to frame her flushed face. Her lips parted soundlessly as she stared at the mess.

"I'm so sorry..." she whispered faintly. "I'll help clean up..." She bent to start doing that, and Joshua flung one hand out to stop her.

"I'd rather you didn't," he told her. "I think enough bedlam has been caused already. Frankly, I'd rather you just went back to wherever you came from."

She stared at him for a second, her face draining of color, her eyes turning glassy—with *tears*? All right, maybe that had come out a *little* unfriendlier than he'd meant it to, but for heaven's sake. His store was a mess, the wretched cat traumatized, and he didn't even know this woman. Besides, everyone in Starr's Fall was used to him being grumpy. It was kind of his thing.

Then, in a split second, as they both simply stood there, staring at each other, her expression changed. It was akin, Joshua thought, to Optimus Prime going from truck to transformer, a total reconfiguration of her expression, her attitude, her whole self. Her shoulders stiffened, her chin lifted, and that alarming glassiness disappeared from her eyes as she defiantly tilted the corners of her mouth up into a breezy smile.

"As it happens," she informed in a light tone that perfectly matched her smile, "that's not very far, because, as you might have noticed, I've just moved in across the street."

Oh. He'd seen her come from across the street, but he hadn't realized she was actually *moving* there. Nobody moved to Starr's Fall. Joshua tried to compose his features into the corresponding expected response of neighborly friendliness, but he was pretty sure he had less success than this woman in his own transformation. He was, he could feel, still scowling, the corners of his mouth turned down as if being pulled by insistent, invisible fingers. "Across the street?" he finally repeated. "Are you opening a store?" Heaven knew Starr's Fall could use some decent new businesses. Thanks to economic downturns and the pandemic, not to mention the town's fairly inconvenient location, currently half the storefronts were empty. Seven miles off the beaten track was a lot when it came to retail therapy, apparently, and it seemed Starr's Fall's population of just over two thousand couldn't support that bustling an industry anymore.

"Yes, a pet store and bakery." Her chin inched a little higher, in seeming defiance.

"Well, that's the most unlikely combination I've ever heard of,"

Joshua replied. He'd meant to sound wry, but it came out grumpy, as usual. It seemed he really did only have one setting.

Her smile faltered for a second before she managed a laugh. "I guess it does sound like it, but the bakery is for pets. For dogs, really. Baked treats and rawhide chews, that sort of thing."

"A... pet *bakery*?" He couldn't keep the disbelief—and even the disdain—from his voice. As far as he was concerned, of all the stores Starr's Fall needed, a pet bakery was not in the top ten. Or top hundred, for that matter.

"Yes." Now her tone was turning steely. "A pet bakery. Because even dogs deserve treats." The way she said this made it sound like it was some sort of life motto, and while certainly unobjectionable, it hardly seemed like the basis of a foundational creed. Still, Joshua supposed he didn't have to understand it, or anything about her. Just because she'd moved in across the street didn't mean he had to see her again. Everyone in Starr's Fall knew he was a recluse, even if some people, like his aunt, refused to accept that fact.

"Well, good luck with that," Joshua said, and it definitely sounded like a dismissal, which it was, so...

"Thanks." The woman paused, clutching the dog to her. "I'm Laurie Ellis, by the way."

He had not, Joshua thought, been angling for an introduction. "Joshua Reilly," he told her, and discovered that yes, it was possible to sound unfriendly while giving your name.

Another beat of silence. From somewhere above him the cat let out a plaintive meow. It was his aunt's cat, named, of all things, Leamhachán, which was Irish for marshmallow. Fortunately, his aunt called her Lea. Joshua just called her Cat. He had, with the utmost reluctance, agreed to look after her for three weeks while his Aunt Maureen was on an Alaskan cruise.

Joshua shifted where he stood, wondering when this woman—Laurie—was going to go. He considered saying something friendlier than he had, but he had no idea what it would be. He hadn't done small talk in years, and he liked it that way.

"Well…" she began, and he nodded in relief. That sounded like a goodbye. Message had been given and received. She nodded toward the books scattered across the floor. "I really am sorry about those."

"I'll clean them up." Hopefully nothing was too damaged.

She still wasn't leaving. Joshua, with effort, held in a sigh. Slowly, Laurie looked around the crowded store. Books, Joshua knew, were everywhere, and in no particular order, but it didn't matter because he knew where everything was. Mostly.

As if reading his thoughts, Laurie asked slowly, "How do people find books in this place?"

Her tone was one of genuine curiosity, but Joshua still gritted his teeth at the implied—or at least felt—criticism. "They don't need to," he informed her shortly, "because they don't come in here. I run a mail order business." Mostly, anyway, since his father had died two and a half years ago. Patrick Reilly had kept a very different store to Joshua and had been a genial and beloved pillar of the town's community. There was no way Joshua could ever follow in his father's footsteps, and so he'd made sure he never attempted to.

Laurie's gaze tracked back to his as she nodded slowly, in seeming understanding. Joshua didn't like the perceptiveness, and maybe even sympathy, that he thought he saw in her gaze. He hoped she wasn't feeling sorry for him because there was absolutely no need, and, in any case, he hadn't given her any reason to.

"Nice to meet you," she finally said, and amazingly, she sounded genuine when, Joshua acknowledged only semi-guiltily, he could not have been very nice to meet at all. He never was.

Scooping her little dog closer to her chest, Laurie turned and left the store, stepping carefully over the fallen books, their pages littered across the floor like yellowed looseleaf. As the door closed firmly behind her, Joshua let out a loud sigh of relief.

Alone again, just as he liked it.

Unwillingly, his gaze moved to the dusty window, through which he could see Laurie Ellis marching across the street, back to her store. It had been empty for a few years now, although it had once sold accessories and jewelry, all of it a bit too niche for the likes of Starr's Fall... just like a pet bakery was. *What on earth?* Joshua gave her six months at the most before she was forced to throw in the towel. Admittedly, there were plenty of dogs in Starr's Fall; lots of people had pets. But a dog bakery? He doubted there was the interest for a such a hoity-toity-sounding place in a town like this.

He felt a flicker of sympathy for her, and he almost wished he'd been a bit nicer. But, no, he decided as he bent to pick up the first of the books that had fallen to the floor—a semi-rare edition of a tome on military history. Better not to give Laurie Ellis—or anyone else—any ideas.

* * *

Laurie kept her calm until she'd closed the door behind her, making sure it was firmly shut, and barricaded the cat flap, and then let Max down to sniff in the dust. Then a sound escaped her— half groan, half shout, half laugh. Technically, that was three halves, but so what? She felt it all—frustration, amusement, *hurt*.

Why did that man—Joshua Reilly—have to have been so darned rude? Yes, she could laugh about it because she'd learned to laugh about a lot of things. To *choose* to laugh, because it was so much better than succumbing to tears. The cup could still be half-full even if it barely had a drop in it, Laurie had told herself more than once. At least it held *something*.

And yet... a sigh escaped her, this one full of only weariness. She'd had so many hopes for her new life in Starr's Fall. Hopes that this would be where she finally felt at home, because she *was* home, in a way. A very distant way, but still. She'd spun dreams of fitting in and making friends, and right from the get-go it had started to go wrong... as life so often did.

No, she was *not* going to feel gloomy, Laurie told herself, as stern as a teacher giving a scolding. She drew a quick, steadying breath, and reminded herself of all the good things that had happened today. Her van had broken down, but someone had rescued her, and Annie Lyman seemed like she could be a friend. She'd even invited Laurie to dinner! She'd met one unfriendly neighbor, but there surely were other people on the street. She loved her little store, and the apartment above too, and could hardly wait to make it all a real home.

So many good things, Laurie told herself again as she picked up the old leaflets from the floor and stacked them on top of the counter. Max, having finished another exploratory sniff, sat in the middle of the store and looked at her plaintively, wagging his tail.

"Yes, I know," she told him. "But we have to wait for the van."

It must have been serendipity, because at that moment a truck rumbled up to the curb outside, her van towed behind it. Laurie found herself grinning. *See*, she thought, *the glass really is half-full.* And in any case, it had just gotten a little bit fuller.

The man who slid out of the truck was tall—about six foot four, his dark hair flattened under a grimy baseball cap, a long gray beard flowing down several inches past his chin. He wore a plaid shirt, very dirty jeans, and red suspenders. Laurie decided she liked him at once.

"Thank you so much," she told him as she came out of the store, leaving Max inside. "You're an absolute lifesaver."

"I'm guessing your van needs a new crankshaft," he stated

without preamble. "Won't run without one. Did you notice the oil looked to be running low?"

"Um, no," Laurie admitted apologetically. She knew next to nothing about cars. "It's a rental, though."

"Hmm." The man—Mike, Annie had said—scratched his cheek. "I'd ask for your money back, if I were you."

"Well, as long as they take the van away, I'm fine with it," Laurie told him cheerfully. She could hardly wait to put her things in her new place, not that she had all that much, but still. It would look a fair sight homier than it did now. "At least I got everything here in one piece."

He glanced at her skeptically, still scratching his cheek. "You can move all that stuff by yourself?"

"I moved it all into the van," Laurie replied with a smile, "so I guess I can move it out again." It hadn't been easy, but she was used to managing on her own.

"Hmm." Mike looked disapproving. "Well, let me unhitch it for you, and then we'll see."

A few minutes later, the van was separated from the tow truck and Laurie had, at Mike's request, opened the back doors. Silently, they both surveyed the van's contents. A mattress, a table and two chairs, one armchair, two lamps and a couple of cardboard boxes and milk crates of clothes and books were the sum total of her possessions.

For a few seconds, Laurie was uncomfortably aware of just how little it all amounted to—but then Mike somehow did not seem like a man too much burdened by material goods. And in any case, she was intending to add to her collection, over time.

"I'll take the armchair and the mattress up for you," he stated, clearly not a matter for debate. "You'll find them tricky on the stairs by yourself."

Laurie decided to accept the offer in the spirit it was given.

"Thank you," she told him, meaning it quite utterly. "That would be wonderful."

* * *

Twenty minutes later, Mike had taken not just the mattress and armchair upstairs, but the table, chairs, and lamps as well, while Laurie had followed with the boxes and crates. The van was empty, and after receiving another heartfelt thank you as well as two hundred dollars, Mike had given her a mock salute, welcomed her to Starr's Fall, and gone on his way.

Laurie was alone in her new home.

She stood in the doorway of the little living room, the late-afternoon sunlight streaming through the window, picking up the golden dust motes that danced through the air. The mattress was upstairs in the bedroom, the table and chairs in the kitchen, and the armchair and lamp by the window, right where Laurie wanted them. Right then, with Max in her arms and her heart feeling full again, Laurie couldn't have asked for anything more.

Except maybe some food.

She hadn't, she realized, eaten since breakfast, which had been a fried egg breakfast sandwich from a fast-food chain that had sat queasily in her stomach for some time. Unfortunately, she had no food in the place, and the refrigerator and oven, ancient as they were, weren't even plugged in. A take-out was on the menu, Laurie decided, and then a big food shop tomorrow.

She decided to take Max for a stroll down Main Street, in the hopes of finding somewhere to eat as she explored. It was after four o'clock when she stepped outside, the air still possessing the warmth of earlier in the day, yet with the barest hint of autumnal chill that made Laurie think of frost-tipped grass and sparkling mornings, with snow heaped on branches like piled icing or falling softly down in great downy flakes. She was looking forward to experiencing all the seasons in Starr's Fall.

The sunlight looked even more golden, pouring over the mellow brick of the buildings, and the quiet street scene seemed like something out of a movie, with the quaint storefronts—at least the ones that were occupied—the wrought-iron benches and the planters bursting with orange and scarlet chrysanthemums. Laurie was the only person out, and she walked slowly, savoring the sights along with the sunshine, while Max trotted beside her.

Interspersed between empty stores, she passed a pharmacy, a women's clothier, a bank, a coffee shop, and an old-fashioned diner named The Starr Light, with deep vinyl booths and a miniature jukebox on every table. Laurie perused the extensive menu in the front window, noting it accepted take-out orders, and decided to return after she'd finished her exploration.

Starr's Fall's Main Street ran gently upwards toward the church, which was on one end of the town green, with a slightly dilapidated playground and bandstand on the other. Laurie walked all the way around, down another street of buildings, including the library, a community hall, and a veterinary practice. Maybe she'd put brochures for her store at the vet's, she mused, although that felt a long way off at the moment. She still had to refurbish the downstairs, obtain all her stock, actually *open...*

It felt daunting, but also exciting. She'd taken an online course on running your own business and she'd secured a small business loan with a bank. She'd ordered most of her inventory and designed a brochure, which she hoped to scatter liberally around the town. She'd looked into advertising and started a website and had arranged with a designer for a sign out front, which would hopefully be ready next week. She'd dipped her toe into the murky waters of bureaucracy in terms of getting the bakery aspect signed off, with all the accompanying regulations. She'd already accomplished a lot, and she was proud of what she'd done as well as excited for the future. She could do this, she told herself, not for the first time. She might be jumping in feet first, it was true, but not over her head. She was optimistic, not insane. Hopefully.

The final two sides of the green were lined with houses interspersed with a few more stores, including a homely looking bakery called The Rolling Pin and an ice cream parlor named The Latest Scoop whose walls were decorated with murals of historic newspapers, both of which Laurie promised herself she'd check out later. She walked slowly along, admiring the flowerbeds and window boxes, the American flags fluttering in the breeze, the general sense of cozy homeliness. In front of one house, a woman was juggling two bags of groceries, her keys, and a towheaded toddler who was charging ahead and nearly knocked right into Laurie.

"Oh... sorry," the woman said breathlessly. She looked young and harried, her brown hair falling out of a ponytail, but also friendly, and Laurie smiled at her warmly.

"Not to worry," she replied. The woman gave her a grateful nod in return before heading into her home, a little brick rowhouse with a red front door festooned with an autumnal wreath of oak leaves and clusters of red berries. Laurie watched her go, feeling a sense of wistfulness mingled with a fluttering of hope.

Was it silly, to wonder who was going to be her friend in this town? To look at the various people now hurrying to their homes and hope that one day she might get to know them? They'd stop and chat, laugh together, plan an evening out or a cozy night in...

A sigh escaped her at the thought. It all felt like a montage out of a rom com or one of those feel-good family movies that had just the right amount of schmaltz... and it could be her *life*, if she let it. If she made it happen.

Of course, she knew it was going to take time. But on Thursday she'd get to know Annie Lyman... and who knew what else might happen? Whom she might meet? She thought of grumpy Joshua Reilly, and then put him firmly out of her mind. There were plenty of other people in Starr's Fall, and they had to be friendlier than he was. With a spring in her step, Laurie turned back toward Main Street.

Bells jangled as she opened the door to The Starr Light Diner, which looked to be about half-full—families enjoying burgers and shakes, an older couple having coffee and huge slices of lemon meringue pie, a couple of farmer types hunched over the lunch counter, cradling mugs of coffee or beer.

"May I help you?" A teenaged girl with a high blonde ponytail and pale blue eyes gave Laurie a quick, professional smile before her expression softened as she caught sight of Max.

"Oh, how adorable! What's his name?" she asked as she crouched down to fondle Max's ears and scratch under his chin.

"Max," Laurie told her with a smile. "Named after the dog in *The Grinch Who Stole Christmas*, because I think he looks just like him."

The girl lifted her head to beam at Laurie. "Oh my gosh, he *does*! I love that story. My mom used to read it to me all the time." She straightened, her smile dropping from her face as, with another jangle of bells, someone came in behind Laurie.

"Speaking of the Grinch," the girl muttered before finding her professional smile once more.

Perplexed, Laurie glanced behind her... and locked gazes with Joshua Reilly.

4

Joshua must have caught sight of her at exactly the same time, because his face flashed with surprise before he adopted what Laurie now suspected was his usual expression—a scowl.

"We meet again," he remarked, sounding completely unenthused by the prospect.

"So we do," Laurie replied, smiling, determined to stay cheerful. The hostess had called him the Grinch; clearly, he had something of a reputation in this town. It was too bad, because despite the scowl, he really was an extraordinarily handsome man—that dark, wavy hair, eyes like melted chocolate, and although he was tall and lanky, his worn t-shirt clearly hinted at some serious muscle definition in the ab area. Not, of course, that she was thinking romantically about Joshua Reilly, considering what a jerk he seemed to enjoy being. Still, Laurie was determined to win him over with relentless friendliness. Either that, she thought wryly, or enjoy annoying him with it. Kill with kindness was surely better than the alternative... to slink away chastened. Or, she thought, smothering a laugh, just kill him for the sake of it.

"I was just going to order something to take out," she told him cheerfully. "Anything you recommend?"

He glanced at her without expression. "No," he stated flatly, and Laurie had to choke back another laugh. It took actual effort to be this unfriendly, she thought, as well as determination. Perversely, it was too blatant for her to be hurt by it.

"Mr. Reilly always gets the same thing," the teenaged hostess helpfully supplied. "So I guess he could recommend that."

A remark which caused Joshua Reilly to scowl all the more.

"Careful," Laurie told him, not even teasing, "or your face might freeze like that. Didn't your mother ever warn you about that?"

His mouth did not so much as twitch in a smile. "That would hardly be the worst thing to happen to me," he replied, before looking pointedly at the hostess. "Eliza? My order?"

"I'll go see if it's ready." The hostess turned away, leaving Laurie and Joshua standing alone by the "Please Wait to be Seated" sign.

"So what *do* you order every time?" Laurie asked after a few awkward seconds. She was genuinely curious. Was he a burger kind of guy, or a closet vegan?

Joshua sighed, as if her question—and his need to answer it— wearied him. "On this occasion, a grilled ham and cheese sandwich, a side salad, and a cup of tomato soup," he replied. "But it's not *every* time."

So he went for well-balanced comfort food. A good choice, Laurie thought. "Do you eat here often?" she asked.

"Often enough." His tone most decidedly did not invite further questions and Laurie, despite her earlier determination to kill with kindness, decided to have mercy on them both and stop with her well-meaning interrogation. If Joshua Reilly didn't want to be neighborly, and it was blindingly obvious that he didn't, well, there were other people in this town... even if she hadn't met them yet.

Eliza came back with a white paper bag that she handed over to Joshua, who took it with a muttered thanks before he headed back outside.

"So is he always that friendly?" Laurie asked Eliza, who rolled her eyes.

"He's basically, like, the town grump. My mom says his dad was really nice, but I don't remember him." She shrugged, dismissing Joshua Reilly in an instant. "Do you know what you'd like to order?"

"I'll have a Caesar salad with chicken and a cup of chicken soup, to go, please," Laurie replied, her mind whirling with this new information. "Thanks."

A few minutes later, her order was ready, and she headed back out into the deepening dusk. The air was decidedly chilly now, the sky violet, the first stars starting to glimmer on the horizon that was fringed darkly by dense evergreens. As Laurie passed lighted windows, glimpsing various people inside their cozy houses— watching TV or setting dinner on the table—she felt a sudden sweep of loneliness, like a cold, empty wind, start to whistle through her, but determinedly, she pushed it back. There was no reason to feel lonely, she told herself. She had everything ahead of her... including all the friends she was going to make, starting with Annie Lyman and *not* Joshua Reilly.

Back in her little apartment, she fished Max's kibble out of one of the boxes and crates piled in the middle of the living room and fed him his dinner before she ate hers tucked up in the armchair by the window. The street below was now dark and empty, but a light had switched on directly across from her—the apartment above Reilly's Antiquarian Books. Gauzy curtains obscured the view, but she saw the silhouette of a man pass in front of the window before heading toward the back.

It had to be Joshua, and she pictured him eating his dinner

alone, just as she was eating hers alone, and for some reason it made her feel both sad and hopeful at the same time, although she really couldn't have said why.

* * *

The next three days passed in a flurry of activity as Laurie cleaned the store and apartment from top to bottom—scrubbing, sweeping, and then polishing and painting. The old, wide floorboards of burnished oak could use a proper refinish, but she did the next best thing and got down on her hands and knees to polish them with a soft rag and a tin of floor wax, heartened by their new, gleaming shine.

She painted the walls of the downstairs a soft cream and spent hours meticulously doing the woodwork and trim in high gloss. Upstairs, she did the same, painting the bedroom a sage green and the living room slate blue. She'd bought all the paint at the hardware on the edge of town, carrying it back with aching arms and a happy heart. The rental company had collected the van the day after she'd arrived, towing it away without apology.

Her life was slowly but surely starting to take shape.

Each afternoon, Laurie went for a stroll through town, hoping to get to know a few people, smiling in a welcoming way that, after a while, was starting to make her feel stupid as well as her cheeks ache, when all she got in response was either a startled look or a wary nod. New Englanders, she reminded herself, could be notoriously reserved. All that small-town friendliness was found in the south of the US, or the Midwest, maybe; not this corner of Connecticut. Still, she hoped.

She thought of what one of her social workers, Callie, had used to say when Laurie had had to start a new school, which had happened several times over the course of her turbulent youth.

Keep showing up, keep smiling, and you will get there. It might take longer than you want it to, but it does happen, sweetheart, I promise.

Well, to be fair, it hadn't *always* happened. Laurie hadn't been able to make all that many friends in high school, no matter how much she'd showed up—day after day—smiling and more than willing to be just about anyone's friend. Foster kids with second-hand clothes and hunted expressions weren't the easiest to befriend, she supposed, and nor did they possess much social currency for the average fourteen or fifteen-year-old. In the end, it hadn't mattered too much. She'd managed to make a couple of friends in her later years of high school and had worked hard enough to get a place at a community college. Once Nadine had taken an interest in her when she'd been fifteen, life at the home had become a lot more bearable, too.

For a second, Laurie let herself feel a wave of grief for the foster mom who had been the closest thing to an actual parent she had ever had. Admittedly, Nadine hadn't even been her foster mom, not technically. She'd just been the supervisor of the care home Laurie had spent three years in, from fourteen to seventeen, but she'd been so kind. Her death had knocked Laurie sideways, even though she hadn't seen Nadine since she'd left the home seven years earlier. That was the thing with foster care; you moved on because you had to, and so did the people who had been so instrumental in your life. Since Laurie had aged out, Nadine had had dozens of kids come through the house. It was amazing she'd remembered her at all.

But why was she thinking about all that now? Her life in Starr's Fall was going to be different. She'd make sure of it.

And it started to feel like it would be when, on Wednesday afternoon, three days after she'd arrived in Starr's Fall, she finally had a visitor.

"Well, doesn't this place look like a breath of fresh air!" Annie

Lyman stood in the doorway of the store, her hands planted on her ample hips as she surveyed the space with obvious approval. "Some fresh paint and floor wax obviously does wonders. I barely recognize the place. When are you having the grand opening?"

"I don't know how grand it will be," Laurie was quick to say, "but I hope by the end of the month? I've got some stock coming in any day now and I need to figure out some advertising…" Instinctively her gaze strayed to the three-page checklist she'd printed out from her online course on how to start a small business. She'd only read to the end of the first page and she knew that if she let it, everything could start to feel overwhelming, but she was doing her best not to stray down that dark path of doubt.

"It's not every day or even every year a store opens in Starr's Fall," Annie replied with a wag of her head. "Of course it'll be grand! We'll get everyone there. Who have you met so far?"

"Umm…" Laurie let out a shaky laugh, because the truth was, three days on, she was starting to feel a *little* lonely. Heaven knew she was used to her own company, but she so wanted this place to be different. She wanted to be different in it. "You?" she told Annie with wry smile. "And Joshua Reilly from the bookstore across the street, although…"

Annie made a face. "Not that Grinch."

Laurie let out another laugh, this one genuine. "That's the second time someone has called him that."

"It's what he's known for," Annie told her. "He cultivates it, I think. Enjoys it, even."

Did anyone really *enjoy* being that grumpy, Laurie wondered. "To be fair," she told Annie, "Max *was* chasing his cat, so he had a right to be a bit Grinch-like."

"His cat? Joshua Reilly doesn't have a cat." Annie frowned, then gave a quick nod of understanding. "That would be Maureen's

Persian. She's a huge beast, isn't she? He's taking care of her for a few weeks, while Maureen's in Alaska."

"Maureen...?"

"Joshua's aunt. His only relative left in Starr's Fall, which is kind of sad. His family goes way back here. Not," Annie was quick to add, "as far back as mine, of course. The Reillys came in the 1850s, I think, after the potato famine in Ireland. Took the O off their name but left it at that. They've been running that bookstore for at least fifty years—first Joshua's granddad, then his dad, and now him."

"What's happened to the rest of his family? I heard something about his father...?" Laurie wasn't usually so nosy, because she certainly understood about respecting the privacy of people's family histories, or lack of them, but when it came to Mr. Reilly, she was more than a little curious. What had made him so grumpy, or was he just born that way?

Annie let out a gusty sigh as she rocked back on her heels. She was wearing a pair of well-worn overalls and a t-shirt that was splattered with paint. Her hair, as wild and curly as ever, was pulled up with half a dozen hairclips. She looked like a cross between a mad scientist and the Farmer in the Dell, but somehow it worked.

"He hasn't had it easy, it's true," she acknowledged. "Which might account for the grumpiness. I remember as a boy he was kind of quiet and shy, but not *grumpy*, per se..." She let out a sigh. "But then Laura, that's his mother, died when he was a teenager. Sixteen, maybe? Cancer. It was very quick, poor woman. And then his dad a few years ago—two or three, now, I'd say. Stroke. Joshua had moved to New York City for college, but he came back to help with his dad and the store and then he never left. I think there was a woman in the picture at one point... a girlfriend, maybe a fiancée? But I suppose when he left New York, it didn't last. I never saw her around here, anyway, but I get the sense he might have had his heart broken. And now there's just Maureen. She's a widow—her husband Pete passed a couple of years ago. He was in the military, never knew much about him."

Laurie nodded slowly, absorbing these pithy yet revealing remarks about the Reilly family. She half-wished she hadn't asked; it felt like too much information to know about a man who seemed, she realized, intensely private. She had a pretty sure feeling that Joshua Reilly wouldn't appreciate her knowing all that about him and his family, and definitely not the heartbroken stuff. What had that woman been like, to capture his heart? Not that it mattered to her, of course.

"Anyway," Annie said, "I'll invite a few people over tomorrow night for dinner. You can get to know some people here a bit more, feel like you really belong."

"That would be great—"

"And then it's the town's Fall Festival on Saturday, on the town green," Annie continued. Her manner, Laurie decided, was that of a friendly steamroller. "Come along to that and you'll meet just about everyone. Maybe even Henrietta Starr!" She let out a rich chuckle as she rocked back on her heels. "She's the matriarch of this place, the last remaining Starr, although hardly anyone ever sees her anymore. Tough as an old boot, though, and had some kind of drama back in the fifties, or so people say, although I don't think anyone knows the details. I certainly wasn't around then!" She let out another chuckle. "I'm not *that* old. She still lives in the Starr mansion, has most of her life. Never married or had children. She's certainly a character." She gave a little sigh before she became brisk again. "Anyway, I'll make sure to introduce you around. Tell everyone to make you feel welcome and that's an order!"

"Oh, that's kind, but you don't have to..." As much as Laurie wanted to make friends, the thought of being paraded in front of the good people of Starr's Fall and having them ordered to be nice to her made her shudder inwardly. She hated being in any kind of spotlight, and she definitely didn't want a welcome born of either pity or duty. How many times had a teacher, with the best intentions, ordered a class to be nice to the new girl? More than once, Laurie had felt a heavy hand on her shoulder as she'd had to stand in front of a class of bored teenagers while a teacher intoned sternly, *"Let's all be nice to Laurie. She's had a hard time recently."*

Thanks, but no thanks. That kind of directive was, Laurie had discovered, almost always doomed to failure.

Hopefully, she could make friends in Starr's Fall the old-fashioned way... by just getting to know people, one by one.

"It'll be fun," Annie replied in the tone of someone who would absolutely not take no for an answer. "Now when is this place opening? Because I talked to Liz Cranbury yesterday, and she was really excited about it. She's got the most ridiculous little dog—Frou-frou is its actual name, can you believe it?" Annie continued without taking a breath, never mind giving Laurie a chance to respond. "When she first told me, I thought she was joking. A Chihuahua. It was her husband's, but somehow after their divorce, he got the house, and she got the dog. Doesn't seem all that fair, but life is like that sometimes, isn't it?"

"I guess it can be—" Laurie began, before Annie launched back into her running commentary.

"Anyway, enough about all that. I told her I'd ask you when, because I think she'll definitely want to be stopping by. It's been hard since the divorce—Greg might have got the house, but Liz wants to stay in Starr's Fall. She's renting by the village green, cute little place at least. He played away, unfortunately. With his PA." She grimaced before continuing in the same breath, "There's also Jenna Miller, who runs the general store, Miller's Mercantile. Have you been there yet? Past the church about half a mile, so a little way out of town, but worth the trek. Lots of great produce and stuff, and the building's from 1807. Really charming. Jenna took it on from her parents a few years ago. They retired to Florida, but she's lived here all her life, like me. Although she did move away for a few years. Don't we all?" She let out a huff of laughter before admitting, "Well, I didn't, but anyway. Jenna and I met when we were kids— well, actually, I used to babysit her, but trust me, I'm not that much older. Well, ten years, but *still*. We became friends when Jenna came back to run her parents' store." Laurie opened her mouth to say something in response, but once again Annie continued without missing a beat. "Her brother Zach helps with the store, too. He's *quite* the charmer, so beware, I'll say that right now. He's already gone through all of Starr's Fall's eligible ladies, and now he's onto Torrington's. But to be fair, he is very nice. I'll introduce them all to you. Anyway," she said again, catching her breath. "Tomorrow, at seven?"

Laurie felt a little bit like her head was spinning. "Yes—"

"Good. See you then. I'll pick you up a little before. My place isn't too far out, about three miles. Don't forget!" She gave a nod as if to say *mission accomplished*, reached down to pat Max firmly on his head, and then strode out of the store, leaving Laurie feeling slightly winded. Annie, she decided, was a true force of nature.

She was just about to go upstairs for a cup of coffee when a van pulled up in front of the store and a young man jumped out, scanned the street, and then rapped firmly on the glass pane of Laurie's door.

"Delivery for a Laurie Ellis?" he asked when Laurie opened it, as he scanned an electronic clipboard.

"That's me."

Soon he was loading box after box into the store—the stock she'd ordered online, from various wholesalers. She'd had so much fun browsing on her laptop and picking out things she thought would be fun to stock, but right now it looked like a *lot*. And she was meant to sell all this stuff? Once again, she felt both daunted and excited, overwhelmed but also hopeful. After years of dreams and wishful thinking, this was really, finally happening…

When the delivery guy had gone, Laurie put Max out in the back, happily sunning himself in the enclosed courtyard, and then propped open the front door to let in some fresh air. It was another warm, sunny day, and she put some pop music on her phone to bop along to as she grabbed a box-cutter and started opening her merchandise.

It was fun to go through all the stuff she'd bought weeks ago—dog bowls and leashes, all kinds of furry and fluffy toys, darling little coats and boots for smaller dogs, plus the usual array of brushes, combs, poo bags, and other accoutrements for the discerning pet owner.

Kneeling down on the floor, she started organizing everything into piles, trying to figure out where she was going to put it all. The toys at the front, she decided, because those were always wearing out, with pet owners needing more, and they looked fun and inviting. She was intending to have the baked treats in a display case in the window, tempting people in. The more practical stuff, collars, leashes, and bowls, could go in the back.

"Oh, hello! Are you opening soon?"

Laurie looked up to see a woman standing in the doorway, a tiny Chihuahua tucked under one arm. She had a sleek gray bob and wore a quarter-zip fleece and skinny jeans, tucked into knee-high leather boots. Laurie realized she knew exactly who she was —Liz Cranbury, who got the dog in the divorce. Frou-frou.

"Hello," she replied as she stood up, brushing the dust from her knees. "I'm hoping to open in about another week or so. I haven't actually set the date yet…" That was at the top of page two of her checklist.

"Oh, you'll have to let me know when," the woman replied with enthusiasm. "Frou-frou here—yes, that really is her name—could use a good groom. You will do grooming, won't you?"

Laurie's heart, so buoyant a few seconds ago, faltered and fell. "I'm not currently set up for grooming," she admitted. She had neither the space nor the training, but that wasn't to say it was impossible... was it? Her optimism came bounding back, with determination. She could fit a grooming station in the back room if she stored stock in the second bedroom upstairs, maybe, and she *had* looked at online courses. They usually only took about three months to complete.

"Oh, that's too bad," Liz said, making a face. "I'm terrible at it myself. I'm not actually a dog person, although I'm trying to be, since it's just Frou-frou and me now." She glanced down at the little dog who was looking, as Chihuahuas often did, unimpressed by everything. "My name's Liz Cranbury, by the way."

"Laurie Ellis."

"Well, let me know when you open and if you start any pet grooming. You'd definitely have a loyal customer in me!" She let out a little laugh before she stepped out of the doorway and, with a waggle of her fingers, set off down the street.

That was a good start, Laurie told herself, and it gave her an incentive to look into offering a dog grooming service, although in reality, she wasn't sure she had the cash for that just now. She'd used up a good chunk of the bequest from Nadine in putting down two months' deposit on this place as well as buying all the stock... a fact which could make her stomach plunge with nerves if she let it.

If this didn't work out... what would she do? It was a possibility she hadn't let herself think about too much, mostly because it was so awful to contemplate. She couldn't bear the thought of slinking back to Trenton, taking up her old job in marketing if it was even available, and eking out an existence like she did before. Life was meant to be so much more than that.

And it would be, Laurie told herself firmly. Time for that optimism again! Joshua Reilly might be something of a Grinch, but she was more like the Grinch's dog, Max, her own dog's namesake: always hopeful, tail wagging and eyes alight, ready for whatever came next.

With a firm, determined smile curving her mouth, she turned back to open another box.

5

"Welcome, welcome, don't mind the mess..."

Annie Lyman led the way into her weathered and fairly dilapidated farmhouse on the edge of Starr's Fall. She'd picked up Laurie and Max—insisting Laurie bring him—in her truck at ten to seven and talked nonstop all the way back to her house, changing subjects with such lightning speed that Laurie struggled to know what—or, really, who—she was talking about. Annie seemed to know everyone in this town, giving Laurie another rundown of various people whose names she knew she'd never remember, their life situations, jobs, and most particularly, how long they'd been in Starr's Fall. It was, Laurie was coming to realize, a town with a whole lot of history.

"So it's just me, my mom, and Jenna and Zach tonight," Annie had informed Laurie after she'd drawn a breath, her tone apologetic, although frankly, Laurie was relieved. With the Fall Festival on Saturday, she'd prefer a smaller event tonight, and four new people felt like plenty. "It's better that way," Annie had continued, "because my mom doesn't do great with crowds anymore. She has Parkinson's—diagnosed four years ago. For a while it was just the standard stuff—shakes, loss of balance, some slurred speech. But in the last few months it's become worse. Anxiety, depression, and, unfortunately, the start of dementia." Annie had grimaced, her lips flattening into a line of grim acceptance. "I thought I ought to warn you, you know, just so you're prepared in case she says something a bit out there."

"I'm sorry," Laurie had replied, heartfelt. "That must be really difficult."

"It hasn't been easy," Annie had allowed, her tone brisk. "But it is what it is. That's life, you've got to make the best of it."

"Yes," Laurie had agreed, petting Max who was nestled on her lap, "that's always been my motto."

"Has it?" Annie had glanced at her a little too shrewdly. "Hmm."

Laurie had braced herself for a barrage of personal questions which fortunately didn't come because they'd turned into the rutted dirt road that served as the driveway and parked in front of a farmhouse that had definitely seen better days, yet still looked friendly somehow. It had a wide front porch that was admittedly sagging in the middle, and the shingles on the roof were curling up at the edges. Although it had once been white, the paint had faded to a dirty grayish color, and the green shutters were in sore need of a new coat of paint; several hung askew. Despite all that, Laurie thought it looked homely and welcoming.

As Annie ushered her in, she stepped inside to a kitchen that was cluttered and cozy, with battered units that looked about forty years old lining the walls, a big square table in the middle. Mess was everywhere—piles of papers, stacks of magazines, a basket of unfolded laundry, and a silver-whiskered black lab who lifted his droopy head from his basket before dropping it down again. Max squirmed, eager to get out of her arms and start exploring.

"Sorry, I'm not very good at housework," Annie confessed unrepentantly as she shed her coat. "The farm keeps me too busy, and

Mom's not up to it anymore... Mom?" she called out. "Are you here?" She glanced back at Laurie. "You can let Max down. George is a real sweetie, and I don't think he'll even move from his basket. And there's nothing here too precious for Max to wreck, I'm afraid. Just a lot of junk!" She poked her head through a doorway that led into a hall that was cluttered with shoes and boots. "Mom...?"

"I'm here, I'm here. Where would I even go?" a woman answered back with good-natured sarcasm. She came into the kitchen slowly, walking with a cane, her bright blue eyes lighting up when she saw Laurie. "Oh, hello! I've forgotten your name, dear, but I know Annie said you were coming."

Laurie stepped forward shyly. "It's Laurie Ellis."

"And I'm Barbara Lyman, but everyone calls me Barb." Although her speech was a little slurred, her smile was warm and twinkly and made Laurie feel instantly welcome. "It's so nice to meet you."

"And you." Laurie liked Barb instinctively. Unlike her daughter, she was fine-boned and petite, barely coming up to Annie's shoulder. Her hair possessed the same flyaway curls as Annie's but was entirely white and tamed back with a headband. Barb shuffled slowly, with faltering steps, toward the table and sat down with a sigh of relief as Max came over to sniff around her feet. She smiled down at the little dog.

"What a cutie! What's his name?"

"Max."

"Hello, Max." With painstaking movements, she reached down to fondle Max's ears with arthritic fingers before she glanced back at Laurie. "Tell me about yourself, dear," she invited as Annie went to check on whatever was bubbling away in the oven—it smelled like lasagna and Laurie's mouth watered. "You're new to Starr's Fall?"

"Yes, I moved here just a few days ago." Laurie pulled out a chair on the other end of the table as Annie bustled around them, setting the table, and Laurie explained to Barb about her pet store and bakery.

"A dog bakery..." Barb's forehead crinkled. "I must admit, I've never heard of such a thing."

Laurie had a feeling she was going to be hearing that a lot. "They have them in cities," she told Barb. "Like New York and Los Angeles."

"But in Starr's Fall?" Barb sounded both kindly and skeptical. "What made you choose this place, wonderful as it is?"

"Well..." Laurie began, unsure how much she wanted to reveal about her reasons so early on. It still felt too precious and private to explain.

"Laurie has family here," Annie informed her mother. "The Ly —what was it again?"

"The Lysanders." It seemed Annie was going to do it for her.

"Have you heard of them, Mom?" Annie asked. "I didn't think I had..." She turned back to Laurie. "How long ago was it they were here?"

"Well..." Laurie said again, clearly hedging. Her throat felt dry all of a sudden. *About twenty-six years*, she could have answered, but didn't. She wasn't ready yet to share the real reason she'd come to Starr's Fall. It felt too exposing, so early on. She wasn't ready to be that vulnerable. "It was a while ago now," she said, and Barb nodded, her face screwed up in thought.

"The Lysanders... That name rings a bell, I must admit, but I'm not sure..." She let out a sad laugh. "My memory's not what it once was." She glanced at Annie. "What was it I did the other day, Annie? Something silly... You got so annoyed with me..."

"I wasn't annoyed," Annie returned quickly. Her face had flushed and for a second, she looked almost unbearably sad, so

Laurie's heart ached for her. It was obvious that Annie and her mother were very close.

"Oh, I know you don't mean to be," Barb replied with an affectionate glance at her daughter. "But it's hard when I'm always doing silly things." She turned to Laurie. "It's the Parkinson's. First it affected my hands, and then walking, and talking, and now this." She tapped her temple with a wry smile. "At least I have enough of my marbles to remember *that*."

"Oh, Mom." Annie sounded caught between humor and tears before she gave herself a shake, went to check on the lasagna, and then banged the oven door with more force than necessary. "Drinks," she announced. "I'm sure Jenna and Zach will be here any second. What can I get you, Laurie?"

"Oh, umm…"

"Wine? Beer? You're not driving."

"A glass of wine would be wonderful, thank you."

Annie was just handing Laurie a very full glass of red when someone tapped twice at the door, causing Max to send up a volley of barking.

"That doesn't sound like good old George." A woman, looking to be in her late thirties or so, stepped into the kitchen, smiling, eyebrows raised in query. She had thick auburn hair that she wore in a long braid down her back, and her broad face was freckled and friendly. She wore a pair of jeans covered in colorful patches and a purple sweater that looked as if it had been stretched all out of shape; together, they made their own likable fashion statement. Laurie liked her at once.

"Not George, but Laurie's dog Max," Annie answered. "Jenna, this is Laurie. Laurie, Jenna. Where's Zach?"

Jenna rolled her eyes heavenward. "Guess what, he had a last-minute date he just couldn't say no to—"

"As he always does!" Annie shook her head, laughing. "What a scoundrel. So he passed us up for something better?"

"He said he might be here for dessert, depending on how it goes."

"Poor woman! I don't envy her."

"My brother isn't that bad," Jenna told Laurie with a good-natured grimace. "But he *does* like to date."

"The women of Starr's Fall know to steer clear," Annie replied as she poured Jenna a glass of wine without asking her; clearly, they were old friends.

"Too true," Jenna agreed, taking the wine with a murmured thanks. "He's had to go all the way to Litchfield tonight." She took a sip of wine as she turned to Laurie with an open and frankly curious gaze. "At least now you've been warned," she told her teasingly. "If you're single, steer clear of Zach Miller, for your own sanity."

"*Are* you single?" Annie asked Laurie with smiling bluntness. So much for that famed New England reserve, she thought wryly. "Because I'm sorry to say, eligible men are pretty thin on the ground here."

"There's always Mike," Jenna teased Annie, who both rolled her eyes and blushed, just a little.

"Mike, who runs the garage?" Laurie asked, feeling as if she was starting to slot a few pieces together.

"That's the one," Jenna confirmed. "He's had a thing for Annie here for ages. Years, if not decades."

"He has not, and you know it," Annie replied tartly. She was *definitely* blushing. "Enough. What about you, Laurie? Have you got a special someone?"

For some reason, an image of Joshua Reilly's scowling face popped into Laurie's head, and now *she* felt herself start to blush. Where on earth had *that* absurd idea come from? "No, definitely not," she replied firmly. "I came to Starr's Fall footloose and fancy-free."

"The best way to be," Jenna approved. "Like Annie and me here. We're not hanging around waiting for a Mr. Right who isn't going to show up."

"And a good thing, too," Annie agreed, although Laurie couldn't help but notice she didn't sound *quite* as certain as Jenna did. Maybe one day she'd hear the story behind their attitudes.

"You just need to find the right man," Barb interjected, smiling. "And be patient."

"Bless you, Barb," Jenna replied, leaning down to kiss the older woman on her wrinkled cheek, "but I'm thirty-eight and I don't think it's going to happen. I'm not even sure I *want* it to happen. I'm set in my ways, and I like my own space."

"Still, you never know," Barb persisted while Annie took the lasagna out of the oven and set it down, bubbling and smelling delicious, on a mat at the center of the table.

"Time to eat," she announced, and that seemed to be the end of the discussion about romance, or lack of it.

The rest of the meal passed in a pleasant haze of wine, food, and boisterous conversation. Often Laurie didn't have much of a chance to get a word in edgewise, but she didn't mind. It was fun listening to Jenna and Annie exchange good-natured teasing, and Barb occasionally make a dry remark, although as the evening went on, Laurie could see that her energy was flagging, and her speech became a bit more slurred. At one point she forgot Laurie's name and then started to look alarmingly confused, glancing around the table with a worried frown as if everyone had suddenly morphed into strangers, which Laurie feared they might have.

"Why don't you put your feet up, Mom?" Annie suggested gently when Barb's chin started to bob toward her chest. Barb smiled tiredly.

"Maybe I should…"

Annie guided her mother into the living room, settling her in a recliner while Jenna and Laurie cleared the table and stacked plates in the dishwasher.

"Poor Barb," Jenna remarked quietly as she rinsed glasses in the sink. "And poor Annie. They only have each other now. Annie's dad passed away about ten years ago. He ran this farm for forty years before he dropped dead of a heart attack, just like that. Annie's doing her best to keep it going on her own, but it's been hard for one woman, as you can probably tell."

"Yes, I can imagine," Laurie replied softly. She certainly knew how hard it could be to try to do everything on your own. That's how she'd had to live most of her life.

"What about you?" Jenna asked, almost as if she'd been reading Laurie's thoughts. "Have you got family back in New Jersey?"

"No," Laurie replied, keeping her tone cheerfully frank. She always dreaded the moment when someone inevitably asked about her family, and then how her ensuing explanation invoked the predictable pity. She'd never, not once, asked anyone to feel sorry for her. "No one, really. Made it easy to leave." She smiled breezily and bent down to put another plate in the dishwasher.

"No one?" Jenna frowned in consternation. "What about your parents…?"

"Not around," Laurie answered, and then with a tiny sigh, admitted, "I never knew them, as it happens. My birth mother gave me up for adoption when I was a baby."

"Oh, I'm…" Jenna hesitated, and Laurie watched confusion flit across her face. *What about your adoptive parents*, she so clearly wanted to ask, but Laurie suspected she wasn't sure if she should, based on what Laurie had said so far. They were clearly not in the picture, and pretty much never had been. Laurie did her best not to think of them at all.

"I don't have any adoptive parents," she explained, deciding to go for the condensed version. "I grew up in the foster system. It was fine." Which was a *bit* of a stretch, but still. She'd kept her voice firm, inviting no more questions, and certainly no sympathy. "I was really lucky in a lot of ways. In fact, the reason I was able to rent the store in town and move here at all was because one of my foster supervisors, Nadine, left me some money in her will, which was amazing."

"Oh, that's..." Jenna looked conflicted, like she wanted to envelop Laurie in a big hug but suspected it wouldn't be welcome, and the truth was, it wouldn't. Laurie liked hugs and she liked friendly people, but she *didn't* like the way people felt sorry for her as soon as she talked about her childhood. She hated how they often looked at her differently, as if she had somehow become lacking. An object of pity, she'd found, could not also be a person worthy of respect. No one could hold both viewpoints at the same time, even if they tried.

"You should join Starr's Fall Business Association," Jenna finally said, her tone turning as upbeat as Laurie's, and she felt a wave of relief that her new friend wasn't going to push her to talk about her past. "We're a small group, and we have a meeting once a month, but it can be pretty fun. There are a few 'characters' involved, if you get my drift, but everyone means well. We have our next meeting in a couple of weeks."

"Sounds great." Between tonight, Saturday's Fall Festival, and this new meeting, Laurie's social calendar was fuller than it had been basically ever... which was both an alarming and exciting thought.

Annie came back into the kitchen, smiling tiredly. "She fell asleep during Double Jeopardy," she confessed, and then let out a sigh that possessed a ragged edge and made Laurie ache for her. "I think tonight took it out of her," she continued as she reached for a dishrag and started wiping the table with movements that were a bit brisker than necessary. "We don't have people over all that much these days. She seemed on pretty good form, though, didn't she?" She shot them both a quick, pleading glance before turning back to the table.

"I thought she was wonderful," Laurie offered with an encouraging smile. "Funny and wise. I liked her straight off."

Annie turned back to give a grateful smile. "And she liked you, I know. She always likes meeting people since she doesn't get out much anymore. I should have people over more often, I know, but I'm usually pretty tired by the end of the day…"

"Hey, you have me over often enough," Jenna replied, giving Annie a quick one-armed hug before turning back to Laurie. "I've just invited Laurie to join the Starr's Fall Business Association. She's going to come to the next meeting."

"Wonderful," Annie replied, brightening. "We could definitely use some new blood in that group."

Jenna rolled her eyes. "That's an understatement. Let's just say," she explained to Laurie, "there are a few older members of the group who might be *slightly* stuck in their ways."

"Betty has been running Midnight Fashion since 1972," Annie explained. "She's a dear but she is pretty behind the times. She still doesn't take credit cards. And don't get me started on her book about the history of the store…" She gave a resigned shake of her head. "But we've had some new people join in the last year— Michael and Lizzy moved here from Hartford with their teenaged twins. They run the bakery on the green, The Rolling Pin. It does the most amazing croissants. And Zoe's always fun—she's only about thirty, and she manages The Latest Scoop."

"Starr's Fall's only ice cream parlor," Jenna filled in.

"I can't wait to meet everyone," Laurie replied sincerely. While it was a bit overwhelming to think of all the new people she'd be meeting, it was wonderful, too. Wasn't this what she wanted—a community to be a part of, friends to count on, or even consider as family? Admittedly, it was early days, and as much as she liked Annie and Jenna and Barb, she barely knew any of them. Still, there was reason to hope, even to believe.

Her optimism had facts behind it this time, Laurie told herself. Finally, this time it was all going to work out.

"Well, I suppose I'd better take you back," Annie announced as she grabbed the keys to her truck. "I've got to be up early in the morning."

After a flurry of goodbyes, Laurie scooped up Max into her arms and headed outside with Annie. The air possessed a chill and when Laurie tilted her head up, she saw the sky was inky black and full of stars.

"Wow," she breathed. "I don't think I've ever seen so many stars." It was as if some giant hand had scattered the sky with diamonds, glinting like bits of promise in a swathe of black velvet.

Annie glanced up, too, to survey the night sky. "Pretty amazing," she agreed softly. "Truth be told, I don't think I could ever leave Starr's Fall."

"I don't think I could either, already," Laurie said, half-teasing, half-serious. "Trust me, it's much better than Trenton."

"What were you doing, in the big city?" Annie asked as they both clambered into the truck and set off down the bumpy road, Max curled up on Laurie's lap.

"I worked in marketing for a pharmaceutical company," Laurie explained, "but very low level... I was pretty much a slightly glorified secretary. All in all, it wasn't very exciting." It had paid her bills and given her something to do, as well as a few people she could be friendly with, which was pretty much all she could say about it.

"Doesn't sound it," Annie agreed. "And you chose Starr's Fall because of the family connection?"

"Ye-es, and because it's such a pretty place," Laurie added quickly. "I've always wanted to live in a small town where everyone knows everyone else."

Annie let out a loud laugh at that. "And yet so many small towners dream of the big city where people mind their own business! Well, like I said, I'll never leave."

They drove in silence for a bit, the countryside no more than a sweep of darkness outside, until Annie turned onto Main Street, its stores dark and shuttered, the only light coming from the old-fashioned iron lamp posts lining the road, a few of them flickering on and off.

"Those streetlights," Annie grumbled. "Always burning out. It will be good to have you on the Business Association," she told Laurie. "We certainly could do with a little more liveliness. Half the stores on this street are empty and have been for years. It's a real shame." She shook her head in regret.

"Do you think that could change?" Laurie asked. "Maybe Starr's Fall needs something to put it on the map."

Annie arched an eyebrow, interested but skeptical. "Such as?"

"I don't know," Laurie admitted. "An event, maybe? A competition or a festival or something?"

"We have our Fall Festival on Saturday," Annie reminded her. "Although I can't see people coming in droves for some fresh-pressed apple cider, delicious as I know it is, a tractor ride, and a cake walk. But who knows?" She pulled up in front of Laurie's place and turned to her with a smile. "Thanks for coming tonight. I'll see you Saturday?"

"Yes, definitely," Laurie promised. She was looking forward to the festival, especially as she didn't actually know what a cake walk was, although it certainly sounded intriguing. Annie waited until Laurie had put her key in the lock and opened the door before she pulled away, honking her horn in farewell, the sound echoing down the empty street.

Out of instinct as much as curiosity, Laurie glanced back at Reilly's Antiquarian Books across the street, but the rooms upstairs were as dark as the store below. Had Joshua gone to bed, or was he out, she wondered, and then wondered why she was wondering. What was it about the man that made her so curious? Was it just the people-pleasing tendency she had to make a grumpy person like her, or was it the possibility of whatever might exist beneath that surly veneer?

She doubted Joshua Reilly would give her much chance to find out. She'd just pushed open the front door when Max, in an uncharacteristic display of energy, leapt from her arms, barking madly, and raced through the store and up the stairs.

What on earth?

"Max!" Laurie called, about to run up the stairs after him, only to then stop on the first step, suddenly unsure. Max was now barking and growling as if he'd cornered something, and the sound was coming from the top floor. *Was someone in her house?*

An icy fingertip of fear trailed along her spine. She'd locked all the doors, but she *had* left the windows open upstairs... but surely someone couldn't scale a drainpipe or something and break in? Not in Starr's Fall, of all places! She'd been diligent about locking everything up back in Trenton, especially as she hadn't lived in the best neighborhood, but here...?

Max was still barking.

With a hand that was not quite steady, Laurie withdrew her phone from her pocket and swiped to dial 911, her thumb hovering over the call button, should she need to press it. Slowly, she crept up the stairs, her heart starting to thud with hard, heavy beats. Potential headlines were dancing through her mind—*Woman New to Area Attacked in Own Home* or *New Business Owner Attacked and*

Killed Before She Even Got to Do Anything. Not the catchiest headline, perhaps, but it was what Laurie was feeling as she rounded the landing and headed up to the third floor.

"Max," she called, her voice sounding thin and papery. "*Max...*"

She came to the door of her bedroom, and stopped. Max was at the foot of her bed, everything in him bristling as he continued to bark at the bed as if his life depended on it.

She took a step in and peeked around the door. There on Laurie's bed—her pillow, even—looking as disdainful as ever, was Joshua Reilly's Persian cat.

6

The knock on the door sounded both hesitant and yet determined. Amazing how a simple knock could communicate so much, and yet somehow it did. Joshua heard the first tentative tap, like an apology, and then the more firm, deliberate knock, like a command. It was ten o'clock at night. Joshua generally didn't get visitors at any time of day, never mind at this late hour. Who could it possibly be?

He raked a hand through his hair as he shut his notebook and pushed away from the table before heading downstairs. His visitor knocked again, this time even louder. Someone was clearly impatient.

He flicked on the downstairs lights, bathing the store in a weak electric glow that sputtered every few seconds. He probably needed to get this whole place rewired, but there was no money for it, as there wasn't for a lot of things.

Joshua moved around the piles and stacks of books with thoughtless ease, stepping over one and swerving another. If someone ever did want to browse, he reflected, they would certainly struggle, but that was okay with him because he didn't want people to browse in the first place.

"Oh, for heaven's sake." The words came out of his mouth in a gusty mutter. Through the frosted glass of the front door, he could see who was standing there. His nosy neighbor, Laurie Ellis, standing with her arms folded and her expression resolute. What on earth did she want at this hour?

He unlocked the door and opened it without bothering to hide his frown of displeasure. "Yes?"

"Good evening," she replied rather pointedly, although she smiled, as if inviting him to share the joke. All right, maybe his greeting had been a little rude, but it *was* ten o'clock at night. "I'm so sorry to disturb you, but your cat is in my apartment, and I can't get it out."

"What..." For a second, he had no idea what she was talking about. He'd been so engrossed in his work, in the haunting world of composing minor chords and melody, that everything else had fallen away, and the first thought in his mind now, like a bubble emerging on the surface of a smooth lake, was *what cat...?*

Then, with the mental equivalent of slamming into a brick wall, he remembered. Leamhachán. Where was she?

"In your apartment?" he repeated blankly, remembering the second part of her sentence.

"Yes, on my bed," Laurie replied with a wry grimace, her nose wrinkling in a way Joshua found unsettlingly endearing. He didn't find *anything* endearing, so to be charmed, admittedly reluctantly and only for a second, by Laurie Ellis' screwed-up nose was... odd. He pushed the feeling away. "I tried to move her," she explained, "but she scratched me."

"Scratched..."

In response, Laurie held out her arm; Joshua realized she hadn't been folding her arms, but rather cradling one with the other. A long, bloody cut ran down from her left elbow to her wrist.

"Dear Lord," Joshua exclaimed faintly. The cut didn't look particularly deep, but it was several inches long and was still bleeding. "Lea did that to you?"

"Well, I tried to remove her from her comfortable spot on my bed," Laurie replied wryly. "I can't really blame her. If someone woke me up so rudely, I'd probably react like that, too." She smiled, as if inviting him to share the joke, her blue-green eyes glinting with good humor, but Joshua found he could not return her smile.

He couldn't see the funny side of it; no, all he felt, he realized, was shame. He'd been snarky in the extreme to this woman both times he'd seen her, and she'd had every right to march over here and *shriek* at him about his stupid cat. His crazy, aggressive cat, as it happened, who scratched people, although, to be fair, Lea wasn't even his.

And yet Laurie Ellis hadn't done any of that at all. Instead, she'd been friendly, far too forgiving, and it made Joshua feel like he was about two inches tall, cringing and penitent.

"I'm so sorry," he managed, and she let out a gurgle of laughter.

"Why do I get the feeling you don't say those three words very often?"

He managed a small smile of rueful acknowledgment even as he struggled not to feel like a complete and utter heel. Which was, he realized, pretty unusual for him; he was accustomed to feeling completely vindicated in batting back people's nosy intrusions into his life, especially by his Aunt Maureen. Although, to be fair, the last few days without Maureen had been... peaceful, yes, but also the *tiniest* bit quiet. Not lonely, mind you. Never lonely.

"I might not," he told Laurie, "but they are certainly justified in this case." He nodded toward her arm. "Have you cleaned that out?"

"No," Laurie admitted. "I'm afraid I don't have any antiseptic."

"I do," Joshua replied. "I'll get it for you, and then I'll go reclaim that darned cat."

"All right. Thank you." She looked surprised by his offer, and he wondered just how big of a jerk she had to think he was, to be skeptical that he'd want to help her when she was injured and bleeding.

Pretty big, was the obvious answer, and she'd be right. He'd given Laurie Ellis no reason to think he was anything but a big, fat jerk with a capital B, F, and J. The real question, Joshua knew, was why that bothered him.

It was something he didn't have to think about now, as he beckoned her inside, closing the door behind her, and then went to find the tube of antiseptic cream in the back of the dented medicine cabinet in the bathroom upstairs. Fortunately, it wasn't past its expiration date—although almost—and he dusted it off before bringing it downstairs.

Laurie was still standing by the door, looking around the store like she was trying to figure it out. All right, it *was* dusty and messy and completely disorganized. So what? He liked it that way. He recognized there was no need to feel so defensive; Laurie hadn't said a word.

"Here it is," he told her gruffly, and handed her the tube.

She brightened, her whole face seeming to come alive, eyes sparkling, mouth curving, as she took it. "Thanks," she said, in a tone of such warmth and gratitude that Joshua felt like he'd stitched up her arm singlehandedly, or heck, even cured cancer.

She started to unscrew the cap of the tube before he interjected, his tone still gruff. "You should wash it first."

"Oh... right." She hesitated, looking a little unsure, and then Joshua said, with obvious reluctance, "Come upstairs to the kitchen. You can wash it there."

He didn't normally invite people into his private space;

Maureen sometimes stomped upstairs without asking and then insisted on running a vacuum cleaner and a dust rag around, washing whatever he'd left in the sink, all of which made him feel equal parts appreciative and annoyed. He never *asked* her to clean up after him, and yet he couldn't deny he was glad when she did.

Now, as Laurie followed him up the narrow stairs to the room above, he was conscious of all its—and therefore *his*—deficiencies. The kitchen units were battered and old, the table small and scarred. The kitchen adjoined the living room which was separated by a pair of bi-fold doors that were pretty much permanently pushed back, and he watched as she glanced at the room, with its sagging sofa, lumpy armchairs, and keyboard. A coffee table was stacked with papers and old coffee mugs. The whole room, the whole *apartment*, looked unloved, almost unlived in, which didn't make much sense considering how much time he spent here, and yet that's how it seemed. How it had felt... since his mother had died fourteen years ago now, and his father nearly three.

His mother had made it a home, had imbued the few shabby rooms with life and love—a soup simmering on the stove, colorful magnets on the fridge, crocheted throws on the sofa. After she'd died, his father had bundled it all up and given it away to charity... without even asking Joshua. He'd come from school one day and found it all gone. When he'd asked about it, his father had said brusquely, "She's gone."

His aunt had said that was his way to grieve, but it hadn't been Joshua's.

Abruptly, he turned away from the sight and went straight to the sink. "Here you go," he said, and he dipped a piece of paper towel under the faucet and handed it to her.

Laurie stretched out her arm, dabbing at the scratch which was, Joshua saw, still oozing blood. It was deeper than he'd thought.

"Do you think you need stitches?" he wondered aloud, and she glanced up at him with a laughing look.

"Definitely not. I doubt I'll even have a scar, although if I did, it would be kind of a cool story."

"Would it?"

She shrugged. "Depends how you spin it. I was mauled by a Persian cat on my own pillow—it sounds kind of exotic, doesn't it? That kind of thing doesn't happen to everyone."

Her cheerfulness was, Joshua thought, Pollyannish and yet somehow not annoying. "Wait... Lea was on your *pillow*?"

"Still is, I imagine. She really, really did not want to move."

Joshua watched as Laurie squeezed some of the ointment onto her fingertip and then began to dab it gently on the scratch. He found himself mesmerized by the whole scene—her slender arm stretched out, her head bent, her golden-brown ponytail falling over one shoulder. The freckles on her nose.

Was he going *crazy*?

He took an involuntary step back, needing to distance himself from this woman, from his feelings. He hadn't so much as looked at a woman since Mia had left him, despite his awful clinging to the remnants of their relationship—something he really didn't like to remember—and he had no intention of doing so now. The bookstore, his music... they were enough. They had to be, because loving people hurt way too much, especially when they left you, whether by death or design.

Not, of course, that he was remotely thinking that way about his new neighbor. He'd just been transfixed, momentarily, by the sight of her. She was, after all, a very pretty woman, in an entirely unpretentious and unselfconscious way. A tendril of hair fell against her cheek, and he had the urge to tuck it behind her ear, let his finger skim along her skin...

Joshua gave himself a mental shake. This was getting ridiculous. Maybe he needed to get out more, which wouldn't be all that difficult since currently he didn't go out at all.

"Umm, Joshua? Here you go."

Joshua blinked and he realized Laurie had finished and was now holding out the tube, and had, it seemed, for at least a few seconds.

"Oh, great, thanks," he muttered and took it back.

She stood there for a moment, and so did he, and it spun out into something awkward. He gave himself another mental shake. "I'll get the cat," he said, and she smiled. It was amazing how her smile transformed her face, lighting up her eyes, making them sparkle.

Stop.

"Lead the way," he told her, and she turned and headed back downstairs. After a second where he gathered the remnants of his composure, Joshua followed her. By the time they emerged out into the darkened street, he was back to being his grumpy self. *Good.*

"This way," Laurie said as she unlocked her front door and led him through the store where she'd clearly been working hard—the walls were freshly painted, the floor buffed to a shine, and she'd started arranging various items on tall wooden shelves. Joshua glimpsed a rattan basket of rubber balls and another one of rope toys. She led him to the stairs that ran along the side of the store, up to the living quarters above. The layout was almost identical to Joshua's place, but that was where any similarity ended.

Laurie's store and home were neat and clean, everything freshly scrubbed and painted. There was a pleasing smell in the air of both paint and polish, with hints of lavender and lemon. As she unlocked the door at the top, her little dog Max hurled himself at her ankles, making her stumble back a little so Joshua instinctively grabbed her shoulders to steady her and keep her from falling down the stairs.

"Whoa." For a second his brain short-circuited as he felt the warmth of her skin through the thin cotton of her shirt, her body pressed ever so briefly back into his. Then she pulled away and quickly scooped up Max.

"Sorry," she mumbled as she cradled the dog to her. "Max doesn't like being left alone. I closed the door to my bedroom so he wouldn't get at the cat."

"Or she wouldn't get at him." Clearly Lea had more vim in her than he'd realized. He stepped into the hall behind her, doing his best to act like that moment hadn't affected him, because of course it hadn't. At least, it shouldn't have. Laurie was already heading up the next flight of stairs, but Joshua glimpsed her living room—an armchair by the window, a bookshelf, and a lamp. That was it. Somehow, he'd been expecting something cozy and decorated, but she had just moved in here, after all. Still, it made him curious in a way he didn't expect, and probably should avoid.

Upstairs, Laurie paused in front of the doorway to the bedroom facing the street. "She's in here," she said. "I'll keep hold of Max."

"For his safety or the cat's?" Joshua asked with the barest flicker of a smile.

An answering smile tugged at Laurie's mouth. "Both."

For a second, they just smiled at each other, and the moment spun out, just as it had before, but this time it didn't feel awkward. It felt... expectant.

Okay, enough of that. Clearing his throat, Joshua turned back to the door. He twisted the knob and stepped into Laurie's bedroom. The first thing he noticed was the lack of furniture in there too. Besides the bed, which was just a mattress on the floor, the only other furniture—if they could even be called that—were a couple of plastic milk crates that held her clothes. Again, he supposed it was normal, considering she'd just moved, and yet...

Something about it felt... off. And not just off, but *sad*. What,

Joshua wondered, was a young woman—he didn't think Laurie could be more than twenty-five—doing, moving to a place like Starr's Fall all on her own? Did she have family here? She didn't *seem* as if she did, and yet he couldn't have said why. But why had she come? Where was she from? And why did she seem so *alone*?

The questions raced through his mind, surprising him, because he tended not to wonder about people. He tended not to care enough to be curious, and yet... with this woman, right now, it was different. He was.

"Umm... Joshua?" Laurie's voice was hesitant, startling him out of his unexpected—and unwelcome—reverie. "The cat?"

Joshua realized he'd been simply standing there, staring at the crates of her clothing like he was some kind of creep. *Get a grip*, he told himself, and giving himself a mental shake, he turned to the bed—and the cat.

Lea was nestled on Laurie's pillow just as she'd said, her plumed tail tucked around her body. Laurie had been right; she seriously looked like she did *not* want to move.

"I hope you're not allergic to cats, after all this," Joshua said, and from behind him Laurie let out a soft laugh.

"I don't think I am, but I haven't really been close enough to one to know. I'm a dog person mainly."

"That's not a surprise," Joshua remarked, with a nod for Max, who was squirming in Laurie's arms, looking very much like he wanted to get down, although to leap on the bed and attack Lea or hide under it, Joshua couldn't have said.

Laurie laughed again, the sound warm and rich, and Joshua struggled not to react. What on earth was going on with him? Why was this woman, who just days ago he'd found only irritating, affecting him like this? It was most unsettling.

"All right, Lea," he stated briskly as he headed for the cat. "Let's get going." He started reaching for her, but Lea let out a hiss as she batted one paw at him. Joshua missed getting scratched the way Laurie had by a mere hair's breadth. Clearly this was going to be more difficult than he'd hoped.

"She really likes my pillow," Laurie remarked, her voice laced with humor. Once again, Joshua was amazed—and humbled—by her unflagging cheerfulness. He was pretty sure if the situation were reversed, and Max was curled up on *his* pillow, he would not be reacting with the same kind of wry humor. Which, he supposed, said as much about him as it did about Laurie.

He reached for Lea again, and this time got nicked on his thumb for his efforts. A bright drop of blood welled up on his finger.

"Oh, I'm sorry," Laurie exclaimed.

"*You're* sorry?" Joshua turned to her with a wry grimace. "It's my cat. Well, technically, my aunt's, but I'm pretty sure you're not to blame for any of this."

"Still…" Laurie murmured.

Joshua glanced back at Lea, unsure how to tackle the contrary beast. Then the matter was taken out of his hands when, with a yap, Max squirmed his way out of Laurie's arms and leapt onto the bed, barking furiously. With a yowl, Lea launched herself from the pillow to the open window, where she disappeared outside, leaping nimbly along the ledge before gracefully jumping onto the maple tree whose branches brushed the building.

"Wow." Laurie grabbed Max from her bed and hugged him to her. "That solves that, I guess."

Joshua let out a rueful laugh as he raked a hand through his hair. "I guess it does. I hope Lea makes it back home. My Aunt Maureen will not be best pleased if I lose her."

"Cats do their own thing, though, don't they?" Laurie replied with a smile and a philosophical shrug. "And at least they know where they're fed."

"True. She's microchipped, so there's that."

They stood there for a moment, Max still squirming in Laurie's arms, Lea long gone, before Joshua roused himself, realizing there was no reason to stand there and stare like some gormless idiot.

"It's late, I should probably go," he said. "Sorry about all this."

"And I'm sorry to have disturbed you so late at night," Laurie replied, smiling.

"It wasn't your fault—"

"Well," Laurie replied with a laugh, "I suppose Lea and I could have shared the bed."

Which made Joshua think, inconveniently and embarrassingly, all sorts of vivid thoughts. It was definitely time to go. "Seeing how she scratched you, I doubt that would have worked out."

He turned towards the door, but Laurie was standing in front of it, holding Max, and they did an awkward side-shuffle dance before, with a slightly breathless laugh, she moved aside. As Joshua walked past, he breathed in the scent of her—what? Shampoo? Perfume? Whatever it was, it smelled of vanilla and almond and it tickled his nose and sparked his senses.

Enough.

He marched down the stairs, determined to get away from her. From this, whatever this was, which was nothing. He didn't like feeling this tangled up inside, a mixture of longing and fear. He was happier on his own. Safer and saner, too.

"Are you going to the Fall Festival on Saturday?" Laurie asked just as he'd reached the front door.

Joshua only half-turned. "The what?"

"The Fall Festival? On the town green? Apparently, there will be apple cider and tractor rides and a cake walk." She laughed. "I don't even know what that is." She cocked her head. "Surely you've gone before, if you grew up here?"

For a second, he could picture it—hazy sunshine, the smell of cinnamon donuts and fresh hay. His mother's laughter floating on the warm breeze. "Maybe when I was a kid," he allowed, "but not for a long time."

"So you're going?" she prompted, and he wasn't sure if she was teasing or not.

"Umm..."

"I'm going to be advertising Max's Place," she told him. "I've made some flyers. You could do the same—"

"Advertise?" He couldn't keep from sounding horrified. "I specialize in rare books of mostly military history," he informed her. "I don't think I'm going to find my customer demographic at Starr's Fall's Fall Festival."

Laurie pursed her lips playfully. "Well, you never know."

"Sometimes you do," he replied, far too grimly, and then, with a parting grimace that wasn't quite a smile, he walked out of the store and into the night.

7

"Laurie!"

Annie's shout echoed across the village green as Laurie stood on its edge, a leashed Max at her feet, his head tucked firmly between her ankles as he warily surveyed the crowds gathered for the town's annual Fall Festival. Various stalls and booths had been erected around the edge of the green, offering plants, baked goods, jellies and marmalades, vintage clothing, and more. Other stalls were set up for old-fashioned games—hook-a-duck, guess the weight of the pumpkin, and corn hole. Amidst all this, people milled around, chatting and laughing—families, friends, couples. There were also a fair number of dogs, which was why Max was seeming so nervous.

"Hi, Annie," Laurie called as Annie came striding toward her, parting the crowd like Moses and the Red Sea. She was an imposing woman, nearly six feet tall, with her springy hair probably adding another two or three inches. She stopped in front of Laurie, hands on her hips.

"Well! I'm glad you made it. And Max, too." She stooped down to pat his head, and he licked her hand, a gesture of cautious affection. "Mom's sitting at the Lyman Farm stall. I'm sure she'd love for you to say hello."

"Of course I will," Laurie replied immediately. It thrilled her to think that already, just a week into her new life, there were people who wanted her to say hello. Who seemed to count her as a friend. It made her feel that moving to Starr's Fall really had been the right decision... even if Max's Place wasn't open yet, and the front of her store was still stacked with boxes of unopened inventory. It would happen. It *was* happening.

"Come on," Annie said, tucking her arm through Laurie's. "I'll show you around and introduce you."

Laurie took a deep, steadying breath as Annie practically towed her around the green, Max trotting behind them. She was jumping in feet first, and she supposed that was the only way to go. And really, everyone in Starr's Fall had been friendly so far... even Joshua Reilly.

Her mind flitted back to Thursday evening, when he'd come over to get his cat. She'd told herself she'd been imagining the tension she'd felt twanging between them at times... a *romantic* tension that she was pretty sure was entirely on her side, because when he wasn't scowling, Joshua was a very attractive man, worthy of any heroine's admiration in the romance novels she read. She'd been close enough to him to see how chiseled his jaw was, how dark his lashes, and she'd breathed in his aftershave which had smelt exactly right—old-fashioned and spicy.

Tension—imagined or otherwise—aside, he'd definitely thawed a little, even if he'd ended leaving rather abruptly. It had been late, after all. The whole encounter, despite the cat scratch, had been inordinately hopeful, and Laurie was holding out for them to be friends. Maybe he'd even be here today, although he had practically sounded repulsed by the notion when she'd suggested it.

Meanwhile, Annie seemed determined to introduce her to just about everyone else in Starr's Fall. Laurie's head spun as her new friend went through what sounded like the town's telephone directory. "This is George Watson... He's the vet, you should get to know him, lovely man, married, three daughters... This is James Finlay, he runs the hardware... This is Elaine Barton, she does Pilates in the church basement, can do a plank for twenty minutes, *honestly...*"

Laurie barely had a chance to stammer a hello before Annie was moving on, seemingly determined to get through as many people in as little time as possible.

"Is the famous Henrietta Starr here?" she asked Annie, curious to catch a glimpse of the so-called matriarch and namesake of the town.

"Oh no," Annie assured her. "She never comes to any of these things anymore, although once upon a time she would have been giving out the blue ribbons and all that jazz. She must be in her nineties now, or nearly. *Anyway.*" She took a quick breath. "I've told everyone about your pet store," she continued as she propelled Laurie along as she tried not to trip over Max, who was keeping as close to her as possible. "What's it going to be called?"

"Max's Place."

"Aww." Annie shot her a teasingly simpering look. "I like that."

"Me too," Laurie replied, grinning. "And thank you for talking it up to everyone. I brought some flyers I made, actually, to hand around..."

"Perfect! Let's see?"

Laurie took one from her bag and handed it over. It was pretty basic, she had to admit, knocked up on her laptop in half an hour, with a photo stock image of dogs bounding across a stretch of grass that could, if you were feeling generous and squinted a little, be the village green. "Max's Place" was written in a playful, curly font at the top, and underneath the address, opening hours, and "Coming soon!" since she didn't yet have a date for her supposedly grand opening... although if Annie had anything to do with it, it would be as soon as possible.

"How many do you have?" Annie asked.

"Just twenty. I ran out of ink."

"Let me take one to put up in the town hall," Annie suggested. "And maybe the church and the library?"

"Thank you," Laurie told her as she handed three over. "Honestly, Annie, I don't know what I would have done if you hadn't rescued me on the side of the road!"

"Good thing your van broke down, huh?" Annie replied teasingly. "Come on, say hello to my mom and have a cup of apple cider."

Barb was sitting in a folding chair behind the counter of the Lyman Farm and Orchards stall, where paper cups of fresh cider and a pile of sugary donuts had been put out.

"We do pick-your-own as well as make cider," Annie told Laurie as she handed her a donut and a paper cup. "We used to have our own cider press, but ours broke last year and I can't afford to get it fixed, so I have to take it across town to Joe's place." Annie's smile was a touch more grim than wry. "We're losing the battle to keep the farm, but very slowly."

Laurie gazed at her in dismay. She hadn't realized it was as bad as that, although Jenna had implied almost as much. "Oh, Annie..."

She shrugged, cheerfully philosophical once more. "Oh, it's not so bad. We'll keep bumbling along as long as we can." She turned to her mother, placing one gentle hand on her shoulder. "Look who it is, Mom!" Her voice took on the cheerful pitch of someone who was determined to seem upbeat. It was a tone Laurie knew well, and she appreciated Annie's help all the more, knowing she had her own struggles.

"Oh, yes!" Barb's face brightened at the sight of Laurie, although her gaze clouded over after only a second, and Laurie realized she must have forgotten her name.

Annie must have realized it too, because she continued in a loud, clear voice, "I was just telling Laurie here that she needs to try some of our world-famous cider."

"Laurie..." Barb repeated, looking relieved. "And your sweet little dog..."

"Max," Laurie supplied, smiling. "And I can't wait to try the cider. I've heard so much about it." She took a sip, savoring its cinnamon-spiced taste, both tart and sweet. "Delicious!"

Barb beamed. "My John always did make the best cider."

"And now Annie, too," Laurie replied. "Like father, like daughter."

"Yes..." Barb glanced at her daughter, her smile touched with sorrow. "He would have been so proud of her."

"I know he would have, Mom," Annie said, her tone turning a little gruff to hide her own emotion, and she stooped to kiss her mother's cheek.

Watching them, Laurie felt the familiar ache of longing for the closeness of a relationship she'd never had. Nadine had been the closest thing she'd ever had to a mother, and while she'd truly been kind, she'd had to maintain a certain professional distance, and in any case, their relationship had dropped off after Laurie had left the foster system. Nadine had too many other kids coming through... and yet she'd still left Laurie that money.

The money to start Max's Place... and to find her family.

Taking another sip of cider, Laurie glanced around the crowded fair. What if someone here was related to her, strolling among the stalls? It was, she knew, an incredibly fanciful notion; her mother might have been from Starr's Fall, according to Laurie's birth records, but she was most likely long gone. She'd only been eighteen when she'd had Laurie, after all.

And yet... Starr's Fall seemed like a place where people stayed. And Barb had said the name Lysander was a little familiar. Maybe there was a reason to hope that someone in her biological family might still be here, or at least that Laurie might find out what had happened to them. The internet searches she'd done had led to dead ends... No social media presence, no tidbits on the back pages of old newspapers, preserved in the nether reaches of the internet. She hadn't been able to find out anything at all about any Lysander in Starr's Fall... which was, at least in part, why she was here... if she could work up the courage to really start digging.

The other reason was the fact that Starr's Fall was really the only place she could ever call home, even before she'd ever been. It wasn't just the family connection, she'd decided, when she'd first looked up the town online, after finding out her mother's birthplace. It had been the place itself... Its air of shabby charm, dilapidated quaintness. Something about it had wrapped around her heart and squeezed. *This* was where she belonged... even if no one here realized it yet.

"Laurie, good to see you again! And Max, too." Jenna strolled up to the stall, grabbing a cup of cider and giving Barb a wave. Her hair was in the same long auburn braid it had been in before, and she wore a long patchwork skirt that nearly brushed the ground, matched with an old sweater that had holes in both elbows and a pair of purple Converse sneakers. Somehow, as before, the whole ensemble worked. "Zach's minding our stall for a bit so I can have a breather." She downed the cider in one gulp. "Have you seen much of Starr's Fall's biggest event of the year?" she asked with a thread of irony running through her voice.

"Not yet, but I'm hoping to find out what a cake walk is," Laurie replied. She took a bite of warm, sugary donut, her eyes widening at the explosion of sweetness in her mouth. Wow, those were *good*. A crumb dropped and Max snaffled it up, seeming to come to the same happy conclusion.

"Oh, our cake walk is famous," Jenna exclaimed. "We all make the same cakes every year, so you know which ones to go for."

"Really?" Laurie was intrigued. "Which ones?"

"Well, my Black Forest cake is pretty delicious, if I do say so myself," Jenna replied with a grin, "and Annie makes a mean Mississippi mud pie." She leaned in closer. "The one to avoid is Wendy Higgins' pound cake. It's as hard as a rock. Always the last one on the stand, poor sweetheart. She means well, she really does. Come on. I think they're starting soon, and you really don't want to miss it." She turned to Annie. "Coming with us?"

Annie glanced at her mother, who was now dozing in her chair. She gave Jenna an easy smile that didn't fool anyone. "Nah, I'll stay here. Leave Max with me, Laurie, to keep him out of trouble. The last thing I need is to eat cake." She patted her stomach while Jenna rolled her eyes.

"I'll bring you back some," she promised. "And Barb, too. She's always liked Liz Cranbury's coconut layer cake."

Leaving Max with Annie, Laurie set off with Jenna across the green, passing various stalls and booths along the way. It seemed that in addition to the plethora of artisanal goods for sale, every organization and community group of the town had a display out —the Scouts, the fire station, the Congregational church, the sewing circle, the running club, and more. For a town whose Main Street was seriously flagging, Laurie was heartened to see that there still seemed to be a lot going on.

The cake walk, as it turned out, was exactly that. A square had been marked out with rope on the grass, interspersed with circles about a foot in diameter, and everyone walked around while music played. When the music stopped, if you had landed on a circle, you got to pick out a cake. Laurie and Jenna gamely paid a dollar each to join the crowd of both excited children and wryly smiling adults who were set to walk around the square in the hopes of winning one of the cakes, of which there were several dozen. Judging by the sheer number, just about everyone who played would walk away with something, even if it was Wendy Higgins' rock-hard pound cake. Laurie wouldn't mind. It was, she reflected, just fun to be part of something.

Soon enough, the music started—John Denver's "Thank God I'm a Country Boy," and when it stopped, a little girl of about five was on the circle. She squealed in delight and picked out the biggest, gooiest chocolate cake on the stand.

"Mary Lee Tomlinson's triple chocolate fudge cake," Jenna remarked with a sigh. "Always the first one to go."

Laurie laughed and shook her head. "Do you know who made every single cake on that stand?"

Jenna looked at her seriously. "I've lived here all my life, bar a year or two in the big wide world. Of course I do."

"I can't even imagine that," Laurie admitted honestly. It was as much as she was willing to say about her childhood; she really wasn't going for the sympathy vote, it was all just so *alien*. Between the ages of four and fourteen she'd lived with seven different foster families, all over New Jersey. At least when she'd been fourteen things had finally settled down; teenagers were almost always put into group homes rather than placed with individual families, due to outcomes generally being more successful that way. A group home had provided stability—and kindness, in the form of Nadine—but it hadn't been a family. It hadn't really been a home.

But maybe Starr's Fall was, or at least it could be.

"Laurie, you're on the circle!" Jenna exclaimed. "You won a cake."

"Oh!" Laurie gazed down at her feet, right bang in the middle of the circle. She hadn't even realized.

"Congratulations," the woman running the stall said. She was tall and dark-haired, in her forties, dressed in a cashmere sweater and loose linen trousers. It was more of a glam look than most Starr's Fall residents had.

"That's Lizzy Harper," Jenna informed her. "She and her husband run the bakery The Rolling Pin. They moved here from Hartford a year ago with their two teenagers, Bella and Samuel."

"Oh, right..." She vaguely recalled hearing their names from the other night at Annie's.

"What cake would you like?" Lizzy asked.

Laurie scanned the offerings, having no idea what to choose. She would have asked for a recommendation from Jenna, but it seemed rude to do so now, considering every cake had most likely been baked by someone everybody knew. Then she remembered what Jenna had said about Barb.

"Coconut layer?" she asked hopefully, and Lizzy nodded in approval.

"Good choice."

Twenty minutes later, all the cakes had been taken and Jenna and Laurie were walking back to the Lyman Farm stall with not just a coconut layer cake, but a chocolate sheet cake as well.

"Everybody gets a cake in that game," Jenna confided as they strolled along in the sunshine. "I hate to admit it, but the whole thing is rigged, and has been for years. Lizzy didn't realize when she took it over last year, and nearly caused a *major* upset. This year, fortunately, she knows the score. Her husband is going to keep track of who is standing where to make sure everyone gets a cake."

"Well, that's fair," Laurie replied. "I guess the real winners are the ones who get to choose the cakes first."

"That's true," Jenna agreed. She hefted the sheet cake. "We didn't do badly, all things considered."

The rest of the afternoon passed in a haze of sunshine and conversation. Laurie couldn't keep track of all the people she chatted to, between browsing stalls, trying her first corn dog, which was disgustingly delicious, and drinking yet more cups of cider. By the time the sun was setting, with a nip entering the air, she felt exhausted yet happy. She'd given out all her flyers, and while some people had been more than a little skeptical about the idea of a dog bakery, other people had seemed interested, even enthusiastic. Overall, it had been a very good day.

She helped Annie pack up her stall and load everything, including the coconut layer cake, into the truck. Jenna had insisted on giving the chocolate sheet cake to Laurie, although she'd protested that she could never eat it all.

"*I* could, which is why I need to give it to you," Jenna replied. "Plus, Zach would eat the whole thing for breakfast and never gain an ounce, which would make me hate him, so you really need to take it."

Laughingly, Laurie had agreed. She hadn't met the mysterious Zach yet; he'd left early for another date. Clearly the man got around.

After saying goodbye to Annie and Jenna, she walked slowly back down the Main Street, watching the other groups of people trickle away—parents with sleepy children hoisted on shoulders, couples with their arms linked, gaggles of teens, giggling and pushing one another. At moments like this, it was hard not to feel a little lonely, despite the many pleasures of the day. She'd give just about anything, Laurie thought wistfully, to be walking home with someone, or to someone. A mother or father, brother or sister, or even just a friend who would call as she opened the door, *"Is that you, Laurie? How was it? Did you have fun?"*

She let out a short, sharp sigh, impatient with herself. She'd had just about the best day ever, and she was going to wish for more? Besides, she had a huge chocolate cake to herself and Max for company, plus the promise of a whole evening of something bingeworthy on Netflix, now she'd got the internet set up. What more could she possibly need?

She was just fumbling with her key, balancing the cake on one arm, when she noticed the light on above Reilly's Antiquarian Books. Had Joshua been home all day and not come to the festival? It had lasted the whole afternoon and been practically right on his doorstep.

Laurie glanced at the light spilling from the second floor of the bookstore, and then the huge cake in her hands. Then, squaring her shoulders, she marched across the street and knocked on the door.

8

He knew it was Laurie by her knock. Joshua didn't know *how* he knew, just that he did; he felt it in his bones. There was something about the sharpness of the raps without sounding demanding... a bit like Laurie herself. Determined and relentlessly cheerful.

And, he realized as he headed downstairs, he wasn't feeling the usual sullen sort of dread that he felt when someone knocked on his door, not that that happened all that often anymore. No, he was actually feeling...

Well, he didn't know what he was feeling, and he had no intention of examining it any more closely. He opened the front door, bracing his hand on the jamb as he gazed at Laurie standing there. She was wearing jeans and a flowy sort of top, Max at her feet, his leash looped around one wrist. Her hair was loose, falling about her shoulders in light brown waves, her eyes sparkling, and he could see freckles on her nose, like a spattering of gold dust.

Gold dust? Had he seriously just thought that?

"Yes?" he asked, sounding as terse as he usually did.

Laurie's smile didn't waver; rather, it widened. "As friendly as ever," she remarked. "I have cake."

"So I see."

"I can't possibly eat it by myself."

"Good thing it keeps."

She blew out an exasperated breath, amusement tugging at her mouth. "Are you being difficult, or just slow?"

He pondered this and realized he wasn't actually sure. "Maybe both?"

"I *wondered*," she said in the loud, deliberate tone of someone who clearly thought you were stupid, "if you'd like to share it with me."

Joshua blinked. All right, he *had* been slow, because he hadn't expected an actual invitation. Maybe an offer of a slice or two of cake, wrapped up in a napkin, a gesture of neighborliness that he would, with reluctant graciousness, accept. But to *share* it?

"Joshua?" Laurie prompted. "This cake is actually pretty heavy, and in a minute, it's going to be on the ground, which would be extraordinarily sad because Jenna Miller said it would definitely be delicious."

"I haven't even had dinner yet," he pointed out repressively, but Laurie was not deterred by his tone.

"Neither have I," she replied easily. "But I think there's enough here for dinner *and* dessert."

A laugh escaped him, an unruly sound that surprised them both. He was as embarrassed as if he'd let out a burp.

Laurie raised her eyebrows. "Well?"

To refuse would be to sink to a level of churlishness that even he wasn't comfortable with, Joshua realized, and the truth was—a truth he did not enjoy admitting even to himself—that he didn't want to refuse.

"All right," he said, opening the door wider, managing to still sound somewhat ungracious. "Come in."

Laurie hesitated. "Is Lea around? I don't want Max to spook her, or for her to spook him. Honestly, I do not understand the power dynamic between those two at all. I think there is some kind of love-hate thing going on. Do they hate to love each other, or love to hate each other? Maybe both?"

"Good question. I don't actually know where Lea is," Joshua replied. He did not, it had to be said, keep very close tabs on the contrary animal. "She keeps her own hours," he told Laurie. "But we can deal with that eventuality if and when it occurs."

"That sounds wise." She brushed past him with a scent he was starting to recognize, of vanilla and almond. He closed the door behind her and then led the way upstairs.

Fortunately, he'd tidied up a little more today. There were no dirty dishes in the sink, and the living room was devoid of its usual mess of half-drunk cups of coffee and old newspapers scattered about the keyboard and coffee table.

Laurie set the cake down, with great ceremony, on the kitchen table, while Max scooted underneath. "Ta da," she announced. "Margery Goldman's chocolate sheet cake. I'm told it's *very* good."

"It is," Joshua confirmed. "I remember from my own cake walk days."

Laurie's eyes narrowed and she planted her hands on her slender hips. "So you *have* gone to the Fall Festival."

He shrugged. "I told you, when I was a kid."

"And not since then? It was so much fun. I'd never done anything like that before."

"Well, you'll have plenty of opportunity in Starr's Fall. Every year, as it happens." Joshua took two forks out of a drawer and handed one to Laurie before going back for plates, only to realize they were all in the dishwasher. This was what happened when he tidied.

"Why bother with plates?" Laurie told him, clearly having assessed the situation. "We can just dig in."

They sat at the table, forks poised above the luscious rectangle of iced chocolate cake in front of them.

"Ready... set... go!" Laurie exclaimed, and then plunged her fork into the cake.

Another reluctant, rusty laugh escaped him as Joshua did the same. The cake was good—even better than he remembered, dense and damp and fudgy. Joshua chewed slowly, savoring the morsel while Max crouched at their feet, clearly hoping for crumbs.

"So," he said once he'd swallowed, "were there no fall festivals where you lived before?" He realized, quite suddenly, how little he knew about her. Basically, nothing.

"I'm sure there must've been," Laurie replied as she stabbed the cake for another bite, "but I didn't go to them."

"Where are you from?" The question felt strange, coming from him, because he was not known to be nosy. In fact, he usually tried to be the complete opposite. Keep yourself to yourself and he would do the same, was generally how he'd lived his life since coming back to Starr's Fall. Since Mia had left him, reminding him of all the good reasons not to get close to people. Not to want to.

"New Jersey," Laurie told him. "I was living in Trenton for the last few years, but I grew up all over—Montclair, Morristown, Elizabeth." She shrugged. "I stayed in Morristown for the longest, though."

There was something about the way she spoke that made it sound as if she'd moved around by herself, without any reference to parents or family—a free agent, even as a child, which surely couldn't be right.

"Why so much moving?" he asked mildly, taking another bite of cake. "Was it for your parents' jobs or something?"

"No." She paused, her chin propped in her hand, her lashes lowered, as she gazed at the cake. "I was raised in the foster system," she stated after a moment, her tone matter of fact. She glanced up at him, her expression resolutely equanimous. "I had a few different placements with families until I was fourteen, and then I went into an adolescent care home. That was in Morristown, so it ended up being the place where I was the longest, until I aged out."

For a second, Joshua had no idea what to say. *Raised* in the foster system? For her whole childhood? He'd heard about such things, he knew, but he'd never met someone who had experienced it, and he found he struggled to make sense of how that could have happened to someone like Laurie, who was so warm and approachable, even if he'd done a pretty good job of resisting her friendly overtures. How could she not have found a family to live with? To love her?

"Your family..." he finally said, his tone baffled, apologetic. He didn't even know what he was asking.

She shrugged and stabbed the cake again, with a little more force than before. "Don't really have one. My mother gave me up for adoption when I was born, and my father's name wasn't on my birth records."

"So you were adopted by someone—"

"Yes, but..." She hesitated and then admitted with a grimace, "It's not something I really like to talk about, to be honest. I don't want people feeling sorry for me, you know? And really, you can't miss what you never had, right?"

"Actually," Joshua replied quietly, the words slipping out before he could think better of them, "I think sometimes that what you never had is what you miss the most."

The words seemed to fall into the stillness and stay there. For several long seconds, neither of them spoke. Laurie stared at him, her mouth slightly agape, her eyes wide—and turning glassy. He shouldn't have said that, Joshua realized with a lurch of both regret and alarm. It might have sounded hugely insensitive and yet he'd meant it...

Then Laurie did what he'd seen her do the other day, that admirable and touching transformation from tearful to determined. Her mouth closed, her chin tilted up, and the corners of her mouth tipped up in a smile.

"You might be right," she agreed in a tone that didn't *quite* manage to sound breezy. "So, what did you never have that you miss the most?"

Ouch. He hadn't been expecting that zinger, although, all things considered, maybe he should have. And based on what she'd already shared, his sad little story didn't feel nearly as tragic and woe-is-me as he knew he sometimes felt it was.

Which was pretty humbling.

"A lot of things, I guess," he finally said, which was the worst hedge ever, and Laurie thought so too judging by the way she pressed her lips together, her eyes flashing briefly before her expression smoothed back into friendly interest. Still, it compelled him, against every instinct and desire, to say more. "My parents being around, I guess," he continued quickly. "I mean, I know I had them, so it's not missing something I *never* had... but I guess I miss what it could have been, but never was." He was sounding, Joshua feared, like a complete idiot.

"I'm sorry," Laurie told him quietly. "Losing your parents has to be so hard. Sometimes I almost feel lucky, that I don't have parents to miss. I mean, I wish I'd had parents, but because I didn't..." She trailed off, shaking her head. "Anyway. What about your parents? I think Annie told me your dad ran this bookstore?"

"And his father before him. The Reilly family has been in Starr's Fall for a century and a half. Newcomers, to some people." She gave a little snort of laughter and he found himself smiling. "I'm actually serious."

"I know, that's what makes it so funny."

And now they were both laughing, accompanied by self-conscious smiles, before they lapsed into a silence that didn't feel awkward *or* expectant, the way it had the other day. It just felt... nice. Companionable.

"Did you like growing up in Starr's Fall?" Laurie asked, and Joshua let himself consider the question honestly.

"I did," he said slowly. "At least, mostly. I think, as a teenager, though, it started to feel pretty small. If you can't drive, you can't get around anywhere. There are no buses here or anything and the nearest movie theater is half an hour away, and all the latest movies came there about six months after they were everywhere else. Not," he qualified quickly, "that watching movies was the most important thing or something. It's just... there wasn't always a lot to do. I had this plan to bust out of here as soon as I could." Looking back, he couldn't even remember why. Had it been the smallness of the town, or the expectation of his father, never spoken but always felt, that he would take over the store after him? The endless Saturday afternoons sitting at the counter, as customers came in, their faces falling when they realized Patrick wasn't the one at the cash register, with his pipe and the cardigan with leather patches on the elbows and the way he chatted so easily to everyone... except his own son.

"And did you?" Laurie asked, startling him out of his thoughts.

It was jolting, Joshua realized, to talk to someone who didn't know every in and out of his life story so well that they would correct him if they'd thought he misremembered something, or contradict him if they thought they knew better. Although, he suspected Laurie knew at least a little more than she was letting on, based on the fact that she'd mentioned talking to Annie Lyman, who knew everyone and everything in this town, and Laurie had been at the Fall Festival all afternoon, so she'd had to have received

an earful of gossip. Briefly, he wondered what people had said—
*such a shame, how quickly Laura went. Six weeks was it all took. Patrick
was never the same. And Joshua... so quiet! Loved his music but a bit of
an oddity, you know the type...*

Or maybe they wouldn't have said anything at all, besides the
fact that he was grumpy and liked to be left to himself. Three years
on, he'd more or less scared off everyone except for his aunt... and
now Laurie.

"I did," he replied slowly, his attention focused on acquiring
another forkful of cake. "Although not when I planned to. My mom
died when I was seventeen, senior year of high school. It derailed
my plans, although obviously that hardly mattered at the time."

He experienced a tightening in his throat that he hadn't felt in a
long time, when he thought of his mother—her quick laugh, her
light step on the stairs, the way she'd drawn him out of himself.
She'd been able to make him laugh, had teased him and he hadn't
minded. His relationship with his father had been entirely different. Joshua swallowed to ease the tightness in his throat. He didn't
normally get emotional about her anymore; it had been fourteen
years, after all.

"I'm so sorry," Laurie stated quietly. She put her fork down.
"That must have been really hard."

"It was." It was more than he usually admitted. He didn't talk
about this stuff, ever. He hadn't back then, either, and neither had
his dad. Beloved by the community, at home he'd been stoic, silent,
isolated in his grief, refusing to let Joshua share it. No one had been
allowed to miss Laura Reilly more than her husband, and so
Joshua hadn't even tried.

At seventeen, he'd been too old for hugs, too proud to ask for
the comfort and affection he'd secretly craved, even if he never,
ever would have admitted it. He and his dad had never had that
kind of relationship, anyway; the weight of expectation and disap-

pointment had been too heavy for both of them. Not, of course, that he was going to go into any of that with Laurie Ellis. He'd already said more—*way* more—than he usually did, and it was making him feel kind of grumpy. He didn't like this whole talk-about-yourself thing. There was nothing fun about *sharing*.

"So when *did* you leave Starr's Fall?" Laurie asked after a moment. "I mean, I know you returned awhile back, but..."

Yet more questions. All this conversation was definitely starting to make him feel twitchy. "When I was nineteen." He kept his tone matter of fact. "My mom died in November, right as I was doing my college applications. I ended up missing all the deadlines and so I applied the next year. Worked here and saved money and then moved to New York the following summer, for music school."

"Music school!" She looked impressed, her gaze flicking to the keyboard in the living room and then back again. "This might be a silly question, but are you a musician?"

Joshua smiled and shook his head. "No, I'm not. Not really, anyway. I try to compose, but I don't get very far these days." When Mia had left him, with her intensity and passion for music, the desire to compose had gone. The threads of music that had always run through his head had been snapped off, silent. It was only recently that he'd finally felt as if he could begin to put notes to paper again, and even then, it had felt like a lot of hard work, not the joyful release it had once been, but at least he was trying.

"So what kind of music do you compose?" Laurie asked, sounding intrigued.

"Oh, just bits and pieces." He shrugged, the movement intentionally dismissive. "Mainly for piano, sometimes for violin." Although not since Mia, star violinist, had left him. "Not that much anymore, frankly."

"Why not?"

"I don't know." He did know, but he really didn't feel like going into it. Joshua felt a sudden compulsion to stop talking about all this stuff. It made him feel itchy and restless, practically twitching with the need to shrug it all off—his parents' deaths, his lost dreams, Mia's rejection, being back in Starr's Fall because, at thirty-one years old, he was starting to fear he'd stalled out in life. "Anyway, that's probably enough grim stuff for now," he stated firmly. "I think we've eaten our main course in dessert. Maybe we should have our dessert be our main course?"

Laurie raised her eyebrows. "What do you suggest?"

"Nothing fancy. I can make us some pasta." The offer clearly surprised her as well as him; he couldn't remember the last person he'd made a meal for, even just a simple bowl of pasta. Mia, maybe, back in New York, something complicated to impress her, which he'd always had a compulsion to do, sensing how hard it would be to keep someone as ephemeral and ambitious as she was interested. Even before it had all gone sour, he'd never felt as if she thought he quite measured up to her, an up-and-coming violinist in the New York Philharmonic, someone who had played in London and Beijing, graduated top of her class at Juilliard, had reviews in the *New York Times* calling her "a prodigy" and "a marvel." No matter how much he'd had going for him, he didn't think it would have ever been enough for Mia.

But besides her...? Joshua tried to remember. He'd had friends, of course, from growing up here, even if he didn't see them much anymore. His best friend Will had moved to San Francisco for a job after college and Joshua hadn't seen him in years. His other high school friends had moved on, as well, over time; for the younger generation, Starr's Fall wasn't so much a place where you stayed as one you left... until you had to come back. And then stayed.

"Pasta would be great," Laurie replied with a shy smile that reminded Joshua—ridiculously—of the unfurling of a flower. He wasn't sure why he was being so nice, at least for him. He didn't know what it was about Laurie Ellis that made him want to make sure she didn't have to assemble her armor the way he'd seen her do—summoning that smile, lifting her chin, throwing her shoulders back. He realized he wanted her not to need to, with him.

"Great," he told her, and he rose from the table to go put some water on to boil.

* * *

Laurie watched Joshua move around the kitchen, filling a pot with water, banging it onto the stove. He wasn't looking at her, and she wondered if he at least half regretted his impromptu invitation. He'd looked as surprised as she must have, to have made it in the first place.

He was definitely acting grumpier than he had all evening, and she couldn't tell if it was because he didn't want her here, or just that it felt disconcerting. She suspected that, like her, Joshua simply wasn't used to having people over. Making dinner that was more than ramen-for-one in front of the TV or maybe, in his case, the keyboard. His musical aspirations were a part of him she hadn't realized before, and they rounded him out in a way that intrigued her. What had he given up, in coming back home when his father had taken sick? Would he ever tell her?

For the first time in their fledgling friendship, she thought that maybe he might. They'd both shared a lot tonight—and maybe that was what Joshua was regretting. But then again, maybe not.

She rose from the table, taking the half-eaten cake and forks to put by the sink while Max trotted behind her, clearly wanting to stick close. "Can I help?" she asked, and Joshua shrugged, his back to her.

"Set the table, maybe? Although all the dishes are in the dishwasher, which I haven't turned on, so..."

"Good thing there's such a thing as elbow grease."

She went to the dishwasher and opened it, taking out two dirt-encrusted plates. Joshua glanced at them with a grimace.

"Sorry..."

"I don't mind," she assured him. It felt weirdly companionable to be in the kitchen together, stepping around each other—as well as Max—while she went to the sink and Joshua rootled around for some vegetables to chop for the sauce. She was pretty sure neither of them was used to this kind of joint domesticity; she knew she certainly wasn't, anyway.

"So a pet store and bakery," Joshua said as he chopped an onion with brisk, precise movements. "What brought that about?"

Laurie let out a self-conscious laugh. "Well, it really started with Max." She glanced down at the little dog who had positioned himself by the fridge, his gaze darting between her and Joshua as if trying to assess the situation. Which she was too, in a way. "I got him from the Humane Society three years ago. He was in bad shape—he'd clearly been abused. Skinny, starving, cowering all the time..." Just the memory of how frightened and skeletal and *sad* Max had been compelled her to go over and give him a good scratch behind his ears.

"That's terrible," Joshua remarked quietly, and Laurie nodded as she straightened, giving Max one last pat, and then went back to the plates.

"It really was. I saw him in his pen and my heart just broke right in half." She paused, because what she'd felt—but wasn't ready to say right now—was that when she'd looked into Max's limpid, chocolate-brown eyes, she'd seen something of herself in them. The fear, the despair, the longing to hope, the terror to let yourself. It had all been there in Max's eyes, and it had all been in herself, even if she had put on a good front and always would. Not, of course, that she was ready to share that sort of stuff with Joshua Reilly.

"So, you went from rescuing Max to deciding to open a pet store... how?" Joshua slid her a smiling glance that reminded her just how handsome he was, or at least could be when he wasn't scowling. But then, he hadn't been scowling very much tonight, if at all.

And when he smiled... his eyes glinted as if they had bits of gold in them, and he revealed a dimple in one cheek that made him seem all the more approachable. Which was a dangerous way of thinking, Laurie knew, because it would be much more sensible to have Joshua as a friend, and not as a romantic interest.

She had enough to be worrying about, getting a business up and running without adding romance into the mix! Not, of course, that there was even any chance of that. Most likely, Joshua wasn't remotely thinking about her that way.

"Well," Laurie told him, launching into the story, "I first got the idea when I once saw a pet bakery in New York. I used to go into the city sometimes, on the train, just for a change," she explained as she dried the plates with a dishrag she'd found in a drawer. Sometimes she'd go in on a Saturday, wander around the Union Square Greenmarket, treat herself to a hot chocolate from the chocolatery Max Brenner's. "And I'll fully admit," she told Joshua, "it was the most ridiculous, ostentatious little place, exactly what you'd probably imagine. It wasn't just rawhide chews or healthy treats... it was all these little dog snacks decorated to look like fancy cupcakes and petits fours and things like that, as fancy as some Parisian bakery! And as for the *customers*..."

A gurgle of laughter escaped her just at the memory. "Well, they were probably exactly what you'd imagine them to be, as well. Elderly ladies dripping with jewelry and designer clothes, their little Chihuahuas with their diamond collars tucked into their

Prada purses... *Not*, of course, that there's anything wrong with Chihuahuas. Liz Cranbury has one and she seems very nice. And so does Frou-frou. The Chihuahua, that is. But..."

She paused, casting her gaze to the ceiling as she tried to verbalize how she'd felt in that moment, when she'd stumbled across that store. The lovely treats, the snooty storekeeper who had looked her and Max up and down, lips twisting into something close to a sneer. "It just seemed like the kind of place for that person, that dog," she said slowly. "And no one else. And they sort of made that clear, not in anything they said but the way they just *looked*..." Those pursed lips and the oh-so predictable side eye. Laurie had seen it plenty of times before—when she'd started school in secondhand clothes, without a backpack or lunchbox. When teachers had whispered *foster child*, as if she couldn't hear them and it explained everything. When parents came for school concerts and bake sales and gushed over their precious children, and she never had anyone come to anything. She glanced at Joshua, who was gazing at her, seeming rapt. "And that made me... sort of mad, I guess." She paused again to take a steadying breath, surprised at how *emotional* she was feeling about the reason for her little store.

She had never, she realized, explained her reasoning to anyone. It wasn't the kind of thing you could include in a business plan to a bank manager. Not like this, anyway. And yet here she was, telling Joshua Reilly all about it. "That place was certainly not for someone like me, or a dog like Max," she continued in a stronger voice. "And so I wanted to create a place that was for us, for *him*. That was special and niche and all the rest of it, but for everybody. For the people and the animals who don't normally get that kind of treatment." She let out a gusty breath, suspecting she'd talked too much. "And I love dogs," she finished. "That's the main reason, actually."

Joshua had been regarding her so very solemnly for the entirety of her impassioned speech, but now he cracked a small smile, his eyes glinting gold. "Well, that's the most important one, obviously."

Laurie let out a laugh that was tinged with relief that he seemed to get it, without making what she'd said a big deal, because toward the end of that speech her voice had started to wobble just a little bit, but maybe he hadn't noticed.

Then again, maybe he had.

"Do you like mushrooms?" Joshua asked as he turned back to the stove and tipped chopped onion into a pan sizzling with olive oil.

"Love them." Laurie set the plates in the drying rack. This was all starting to feel cozily normal... and she *liked* it. A lot. Time to give herself a mental shake. She turned to him with a brisk smile. "What else can I do to help?" she asked.

9

Laurie had been in Starr's Fall for just over two weeks when the sign went up over the store. Max's Place, written in a friendly red font, with a cartoon picture of a dog bowl and bone next to it. The last week she'd been flat out, getting the store ready for its grand opening at the end of the month, at Annie's insistence.

"Why wait?" she'd told Laurie when she'd dropped by one afternoon while Laurie had been having the cash register delivered. "There's no time like the present, and you can't work out the kinks until you have something going. Learning on the job is always better."

"Is that what you did?" Laurie had asked, and Annie had let out a huff of laughter.

"Yes, if you count when I was just a kid, learning how to manage a farm around the age of six. But since then..." She'd paused, her expression clouding briefly. "It was a steep learning curve, after my dad died, even with all that training. Nothing prepares you for jumping in and just doing it, so why dither? *That's* my point."

Laurie had decided her friend was right. There was no time like the present, and she had a business plan in place. There was no reason not to enact it, and in any case, her savings were steadily dwindling, so bringing in some income—*any* income—would be welcome. And so she'd had a week of rushing around, determined to get things done—shelving stock, finishing the design of the website, placing adverts in the local newspaper and online, and filling out myriad forms with the FDA to qualify for the bakery side of the business, which involved reams of red tape that she duly waded through.

All in all, it was exciting to get to this moment, when the sign was actually up. Over the last week, it had all started to feel a lot more real, but this felt the most real of all. Max's Place was a real place. A real thing. She could look up and see the words, the reality, right there.

"Looking good, Laurie."

She turned, Max in her arms, to see Joshua smiling at her from across the street, his hands thrust into the pockets of his worn jeans, which had the noticeable and pleasing effect of stretching his t-shirt across his impressive shoulders.

Laurie's heart did a silly little flutter at the sight of him. She hadn't seen him since their impromptu and enjoyable cake and pasta—in that order—a week ago, although she'd certainly looked out for him, hoping to run into him, say hello, maybe even chat for a little while. Hoping, or even half wondering, if *he* might stop by and say hello. Now he finally was, although he hadn't crossed the street. He stood on the curb, gazing up at the sign with a faint smile on his face.

"Thanks," she called back to him. "I was just thinking it's starting to feel real. A little scary, too."

He gave her that crooked quirk of a smile she was already starting to recognize. "Good scary, though?"

"Yes, definitely, good scary. Kind of like how Max views Lea."

He let out a huff of genuine amusement, which made her grin. When they'd had dinner last week, they'd spent the rest of the evening chatting about innocuous things, having both decided, by mutual, unspoken agreement, that they'd had enough of the heavy stuff. It was ten o'clock before Laurie finally stirred herself to go home, and when she went to find Max, who had managed to sneak away without her noticing, she discovered Lea royally perched on an armchair, with Max curled up underneath, looking, Laurie thought, like a supplicant to the throne.

"They seem to have reached a truce," Joshua had remarked, only for Max's little ears to perk up. He'd scrambled up and started barking at Lea, who had lazily swiped a paw toward him. Max had easily ducked it, but it had been enough to send him, chastened, back to Laurie, his head tucked between her ankles.

"Clearly it's a complicated relationship," she'd remarked wryly.

"With a dog and cat," Joshua had replied, "how can it not be?"

The whole evening had been enough to make her think, or at least hope, that she and Joshua were friends. At least, they were *becoming* friends, but then she hadn't seen him for a week and now she wondered why he wasn't even bothering to cross the street.

"So when's the grand opening?" Joshua asked, and now he did stroll across the street, which made her heart flutter *again*. She really needed to get herself under control.

"Saturday after next. Which I kind of can't believe I'm saying."

He nodded toward the storefront. "Looks like you're pretty ready to me."

Laurie glanced toward her little store, with its shelves of dog food, bowls, and leashes, the rattan baskets of toys and treats, the endearingly old-fashioned cash register on the newly polished mahogany counter. "Thanks," she told him, "but unfortunately there is still a lot of admin stuff to do, especially for the bakery part." She gave a wry grimace. "I think it would be easier to open a bakery for humans rather than dogs."

That earned her a small, slow smile. "Sounds about right."

"Anyway." Laurie found she had to look away from him, because she was afraid she was going to blush. "I'm sure I'll learn on the job. At least, I hope I will."

"That's the best way to learn, I find," Joshua replied. "When I had to come back here three years ago, I had to learn fast. And I did... on the job. It wouldn't have been the same, learning from a book."

It was an intriguing little glimpse into his life. "Even though you're selling books."

He gave a little laugh and then a nod. "Even though."

"Well, I've got the members of the Starr's Fall Business Association to help me," she remarked. "There's a meeting next week, after the opening—are you going?"

Joshua shook his head. "Nah." He left it at that, but it made Laurie wonder. He had a business in Starr's Fall. Why wouldn't he attend the meetings? Why had he decided to be such a hermit, as well as a Grinch? She suspected it had to do with coming back to Starr's Fall, and the life—and maybe the woman—he'd left back in New York City. She wondered if he'd ever tell her.

The workman who had been putting up the sign climbed down the ladder. "Look okay?" he asked Laurie, and she nodded.

"Perfect. Thanks!"

He smiled and gave her a thumbs up, and after saying goodbye, she turned back to talk to Joshua... only to find he'd gone back to his store.

Laurie tried—and failed—not to feel dejected, but she firmly pushed the feeling away. Joshua had to get back to work... and so did she. With a determined spring in her step, she headed back inside.

* * *

It was late afternoon when Laurie finally decided her back needed a break from bending and straightening as she continued to organize the store. Max was getting antsy, standing by the door and letting out the occasional woe-is-me whimper that had Laurie finally relenting.

"All right, all right," she told him. "We'll go for a walk."

She glanced around the store, feeling a sense of satisfaction at all the work she'd done, but also a tremor of trepidation for all that was still to come. And, more than that, she realized, was a sweep of loneliness that annoyed her, because why should she feel lonely now, when she was finally in a community that was welcoming her?

Maybe it was the presence of friends, Laurie reflected, that was making her realize afresh the lack of them before. She'd had *friends*, of course, of a kind—work colleagues she chatted to or went out with for the very occasional drink; some fellow students from her two years at college, although they'd all dispersed throughout the mid-Atlantic; a couple of girls from the care home days, although again, their paths had diverged fairly significantly. But all that aside, she hadn't had *real* friends. The kind of people you could be silly or weird with, who you could call up in the middle of the night, who you didn't mind seeing you ugly-cry. Those kinds of friends Laurie had never had, and she'd half-convinced herself they only existed in romcoms and chick-lit novels, but now she wondered... or at least, she hoped.

Maybe they were here in Starr's Fall.

And yet it was exactly that sense of hope that perversely brought the loneliness rushing in. She hadn't expected it, which made it harder to handle. Because it was in moments like this— when the sun was setting, spreading its long, golden rays over the town, and people were hurrying back to their homes, lights coming on in houses and curtains being drawn—that Laurie was forced to acknowledge she didn't know Annie or Jenna or anyone well enough yet to call them and ask them over for a meal, or even just to chat. She didn't think Annie would mind if she did, but she still didn't feel comfortable doing it. And who else was there?

Admittedly, she had knocked on Joshua's door, in a moment of reckless impulse, but the following week of *not* seeing him and the ensuing two minutes of chitchat hardly constituted a meaningful friendship. *Keep showing up*, Laurie told herself as she pulled Max along. *Just keep showing up*.

But sometimes, she thought, she wanted someone to show up for *her*.

She'd meandered down a side street off the green that she hadn't gone down before, filled with gracious Colonial and Federal-style homes, some of which looked like they'd seen better days a decade or more ago, others that were in better shape.

In front of a distinguished but somewhat dilapidated house, a woman, white-haired and elegantly dressed, was walking slowly with the help of a cane. As Laurie walked by, the woman carefully mounted the sagging steps to the house. Laurie hesitated for a second, because the steps were steep and looked half-rotting, and the woman seemed—not quite frail, no, but a little unsteady on her feet.

She managed the first three steps and Max, impatient, tugged on his leash. Laurie turned back to him and started walking again, only to hear an awful, almighty clatter and then a short scream.

She whirled around, her heart seeming to go into free fall at the sight of the woman collapsed at the bottom of the steps.

"Oh, miss! Miss!" Laurie hurried to her and knelt down on the sidewalk. "Are you all right? I can call 911—" Panicked, she fumbled for her phone.

The woman was lying at an awkward angle, her tweed skirt rucked up about her bony knees, her thick lisle stocking dirty and torn. She blinked Laurie into focus and then intoned in arctic tones of great asperity, "Do not call any kind of emergency service, thank you very much. I am perfectly fine." She started to move, and then winced.

"Wait," Laurie implored. "You might have broken something." The woman had to be in her eighties at least and was as slender as a twig, the points of her wrists and collarbones jutting out sharply, her skin seeming paper-thin. Her bones might snap just as easily as if she really was made of twigs, Laurie feared.

"I assure you," the woman replied with stiff dignity. "I have not broken anything." She paused before continuing as if it cost her something, "But if you could help me to my feet, I would greatly appreciate it."

"Of course." Laurie looped Max's leash around the steps' railing before turning back to the woman. She didn't *think* the woman had broken anything, but what if she'd had some sort of spinal injury and moving her made it worse? That was the last thing Laurie wanted to do, and yet it was clear the woman was going to move herself whether Laurie helped her or not. Already she was attempting, laboriously and with obvious pain, to get onto her hands and knees. "Wait," Laurie said again. "Wait, let me help you."

Carefully, not wanting to hurt her any further, Laurie put one hand beneath the woman's elbow and another around her waist. She felt fragile beneath her hands, her bones as light and hollow as a bird's. If she hadn't broken anything, Laurie thought, it would be a miracle.

Somehow, with a wish and a prayer, she managed to get her to standing.

"My cane, if you please," the woman asked, holding out one

hand in a manner that was decidedly imperious yet somehow without seeming rude.

Laurie fetched the cane, which was lying on the sidewalk. From his impromptu prison, tied to the railing, Max whined.

"What an unusual little dog," the woman remarked, and, with her cane in hand, she took a step—and then staggered. Laurie lunged forward, steadying her with a hand to her elbow.

"Let me walk you inside," she suggested. "If you don't mind. It would make me feel better, at least."

The woman looked as if she minded very much, but after a second's hesitation she gave a regal nod.

"Very well."

Step by painstaking step, Laurie managed to help the woman up the house's dilapidated steps, to the front door. By the time they reached it, the woman was leaning heavily against her, and her face, underneath its liberal application of powder, had gone very pale. Laurie knew there was no way she could simply leave her there.

"Your key," she asked gently, and the woman gestured feebly to the impressive and ancient handbag of crocodile-patterned leather dangling from one thin wrist. As carefully as she could, Laurie took the bag from the woman and, feeling a little like a snoop, riffled through it for the key. She glimpsed a lace-edged handkerchief, an ancient-looking checkbook, and then, thankfully, the key. From the bottom of the steps, Max whined again, clearly alarmed that his mistress was leaving him.

"I just need to sit down for a moment," the woman murmured. "If you don't mind... Bring your dog, if you like..." Her voice trailed away as she sagged against Laurie, who had a panicky suspicion that she might have fainted.

Somehow, while half-holding the woman, Laurie managed to unlock the door and push it open, ushering the woman, who had roused herself enough to stumble along, into a dark hallway that looked a bit like something off a set for Miss Havisham's house—ancient wallpaper decorated with cabbage roses that was, in certain places, peeling off in long strips; heavy, dark furniture that cluttered the hallway, and a few frowning oil paintings of people from a century ago or more.

She helped the woman through a set of double doors inset with frosted, beveled glass, into a drawing room that was elegantly furnished, but just as fusty and dusty as the hall. Gently, she sat the woman on a slightly moth-eaten velveteen loveseat with elaborately carved legs and arms, before hurrying back outside to collect a mournful Max. He tucked his head so firmly between her ankles that Laurie had to pry him out and into her arms before she headed back inside.

"Sorry, Max," she whispered. "But right now, someone needs me more than you do." Which was a novel thought.

Feeling equal parts curious and apprehensive, Laurie headed back inside.

10

Back in the house, the woman had roused herself and was now sitting upright, her ankles neatly crossed, her expression so imperious that Laurie faltered slightly as she came into the room.

"Sorry..." she began for no good reason, except the ferocity of the expression on the woman's face.

"Thank you," the woman said in a tone that was equal parts frosty and gracious, "for assisting me. I have been meaning to get those steps repaired for some time." She spoke in a way that made Laurie feel as if she should leave, and yet something compelled her to stay. Maybe it was the fact that this house seemed so empty and abandoned, even with the two of them standing right in it. Maybe it was that she suspected that the woman's frosty demeanor hid a loneliness as deep and pervasive as her own. Everyone, Laurie supposed, had their own kind of mask. Or maybe it was just because she was curious... and, it had to be said, feeling a little lonely herself.

In any case, she stayed.

"May I get you something?" she asked. "A drink of water, or a cup of tea?"

The woman opened her mouth and Laurie braced herself for a firm, and maybe even cutting, refusal, only to have her close it, give a brief nod, and then say stiffly, "A cup of tea would be very welcome. Thank you. The kitchen is at the back of the house." She paused, and then gave a regal nod towards Max, who was pressed against Laurie's chest. "You may leave the dog here, if you like."

Laurie had a feeling Max *wouldn't* like, never mind how she felt about it, but again she had a sense of something hidden behind the woman's cool self-possession, and she set Max gently on the floor and looped his leash around one of the intricately carved legs of the sofa. Hopefully he wouldn't pee on the floor in his agitation. He had been known to do so, on more than one unfortunate occasion.

Max whimpered as Laurie started to leave the room, but when she glanced behind her she saw the woman was slowly, with careful, and clearly arthritic, movements, bending down to fondle his ears with her gnarled, beringed fingers. Max, after a panicky second, submitted happily to the caress, and Laurie went in search of the kitchen.

The kitchen was in as derelict a state as the rest of the house, with appliances that looked to be from the 1950s, and some *very* questionable wiring. At some point in time, someone had more or less chopped a hole in the wall to hook up a dishwasher, and a fistful of black wires were dangling from the hacked-open space.

Laurie took a deep breath, let it out, and then started opening various cabinet doors to look for tea. She found it a few minutes later—a few desiccated-looking teabags in the bottom of a ceramic pot in the shape of a Toby jug. The kettle was a dented copper one that looked as if it had been through the wars, and when Laurie turned on the gas for the ancient stove, she braced herself for an imminent explosion.

Fortunately, none was forthcoming, and she managed to boil water and make a cup of tea without mishap. She added a cube of sugar—wasn't sugar good for shock?—but no milk, because when she opened the fridge, it was empty save for a thin wedge of hardened cheddar and half a tomato that had shriveled to a quarter of its size.

At the sight of those two items in the empty expanse of the wheezing fridge, Laurie's heart gave a painful little twist. How was this woman, whoever she was, surviving? And how could Laurie help her?

Realizing she'd been gone awhile by that point, Laurie hurried back to the living room, stopping short when she saw the woman sitting on the loveseat, with Max nestled comfortably in her lap.

"He obviously likes you!" Laurie exclaimed as she came forward with the cup of tea. Max didn't cuddle up to just anyone.

The woman smiled faintly. "I don't believe I have introduced myself. My name is Henrietta Starr."

Laurie nearly dropped the cup of tea she was holding. *This* was Henrietta Starr, the grand matriarch of Starr's Fall? The way Annie and Jenna had described her, Laurie had pictured a woman dripping in jewels and designer clothes, living in a grand mansion with an army of servants. Admittedly, this house might have once been grand, but it hadn't been for a long time, and there clearly wasn't a servant in sight. The Starrs must have fallen on hard times at some point.

"I'm Laurie Ellis," she said after that second's startled pause. "I just moved to Starr's Fall." She put the cup of tea on a table by the sofa and then gingerly sat opposite her, in a spindly chair that looked as if it had had a battle with woodworm and not quite emerged the victor.

"I am very pleased to meet you, especially considering the circumstances." Henrietta Starr spoke as if she was meeting Laurie at a formal ball. Now that she thought about it, Laurie could believe she *was* the matriarch of Starr's Fall. No matter how hard the times she might have fallen on, Henrietta Starr was clearly a woman of great class and style... and she knew it.

"Are you feeling better?" Laurie asked.

Henrietta brushed the question aside with an imperious sweep of her hand. "Tell me, young lady, why have you moved to Starr's Fall?"

"To open a pet store," Laurie replied, to which she received the eloquent response of a single arched eyebrow.

"You might be opening such an establishment," Henrietta stated after a moment, "but that does not explain why you chose to move to Starr's Fall."

Which brought Laurie up short, because it was a perceptive observation, as well as a revealing one. She could have opened a pet store anywhere—back in New Jersey, in any of the towns where she'd grown up and spent at least a little time. How had Henrietta Starr realized so quickly and astutely that there was another, deeper and more important reason to move to Starr's Fall?

Laurie swallowed. She looked around the room in all its faded, peeling glory, and then back at Henrietta Starr, who was gazing at her with a shrewd expression, and she decided to tell the truth. "I came to Starr's Fall," she admitted quietly, her voice trembling a little, "to find my mother." If she was brave enough to actually start looking.

Henrietta's pale blue eyes widened only slightly before she asked, her voice raspy, "Has she gotten lost?"

And for some contrary and unfathomable reason, that question made tears fill Laurie's eyes before she hurriedly blinked them back and sat a little straighter. "I think I'm the one who was lost, maybe," she replied. She'd meant to sound lightly wry and had failed miserably. "My mother gave me up for adoption when I was born. But she gave Starr's Fall as the place of her residence. That, a name, and an age is all I have of her."

Henrietta was sitting very still, her gaze transfixed on Laurie. "And what, if I may be so bold as to ask," she commanded, "is her name?"

Laurie took a deep breath, let it out slowly. "Helen Lysander."

"Lysander…" Unlike either Annie or her mother, who had both considered the name for a few seconds, at least, Henrietta shook her head very firmly. "There has never been a family by the name of Lysander in Starr's Fall."

Laurie opened her mouth, then closed it. From the old lady's lap, Max perked his ears, looking alarmed, no doubt sensing her mood. "But there must be," she finally said. "Since she put it down." She decided to be polite and not point out that Henrietta Starr, no matter her eponymous name, could not know every single family in Starr's Fall, a town of over a thousand people.

"No." If anything, Henrietta sounded even firmer. "There is not."

"But twenty-six years ago…?" Laurie pressed, feeling a bit desperate as well as annoyed. Why did she have to sound so *certain*?

"My dear, I have lived in this town all my life, save for two unfortunate and wonderful years when I lived in New York City. There are no Lysanders in Starr's Fall. Never have been." The words *and never will be* seemed to hang in the air.

"Then why would she have put Starr's Fall down?" Laurie burst out. She sounded angry when what she really felt was afraid. What if she could never find out anything about her mother? She'd been depending on learning *something*, no matter how small, from the fact of her name.

Henrietta was silent for a long moment as she stroked Max, who, traitor that Laurie was now thinking him to be, curled up all the more in the old lady's lap.

"Either your biological mother lied on your adoption record

about her own place of birth," Henrietta stated finally, "or she lied about her name." Her faint smile was tinged with sympathy as she added, "I know which one I think would be more likely."

Laurie sat back in the chair, which creaked alarmingly underneath her. "Can you even do that?" she asked. "Lie on an official document? A record of birth?" Surely not.

"I believe it is frowned upon," Henrietta replied dryly. "As well as potentially illegal. But can you? Yes." Once again, she sounded frustratingly certain. How could she possibly know for sure? Of course, a quick search on the internet would give Laurie the answer she needed, but she wasn't about to whip out her phone right now. It had never even occurred to her that her mother's name might be false. She didn't know why it upset her to think that it might be, only that it did. A lot. And she, rather suddenly, wanted to be alone so she could think about why.

"You seem to be feeling better," she remarked, summoning a smile even though she felt closer to tears. "I should probably leave you in peace."

She rose from the chair and went to scoop up Max from Henrietta's lap. He came with some resistance, which made everything worse. Why had Max bonded with this woman so suddenly? He was more at home in Starr's Fall than she was, Laurie thought bitterly, knowing she was being entirely unreasonable and yet feeling it anyway.

"My dear, I fear I might have upset you, with my observation," Henrietta remarked as Laurie set Max on the ground, looping his leash around her wrist. "These things are very emotional, aren't they? Were you hoping to find your biological mother here in Starr's Fall?" Although her tone was kindly, it suggested a certain amount of disbelief that Laurie could have considered something so unlikely, after so much time.

"I don't know about finding her," Laurie replied stiltedly. "But

learning more about her, yes." Which would, she realized, be virtu-
ally impossible if her mother had given a false name. Yet even that
wasn't what really upset her, she knew. She could handle a chal-
lenge. She certainly had before.

"I do hope you'll visit me again," Henrietta said. "Along with
your dear little dog. What did you say his name was?"

"Max. And I will visit you, if you'd like me to." Any annoyance
she'd felt at Henrietta Starr for wrecking her fledgling dreams was
mitigated by the obvious fact that the woman was old and lonely,
moldering away in this ancient and decrepit house. It wasn't her
fault for pointing out what should have been obvious, and really, it
had been a help. At least now Laurie didn't need to track down all
the Lysanders in Starr's Fall, since it seemed there weren't any.
She'd still check the town records but, based on how little she'd
found on the internet, she doubted there would be anything. There
was a reason, she realized, why she hadn't been able to dig up
anything online about a Helen Lysander of Starr's Fall... because
she might not even exist.

After saying another farewell, Laurie headed outside. The sun
had sunk behind the trees and the sky was violet, the first stars just
starting to glimmer on the horizon. She walked slowly, Max trotting behind her, feeling a heaviness inside her that she couldn't
shift, and she wasn't even sure she wanted to.

What was the point of being Pollyanna-positive, if she wasn't
even going to be able to find out anything about her mother? Didn't
even know how to begin? She'd reached a dead end before she'd
even begun, and while that was certainly depressing, what was
worse was the realization that her mother couldn't have *wanted* to
be found. Couldn't have wanted her daughter ever to find her.

That was what was upsetting her so much now. She'd done her
best to keep herself from embroidering the inevitable fantasies of
any adopted kid, that their biological parents had been tragically

separated from them at birth and had been looking for their long-lost child all their lives. She'd even prepared herself—or so she'd thought—that her birth mother might have distinctly ambivalent feelings about her existence. She'd accepted that she might not find her, or her mother might not want contact, at least not at first, but she hadn't taken into account that she might never get anywhere at all.

Laurie's steps slowed as she came to Max's Place. The sign was up, the shelves were stocked, the brass cash register gleaming from a coat of polish. Upstairs, her cozy little apartment—admittedly with a decided lack of furniture—waited for her. She even had a chicken chili bubbling away in a crockpot she'd found at the Goodwill store on the edge of town ready for her dinner. Normally, all of that would be enough for her to head cheerfully home, but tonight it wasn't. Just like after the Fall Festival, she felt as if an empty wind was whistling right through her. She didn't want to be alone.

Instinctively she glanced at Reilly's Antiquarian Books across the street. The store was closed, the windows above lightless. It looked like Joshua wasn't home, and in any case, she didn't feel as confident as she wished she was to march over there and check.

What she should do, Laurie told herself, is go home, eat dinner, feed Max, spend an hour or two wrestling with the wretched FDA forms, and then read a book and go to bed. That all sounded sensible, even enjoyable to some degree... and right then she simply couldn't do any of it.

She came to a stop right there on the sidewalk, so Max sat down, let out a whimper, and then tucked his head between her ankles. Laurie sighed.

"Come on, Max," she said as she gently nudged him out from her ankles. "Let's go home."

Just then the loud beep of a car horn had Laurie nearly

jumping out of her skin. A beat-up station wagon slowed on the street, and Jenna poked her head out of the window.

"Hey, Laurie!"

"Hi." Laurie pressed her hand to her chest, her heart still beating hard from the surprise.

"Sorry, did I startle you?" Jenna asked with a laugh. Her auburn hair was in its usual long braid, her freckled face screwed up into a wide smile. "Sign looks great," she said with a nod towards Max's Place. "Not long now, I guess, right?"

"Right." Laurie let out a little laugh. "A fact which makes me feel pretty nervous."

"It's going to be great," Jenna assured her. "Have you had dinner? I was just going to order something from the diner if you want to join me?"

"Actually, I've made some chicken chili in my crockpot, and it should be ready just about now." She hesitated and then added a bit recklessly, because she didn't know Jenna as well as she did Annie, "Do you want to join me?"

Jenna's answer was as easy and open as everything else about her. "If you have enough, sure, that would be great! I'll just park."

So she didn't have to be alone, after all. The optimism that had taken a serious beating earlier came back in close to full force. Life really was good. She could deal with this setback and what it meant. She wouldn't let it defeat her.

Laurie waited by her front door while Jenna parked her car on the street, and then came strolling to her, keys in hand. She was wearing another one of her usual funky ensembles—this time a pair of wide-legged jeans in a brown and white zebra pattern and a dark green cardigan with leather buttons that looked like it should be worn by a grandad, thrown over a faded rock band t-shirt.

"I haven't been in your apartment yet," Jenna told her. "I bet it's really cute."

"It's really bare," Laurie confessed. "I haven't done too much on the furniture front."

"Do you need furniture?" Jenna asked as Laurie unlocked the door and led her inside. "Because we've got a barn full of antiques behind the store that we haven't gotten round to throwing out. They're not real antiques, like actually valuable ones. Just a lot of old furniture, basically."

"Don't you want it yourself?"

"Absolutely not," Jenna replied firmly. "The house is already full of stuff. My parents were collectors. You'll have to come over sometime, and you can take whatever you want."

"Well... okay," Laurie replied on an uncertain laugh. She wasn't sure whether Jenna was really being serious; it was certainly a generous offer. "Thanks."

Jenna waved her thanks aside. "Honestly, you'd be doing me a favor."

As they stepped inside the apartment, Laurie set Max down and went to the kitchen to check on the chili, and Jenna ambled around, unabashedly snooping, not that there was much to see. She really didn't have much furniture, so maybe she would take Jenna up on her offer.

"So has your family been in Starr's Fall for centuries, too?" she asked as she got out plates. Jenna opened a cabinet door and took out two glasses, setting the table alongside Laurie with a natural ease.

"Nope. My parents are transplants, which means maybe my great-great-grandchildren will be accepted as residents, but I doubt it. Not," she clarified quickly, "that I plan on having children."

Laurie recalled Jenna's comment about not waiting around for Mr. Right and wondered what hard history lay behind that comment. "Where did your parents move from?" she asked.

"Boston. They did the whole big city grind and then decided to up sticks and come out here. Took over the old general store, which was *seriously* struggling, and kept it going. And then I took it over from them four years ago."

"Have they retired?" Laurie asked, vaguely remembering Annie saying something about this, and Jenna confirmed this with a nod.

"Living their best lives on the Gulf Coast of Florida. Golf," she stated succinctly, "has become their obsession. Not sure I understand it, but..." She shrugged.

"And what about Zach?"

"Zach?" Jenna let out a huff of laughter. "Well, Zach and I technically co-run the store, but I definitely do more work than he does." She was smiling as she said this, in a way that suggested she wasn't entirely serious.

"Is he out on another date?" Laurie asked teasingly. She had yet to meet or even glimpse the notorious Zach.

"Probably. Although he must surely be running out of women in all of northwestern Connecticut, if not the entire state." She paused, her expression turning thoughtful, even sad. "The truth is, Zach needs to find a good woman or give up. I've already given up." She softened this statement with a breezy smile. "Anyway. This chili smells delicious."

"Thanks." Laurie started doling it out. "Do you know anything about Henrietta Starr?" she asked a little abruptly, although she'd meant to sound casual.

"Henrietta Starr!" Jenna sounded completely bemused. "Why are you asking about her?"

"I met her earlier today."

"You did?" They both sat at the table with heaping plates of chili. "I thought she was kind of a recluse and had been for years. Decades."

"She might be," Laurie allowed. "But I guess she has to leave the house to shop and stuff like that."

Jenna shrugged. "I assumed she had a housekeeper or something to do that."

Laurie thought of the empty fridge, the decrepit house. "I don't think so."

"Well, I don't know much about her at all. The Starrs founded the town, hence the name. The fall is the waterfall on Lambert Hill above the town—have you done that hike? It's really pretty, especially this time of year. But as for Henrietta... I know she never married or had children, and she lived in New York City for a little while but came back a long time ago. And that's about it." She shrugged. "She used to give out ribbons at the festival or appear at the Veterans' Day parade and stuff like that, but she hasn't since I was a little kid. To be honest, I think most people have forgotten she exists."

Laurie pictured Henrietta Starr sitting on that motheaten sofa, looking both regal and lonely. She'd left in a hurry, because she'd been upset, but it was ridiculous to let such a remark keep her from seeing her again... especially when she understood all too well how she suspected Henrietta felt.

Henrietta Starr seemed as if she could use a friend... and so could Laurie.

"Yes," she told Jenna with a small, sad smile. "I think most people probably have."

11

———————

"Joshua, why are you staring out the window?"

Joshua tensed at the sound of his Aunt Maureen's voice, her tone both curious and demanding. Sixty-five years old, widowed and nosy, she liked to have a minute-by-minute account of his life, and he did his utmost not to give it to her.

"It's the opening of that pet store across the street today," he replied, turning around. "Max's Place."

"Oh, yes." Maureen wrinkled her nose. "Wasn't it started by some woman from New York?"

"Trenton, actually."

Correcting his aunt was clearly a mistake because her eyebrows rose toward her hairline. "And how do you know she's from Trenton?" she demanded.

Joshua suppressed a sigh. "Because we chatted once," he admitted, knowing his aunt would make a meal of it, wanting to know when, where, what they talked about, maybe even what he'd been wearing. Or what Laurie had been. Basically, everything.

"You *chatted*?" Improbably, his aunt's eyebrows inched even higher. "When? Where? What is she like?"

"Just after she moved in, at her store, and she's fine." He kept his responses as brief as possible, to discourage any further questions, and far worse, any potential speculation. Since things had ended with Mia when he'd moved back to Starr's Fall, his aunt had been desperate to set him up with some worthy Starr's Fall female —or really, *any* Starr's Fall female—and so far, he'd managed to avoid any kind of introductions, but the threat was always looming.

"Fine?" Maureen repeated, sounding pleased. "Oh, my."

Clearly, he should have said Laurie *wasn't* fine. If he'd been smart, he would have told his aunt that Laurie Ellis was the most unpleasant person he'd ever come across, or maybe just the most boring, but that would have maligned her character, and Joshua knew he couldn't do that.

Firstly, because Laurie didn't deserve such treatment, and secondly, because the truth was, he actually *liked* her. As a person, that was, not as anything... *romantic*. He'd sworn off romance three years ago, after his engagement had gasped its way to a slow death, to the point that the woman who had worn his ring had felt it sufficient to break up with him by text, although admittedly he should have seen the warning signs loud and clear before then and stopped trying so darn hard.

In any case, just the fact that he liked Laurie would be enough to send wedding bells clanging through his aunt's head.

"Anyway, aren't you taking Lea?" he asked his aunt. It was the reason why she was here, at nine o'clock on a Saturday morning. The imperious and unfathomable Leamhachán was finally going home. Joshua wouldn't miss her... much, anyway.

"Yes, yes..." Maureen, who had been standing at his sink, doing his breakfast dishes much to his shame, glanced around the apartment. "Where is she?"

Joshua shrugged. "I have no idea." As he hadn't had for the

three weeks he'd had the wretched beast. Lea was a law unto herself.

Frowning, Maureen peeled off her yellow rubber gloves and headed toward the living room. "Lea..." she called, her voice turning soft and cajoling as she clucked her tongue. "Lea, my little marshmallow..."

Shoving his hands into the pockets of his jeans, Joshua only just managed not to roll his eyes.

"Ah!" His aunt gave a crow of delight. "*There* she is. How perfect. Now I'll have to go over and introduce myself."

"Wait—what?" Joshua started forward, only to glimpse Lea leap nimbly onto the windowsill of Laurie's apartment and disappear through the open window.

His aunt was already heading downstairs.

"Aunt Maureen," he called, half in exasperation, half in alarm. "Do you have to? Laurie's probably really busy right now—"

Maureen was already halfway across the street by that time, and Joshua felt he had no choice but to follow her. If he couldn't mitigate any awkwardness, he could at least assess its damage. But, he acknowledged as Maureen headed toward Max's Place like a ship in full sail, he really hoped he could do some serious mitigating.

"Hell-*o*!" His aunt's voice, a booming trill, could be heard all the way down the street. Joshua winced as he took in Laurie's uncertain smile and his aunt's speculative, narrow-eyed gaze.

"Hi..." Laurie began just as Joshua joined his aunt on the sidewalk.

"Laurie, hi," he chimed in quickly. "This is my aunt, Maureen Patterson. Aunt Maureen, Laurie Ellis, owner of Max's Place."

"Of course!" Laurie's hesitant smile became a full-wattage beam. "How was Alaska?"

"You knew I was in Alaska?" Maureen shot Joshua a noticeably significant look and he suppressed a groan. Damage control definitely needed to happen... and fast.

"I might have mentioned it," he told his aunt. "This isn't the first time Lea's gone exploring."

"Lea's here?" Laurie surmised with a laugh. "Honestly, I'm not sure whether she wants to cuddle Max or kill him."

"Probably both," Joshua replied. Kind of like how he felt about his aunt sometimes, including right now, although he was veering toward the latter. "She went in through your window upstairs."

"You're welcome to come in and find her," Laurie replied as she stepped aside to let them enter. "Sorry for the mess. I realized this morning there were about a thousand last-minute things to do before I open in..." She checked her watch with a grimace. "One hour."

"Isn't that always the way," Maureen agreed. "But what a cute little store! I love it." She widened her eyes as if she'd only just that very second had the most wonderful idea. "Joshua, why don't you help Laurie get ready for her grand opening? I'll grab Lea and be on my way."

His aunt could matchmake on the moon by herself, Joshua thought in exasperation. And what was worse was she did it so *obviously*. A smile was lurking in Laurie's eyes, playing about her mouth. Clearly, she found the whole thing funny, which was better, he supposed, than her finding it awkward and embarrassing.

As he was... except, he realized with some surprise, he *wasn't*. He was... not quite enjoying this, but something close to it. How novel. How *strange*. "Sure, I can help out," he told Laurie. "What do you need doing?"

"Oh... well..." She blew a strand of hair away from her eyes. "There are a bunch of cat toys that came in yesterday that I forgot to put price tags on." She gestured to a box by the cash register. "You could do that. The pricing tag gun is on the counter." She turned to Maureen. "I'll show you upstairs if you want to look for Lea."

"Wonderful," Maureen replied, a decided gleam in her eyes. Inwardly, Joshua braced himself for whatever came next. He couldn't exactly offer to go upstairs as well, but he feared his aunt would be remarkably unsubtle in her grilling of Laurie as a potential niece-in-law.

As they headed upstairs, he reached for the box of cat toys Laurie had indicated and the pricing tag gun. He was putting a price on a squeaky rubber mouse when he heard his aunt's voice float down the stairs.

"So are you single, dear? How long have you known Joshua?"

Wow. Maureen was taking the art of not being subtle to dizzying heights—or really, plunging depths. Hopefully Laurie would take it in her stride and realize his aunt's attitude was not indicative of his own.

Except... wasn't it? At least a little bit? The thought had Joshua go still, pricing gun in hand as he stared blankly into space. *Was* he interested in Laurie that way? He'd certainly been thinking about her a lot lately. Had been aware of her presence even more, even when they weren't together. The number of times he'd glanced across the street to see her moving about her little store and thought about ambling over...

Except he wasn't sure he was an ambling kind of guy, the sort of person who dropped in for a chat, a cup of coffee or a glass of wine...

In any case, thinking about someone didn't necessarily mean he wanted to wade into the dating pool again, did it? Three years on from his breakup with Mia, he wasn't feeling hurt anymore, just weary, because it took so much emotional effort to invest in a relationship, and after his dad's death, he just didn't know if he had it in him. Too much risk, maybe, for too little reward... right?

"Joshua, you have to come up here," Laurie called down the stairs, her voice full of laughter. "You've *got* to see this."

With deepening apprehension as well as curiosity, Joshua headed upstairs. Neither his aunt nor Laurie were in the kitchen or living room, so he headed up to the bedroom, where they'd found Lea before. Sure enough, Laurie and Maureen were standing in the doorway of her bedroom, laughing and shaking their heads. As Joshua stepped into the room, he saw why.

Lea and Max were cuddled up together in the middle of the bed, like the proverbial peas in the pod. Joshua let out an incredulous laugh. Max was snuggled in close to Lea, and the cat had one velvety paw laid possessively over him, her plumed tail fanned over them both like a blanket.

"It must be love," Maureen trilled, and then, to top it off, gave both him and Laurie a significant look.

Enough already, Joshua decided. The cat-and-dog thing was cute, but he didn't need Maureen making any more inferences than she already had.

"Well, glad you found Lea," he said in the firm sort of tone that implied his aunt should be leaving *now*.

Maureen gave him a saintly smile. "Isn't it wonderful? I'll leave you two to it." Another meaningful look that made Joshua almost choke. Then, finally, *thankfully*, Maureen took Lea and headed back downstairs. Without meaning to, Joshua glanced at Laurie, who gave him a teasing look back. At least she was still finding this funny.

They followed Maureen down the stairs, and as his aunt left the store, Joshua picked up the pricing gun once more. "Sorry about that," he felt compelled to say. "My aunt means well, but she can be a little much."

"Well, she's not subtle," Laurie replied with a laugh. "I think she was about to inform me of your bank balance and the state of your teeth."

A laugh erupted out of him, and he shook his head. "And how much is in my 401(k), probably."

Laurie raised her eyebrows. "You have a 401(k)?"

"No," Joshua admitted, and Laurie let out a laugh that sounded like a bell pealing, merry and infectious. He found himself grinning back at her.

"Well, she obviously loves you very much," Laurie remarked as she headed back to the stockroom to bring out another box of merchandise. "And she wants you to be happy."

"Yeah." Joshua stuck a price tag on a floppy rubber fish. "I think she feels a little guilty though, too," he found himself saying, which surprised him, because he didn't usually talk about this stuff. There was something about Laurie that made him feel like being honest. Maybe it was because she was so honest and open herself.

"Guilty?" Laurie frowned. "Why?"

He shrugged. "She wasn't around when I was a kid. When my mother got sick and died, Aunt Maureen was in Germany. She married an army guy, and she didn't come back to Starr's Fall until after he'd died. I think she feels like she should have been here, back then, because it was... hard." Which was something of an understatement, but he was pretty sure Laurie understood that.

She was slowly unloading colorful dog leashes from a box and hanging them on an antique coat stand, which was, Joshua decided, a quirky but fun look. "I'd assumed she'd spent her whole life in Starr's Fall," she admitted. "Like just about everybody else in this town."

"She was born here, but she couldn't wait to get away, or so my dad said. She's his sister."

"So she's making up for it now?" Laurie surmised.

"If you call her trying to set me up with every eligible female in Starr's Fall making up for it."

Laurie pretend-pouted, one hand pressed to her chest. "And here I thought I was special."

To his chagrin, Joshua found himself flushing. "Nope," he half-muttered, turning back to the box of cat toys, which he saw was empty. "Afraid not."

A silence descended upon them which didn't feel quite as companionable as other ones had. It had been his instinct to back off, because that's what he did, but maybe it shouldn't have been… especially if he did feel about Laurie the way he thought he was starting to.

"All done with the cat toys," he said into the silence. "Where do they go?"

"I'll get a basket." She went back to the stockroom and returned with a rattan basket; the shelves lining the walls were full of them, each one holding a different type of toy, another quirky, cheerful aspect to the little store.

As Joshua looked around properly, he saw just how cozy and welcoming it looked—the colorful braided rug on the floor, a big, squashy armchair in the corner by the window with a coffee table holding a selection of books about training your puppy or understanding your cat's behavior. With the leashes hanging from a coat stand, and a pick 'n' mix stand for different dog and cat treats, the place had the look of a country store crossed with a living room. It was, he decided, a nice vibe, laid back and welcoming, with that endearing bit of quirk.

"You've done a really good job here," he told her. "This place looks… inviting. If I had a pet, I'd want to hang out here."

"Would you?" Laurie beamed. "Because that's what I want. That's why I called it Max's Place. I don't just want it to be a store, but a meeting point for the community. I know that probably sounds a little sappy, but—"

"It doesn't sound sappy," Joshua interjected quietly. He could understand why Laurie would want to create such an environment. She was, he realized as he looked around the store once more, making a home out of a store. Out of an idea. The kind of home she probably had never had. "I think you've done a really good job," he repeated firmly. "This place is going to take off."

"You could do something similar," Laurie blurted.

Joshua, in the process of emptying the cat toys into the basket, stilled. "What?" he asked, a little stupidly, because he suspected he knew what she meant even as he found he couldn't fathom it.

"With Reilly's Antiquarian Books," she explained. "That place is crying out for a major refurb. It's got so much possibility, with those big windows and all that space... You could do so much with it. Armchairs tucked in corners, tables with the latest books or personally recommended reads, even a little café or bakery in the corner? Or, if you didn't want to go to that much trouble, just have a little cart and offer free coffee and tea. Donations accepted, of course. Maybe even bring your keyboard down, or find a piano... You could have a music thing going too..." She smiled, inviting him to share the dream, but Joshua felt himself recoiling.

"No," he said shortly, as he shoved the basket onto the shelf. "I don't think so." His tone was firm, repressive, but Laurie was too wound up to take the hint.

"Why not? You could do so much with it, it could be such a neat place for people to—"

"I specialize in antiquarian books," he cut her off in the same terse tone. "Most of my orders are from people with very specific interests from far away. It's more of a mail service than anything else."

She stared at him, her nose crinkling, her eyes becoming shadowed with confusion. "But it doesn't have to be that," she pointed out.

No, it didn't. And once upon a time, it hadn't been. It might not have had the armchairs or free coffee or even the keyboard that Laurie had been suggesting, but it had been a meeting point for the town, a hub of conversation and community, just as Max's Place undoubtedly would be.

And Reilly's Antiquarian Books would not. It would not, he thought, be a place to live out his dreams.

"It works for here, but not for my store," he stated as firmly as he could. "What else needs doing?"

Laurie stared at him for a moment, her forehead crinkled, her eyes narrowed thoughtfully. "This conversation isn't over," she told him in a warning voice. "I'm going to ask about it again. But not half an hour before my grand opening." She looked around the store. "I have some lemonade I made upstairs that I was going to serve—"

"I'll get it." He turned toward the hall, needing a break from Laurie's assessing stare. He felt like he'd revealed something without meaning to, and it annoyed and aggrieved him in equal measure. This was what happened when you started letting people close. They got to *know* you.

And he wasn't sure he was ready for that.

He found several pitchers of homemade lemonade in the fridge, and as he came downstairs, he heard a loud peal of laughter that he suspected belonged to Annie Lyman. She must have stopped by, and he braced himself for more speculation.

"Joshua Reilly, as I live and breathe!" Annie exclaimed with a wicked glint in her eye as he came into the store bearing lemonade. "Well, well, well."

"Hello, Annie," he replied as he set the lemonade on the counter, hating how stiff he sounded. "How are you?"

"I'm fine, but the bigger question is how are *you*?" Her eyes gleamed and her smile was all too knowing.

"Fine," he answered a little shortly. Enough with the speculation already. Unfortunately, his reply had the effect of plunging them all into an uneasy silence. Way to kill the mood.

"Annie, these muffins look fantastic," Laurie finally said, nodding to the tray of muffins Annie had brought. "What are the flavors?"

"Double chocolate, lemon, banana, and raspberry and white chocolate," Annie replied. "From The Rolling Pin. They're scrumptious, and I figured you could offer them with your lemonade."

"You're too kind," Laurie murmured. She glanced at her watch. "Twenty minutes to go! How does everything look?"

"Absolutely amazing. You've got this, girl." Annie clapped a hand on Laurie's shoulder, hard enough to make her stagger slightly.

Joshua decided this might be a good time for him to go. He made a show of glancing at his own watch, belatedly realizing he wasn't actually wearing one. "I should probably make a move..."

He didn't miss the flash of disappointment across Laurie's face before she rallied with a smile. "Thanks so much for helping me out, Joshua..."

"You're going?" Annie's voice rang out in disbelief. "Right as Laurie is about to have her grand opening? That's too grumpy even for you, Joshua Reilly. You're staying." Annie's tone brooked absolutely no argument, but to soften the blow, she held out the tray she'd brought. "Have a muffin."

12

A small crowd was already forming as Laurie went to open the front door to Max's Place and officially flip the old-fashioned sign she'd bought from "closed" to "open." As she did so, a cheer went up, and her heart felt like a balloon in her chest, floating toward the sky. She recognized only a few of the faces, but everyone was smiling and looking supportive.

Then she glanced at Joshua, who was hanging back, his arms folded. He'd refused Annie's offer of a muffin, and he wasn't smiling.

Laurie's heart sank a little before she pushed the feeling away. Things had clearly become a little too awkward between them, and she wasn't sure why—had it been his aunt's relentless matchmaking, or Annie's obvious interest, or her suggestion that he refurbish his store? Maybe all three... or something else entirely?

She didn't know, but she intended to find out... just not right now.

"Welcome to Max's Place," she called out merrily. "Please do come in!"

As townspeople started streaming into the store, Laurie knew she no longer had the headspace to think about what was going on with Joshua. All around her, people were chatting, exclaiming, asking questions. The muffins were already almost gone, and half a jug of lemonade had been poured out into glasses by Annie. She should have brought in more refreshments...

"These are so cute," Liz Cranbury, holding Frou-frou in her arms, exclaimed, turning to Laurie with a squeaky pink mouse. "And made of sustainable fibers, too." She smiled wryly. "Although Frou-frou might rip it to pieces in seconds."

Laurie barely had a chance to reply before the questions started coming thick and fast—were the toys safe for cats? (Yes.) Were the dog treats organic? (Some of them, yes.) Did she carry extendable leads? (Yes, but they weren't recommended for all types of dog.)

At some point, Michael and Lizzy Harper arrived with another tray of muffins as well as one of croissants, and the lemonade was replaced by jugs of Lyman Orchards' apple cider that Annie had brought. Laurie realized she should have employed someone to help her; she ended up spending most of her time behind the counter, operating the cash register, when she'd wanted to be out circulating among the good people of Starr's Fall, most of whom seemed to have turned up for the opening of her little store.

Max's Place, Laurie decided two hours in, much to her amazement and joy, was turning out to be something of a success. At least on its first day... but hopefully it was a harbinger of things to come.

By noon, the original furor had died down and most people, having wished Laurie well, had gone on their way. Annie had gone back to see to her mother, promising to bring her later, and at some point in all the busyness, Joshua had slipped out without Laurie noticing. She could hardly blame him; for someone who seemed to spend most of his time alone, being in a small space with a good portion of the town's population had to have been challenging. Still, she felt an uncomfortable prickling of unease when she thought of how their last conversation had ended. Everything had seemed so companionable... until it hadn't.

Still, she didn't have time to dwell on it, because soon enough she had another couple of customers come in—a family with two children who wanted to see puppies, but were happy enough with Max. Her little dog had coped admirably with the crowds, and wagged his tail and sat obediently as he was petted and fondled over and over again.

"This place is so cute," the children's mother enthused as her three-year-old sat sprawled on the floor in front of Max.

"Thank you," Laurie replied as she glanced around the store with pride. It did look nice, just as Joshua had said. And there she was, thinking about him again. She turned back to the woman. "Have you got a pet?"

"Besides these two, you mean?" the woman joked. "Not yet, but we're thinking about a puppy, or maybe a rescue dog. Apparently the Connecticut Humane Society has been overrun lately, which is so sad."

"It really is." Laurie's heart ached for all the dogs who were in need of a loving home—lost souls like her, who only wanted a family to belong to. At least the Connecticut Humane Society was a no-kill shelter, but it still made her sad, to think of dogs in kennels who longed to be in proper homes. Basically it was how she'd grown up, which was why she felt so strongly about it all. "Well, when you do get a dog," Laurie told the woman, "let me know and I'll put together a 'Welcome Home' package with all the necessities, as well as a few treats." It was an idea she'd just thought of, but she liked the sound of it, and the woman's face brightened.

"Oh, would you? That would be amazing." She glanced at her husband, who had been leafing through one of the puppy-training books. "Maybe we should visit the Humane Society sooner rather than later."

Half an hour later, after they'd gone, Annie came by with Barb, who, Laurie saw with a lurch, was looking frailer than even a few weeks ago. Her alarm must have shown in her face because Annie gave a little sorrowful grimace as she helped her mom to sit in the armchair.

"Isn't Laurie's place amazing, Mom? Or really, I should say Max's Place. I wish I'd brought George to have a sniff around now, but I'll bring him another time."

"It's so good to see you, Barb," Laurie said, coming forward to touch the older woman gently on the shoulder. "May I get you a drink? A cup of apple cider or tea?"

Barb glanced up at her, her forehead crinkling, her eyes clouded with confusion. "I don't know..."

Laurie glanced at Annie for instruction, and for a second her friend looked despairing, her face collapsed in sadness. Then she rallied and gave Laurie a bracing smile. "I'm sure Mom would love a cup of tea. Milky and not too hot, if you don't mind. I can manage down here if you like."

"Great." Laurie shot her a quick smile in return before heading upstairs. Despite the joys of the day, her heart felt heavy as she made Barb a cup of tea. She couldn't imagine how hard it had to be for Annie, to be managing a farm by herself as well as taking care of her beloved mother, when her health was so clearly and swiftly failing. Maybe it really was better that she hadn't had those kinds of people in her life. At least she'd never had anyone to lose.

For some reason, this made her think of Joshua... *again*. Did he hide away from life for the same reason? To keep from being hurt by people he'd come to love?

"Better to have loved and lost than never loved at all," Laurie murmured softly. She didn't know whether that was true or not, but she wouldn't mind at least having a chance to find out.

She headed downstairs with the cup of tea, only to find Barb had dozed off in the armchair and Annie was looking near to tears.

"Sorry," she said with a sniff as she wiped her sleeve across her eyes. "I really don't mean to rain on your parade today."

"You're not," Laurie assured her. She put down the cup of tea to give her friend a slightly clumsy hug, which Annie returned before wiping her eyes again.

"The thing that's hard," she said with an audible tremor in her voice, "is that it's only going to get worse. There's *nothing* to look forward to." Her voice broke and she drew a quick, clogged breath. "And I know Mom is scared about that, too. She doesn't say as much, but I see it in her eyes..." She trailed off, biting her lip to keep from breaking down.

"Oh, Annie." Laurie had no idea how to comfort her friend. What comfort was there, besides standing in solidarity and agreeing that it was hard, it was *terrible*? "I'm so sorry," she said. "Your mom is so wonderful. And she always will be, no matter what happens."

Annie nodded, her eyes bright with tears, her expression resolute. "Yes," she agreed. "She will be."

By late afternoon, the store was empty save for Laurie and Max, and the weather had turned, reminding Laurie that it was almost October, the sky slate-gray with the occasional spattering of rain against the storefront. Laurie had kept the door propped open for most of the day but when a gust of chilly wind blew through along with a few damp leaves, she decided to close it.

"Looks like we might close for the day, Max," she told her dog, who was curled up in his dog bed by the cash register, snoozing gently. All the excitement had clearly tired him out. She decided to tidy up the refreshments and straighten the merchandise, as well as restock a few of the rattan baskets. She'd done a brisk business in chew toys.

By the time she'd finished, it was close to five o'clock, and Laurie supposed there was no good reason to stay open any longer; no one had come in for nearly an hour. Yet for some reason, the thought of flipping the sign to closed made her feel a little sad, a little lonely. It had been an amazing day, and yet now that it was at an end, she came bumping up against the unrelenting fact that she still wanted something more.

Or, really, not so much *something* more as someone.

Maybe even someone in particular...

No, she decided, she couldn't think like that. Not yet, anyway, and especially not after the abrupt way things had ended between her and Joshua this morning. She went to the door and was about to flip over the sign when an imperious voice had her stilling.

"I hope, young lady, that you are not intending to close this store of yours the very moment I have arrived?"

Laurie turned to see Henrietta Starr walking slowly down the street with the help of a cane, as regal as ever. She had her ancient handbag looped over one wrist and her snow-white hair was covered with an old-fashioned rain bonnet.

"Miss Starr!" Laurie exclaimed. "I'm so glad to see you." She'd been meaning to visit Henrietta again, but what with all the things that had needed doing with Max's Place, she hadn't found the time. "Please come in."

She held the door open as Henrietta Starr walked slowly and painstakingly in. She stopped in the middle of the store to slowly inspect it, her narrowed gaze so assessing that Laurie felt the need to brace herself for the verdict.

"What a charming establishment," Henrietta finally remarked.

With gnarled fingers that trembled a little, she undid her rain bonnet. "It has a great deal of character."

"Thank you," Laurie replied. "May I take that?" She held her hand out for the bonnet. "And your coat, if you'd like? Would you like a cup of tea?"

Henrietta's lips twitched in the approximation of a smile, her pale blue eyes glinting with shrewd humor. "It is not at every establishment in this town that I'm offered a beverage, but yes, I will accept. Thank you."

"Come, sit down," Laurie invited. She took Henrietta's rain things and helped her to the armchair while Max raised his head from his basket to regard them with sleepy interest. "How have you been?" she asked.

Henrietta gave her another pointed yet humor-filled glance. "My dear, I am ninety-one years old. How do you suppose I've been?"

Laurie wasn't sure how she was meant to respond to that, so she settled for a smile and murmured, "I'll get you some tea." She hurried upstairs to boil the kettle, marveling that Henrietta had made it all the way to her store. She hadn't even told her when the grand opening was and hadn't remotely expected her to show up. It made her feel quite affectionate and even protective toward the old lady, although Laurie doubted Henrietta would appreciate either sentiment.

Back downstairs, Henrietta was sitting up very straight in the armchair, her hands resting on top of her cane as she continued to inspect the store. Max, Laurie saw, had come over to lie beneath the old woman's feet, his chin resting on her right ankle. Laurie couldn't tell if Henrietta noticed or not.

"As you might have already deduced, I do not have a pet," she announced as Laurie put the cup of tea on the table next to her. "And I am in no position to care for one."

"No," she agreed in a commiserating tone. "Lots of people aren't. But you can still enjoy animals, I think. There are community centers that offer pet therapies—afternoons visiting with a dog, for example..." She trailed off because Henrietta was looking at her as if she'd grown another head. "If you wanted," she finished with a small, apologetic smile. It looked very much like Henrietta *didn't* want.

"I am not aware of any such *programs*," Henrietta replied with asperity, "and I assure you, I am in no need of some kind of *pet therapy*." She made a little moue of distaste before glancing down at Max, whose head still rested on her foot. Her expression softened slightly. "This little one is quite enough interaction with a pet for me."

"He really has taken a liking to you," Laurie replied with a smile. "And that's saying something, because he's normally pretty shy."

"Well, perhaps he senses a kindred spirit," Henrietta replied. Her tone was wry, but Laurie thought she heard a trace of sadness behind it and wondered at it. Henrietta Starr seemed neither timid nor shy to her, but who knew what she'd been like as a girl or a young woman?

"I've been thinking," Henrietta announced after a moment, "about our last visit."

Their *only* visit, but Laurie wasn't about to point it out. "Oh?" she asked cautiously.

"About the suggestion I made that your biological mother might have used a false name."

Laurie did her best not to wince in memory. What with the store, she hadn't had the head—or heart—space to think too much about her biological mother and her potential—*probable*—name change. Now it all came rushing to the fore—the knowledge, the disappointment, the sadness, the fear that she'd never find anything out about her mother at all. How could she, if she'd used a fake name? But worse than that was the growing certainty that her mother hadn't wanted to be found... and maybe still didn't.

"I think," Henrietta continued when Laurie hadn't spoken— because she really had no idea what to say—"that I might have spoken out of turn."

Laurie blinked at her. "You mean... you think my mother might not have changed her name?"

"No," Henrietta replied gently, "not that. But I think she could have had good reasons to have changed her name... reasons you shouldn't necessarily judge her for. Reasons that might not be what you think they are or have the effect you think they do."

That felt like a lot to untangle. "I haven't thought about the reasons very much," she admitted. "Beyond her not wanting to be found... by anyone." *By me*, was what she really meant, but wasn't willing to say.

"Well, it might not be as simple as that," Henrietta replied after a moment, her lips pursed. "What someone feels in the moment... the decision they make at the time, under pressure or out of fear..." She paused. "It might not reflect how they feel later, for the rest of their lives. Which," she added with a touch of wry humor, "can be a very long time."

Laurie smiled in acknowledgment, but her mind was racing. Henrietta almost sounded as if... as if she was speaking from experience. As if *she'd* made a similar decision, once upon a very long time ago. Yet there was no way, Laurie felt, she could ask such a personal and invasive question.

And yet...

"You sound like you know what you're talking about..." she ventured uncertainly.

Henrietta was silent for a long moment. One gnarled hand rested on the knob of her cane as she reached down to give Max a few gentle strokes. "Yes," she finally said, quietly. "I do." They both lapsed into a thoughtful silence then; Laurie struggled with what to say, what to ask. She was still deliberating when Henrietta began getting to her feet. "I should go," she announced, "before it gets dark."

"Oh..." Laurie gazed at her in apprehension. "Do you want me to walk you back? It's such a long way..." It was only ten minutes, but still. It would take Henrietta twice that time, or more.

"Certainly not," Henrietta replied with her usual sharpness. "I am not, despite assumptions and appearances, that decrepit. But perhaps you will visit me one day... with this little one?" She glanced down at Max with a smile.

"Of course!" She really should have visited her sooner, Laurie thought with a rush of guilt. "I could come one afternoon this week...?" Even if it meant closing the store for an hour or two. She'd be glad to do it.

"I am quite certain I will be at home," Henrietta replied, as imperious as ever, but with the hint of a smile lurking about her mouth and eyes. "Good day."

Laurie hurried to fetch her coat and rain bonnet, which Henrietta tied with great ceremony, and then went to open the door of the store for her. She held it as Henrietta walked slowly and regally out, and then down the street, until the oncoming twilight and the drizzling rain swallowed her up.

Well. Laurie let out a gusty sigh as she flipped the sign on the door to closed with something like relief. Her mind was whirling after that visit, but at least she wasn't feeling quite as lonely anymore. Her mind was too full for that.

And yet... as well-meaning as Henrietta Starr had been, did it really change anything? Laurie stood there, staring into space while Max sniffed about her ankles as she considered the implications of what Henrietta had said. Her mother might have regretted her anonymity with the passing of years, but... it didn't mean she could be found.

And if she couldn't be found... what was Laurie even doing here? Why had she come to Starr's Fall at all?

No. She wasn't going to give in to that gloomy kind of thinking. Not now, and not ever, if she could help it. With a sigh, Laurie turned toward the stairs, Max trotting next to her, her faithful friend. She'd make some dinner, Laurie decided, and add up the receipts to see how much she'd made today, and let that knowledge buoy her spirits. More importantly, she'd let it be enough.

With a spring in her step, she took the pile of vendor receipts she'd stacked next to the cash register and started for the hallway to the upstairs.

She'd just reached the first step when she heard a rapping on the door, a tentative *rat-a-tat-tat* that sounded like a question.

She turned back to the store, and then through the rain-spattered glass she spied Joshua standing there, holding a pizza box.

13

He felt stupid. The look of blatant shock on Laurie's face as she came to unlock the door made Joshua wonder what on earth he'd been thinking, showing up here unannounced with a whole pizza, extra-large. He didn't even know if she *liked* pizza. But then, he reminded himself, she'd showed up at his door with cake. Surely it wasn't *too* off piste, although admittedly it was for him, and Laurie must know that.

Then, as she opened the door, the look of surprise morphed into one of obvious pleasure. The smile she gave him had to be genuine, making her eyes sparkle. "You brought pizza!" she exclaimed, sounding so happy about it that suddenly Joshua didn't feel stupid at all.

"I thought you might be hungry after your big day." He sounded gruff, but only because he felt happy too, and his instinct was to hide that unsettling emotion.

"I'm starving," she admitted. "Come upstairs. That is..." For a second, uncertainty flashed across her face. "If you want to share it with me?"

"I'm not so altruistic as to bring a pizza over and not have any," Joshua replied wryly, and Laurie smiled in relief. He knew why she sounded so unsure; after he'd shut down the idea of refurbishing the bookstore, and then attempted to beat a hasty retreat, and *then* left the opening without saying a word to her... well, if he were in her shoes, he'd be feeling hesitant, too.

But this was an attempt to make up for all that if he could.

"The opening seemed to go really well," he remarked as he followed her upstairs, Max trotting so closely behind him that he almost tripped over the little dog.

"It did," Laurie confirmed. "The people of Starr's Fall showed up in a way I really hadn't expected, considering I've only been here for a few weeks." She went to the kitchen cabinet for plates while Joshua put the pizza box on the table, Max tangling around his ankles as he sniffed hopefully.

"Sorry, Max's favorite place to be is between someone's feet," Laurie explained with a laugh. She scooped up the dog in one hand and put the plates on the table with the other. "That smells absolutely delicious. I didn't even know there was a pizza place in Starr's Fall."

Which had Joshua admitting a bit abashedly, "There isn't. I had to go to Torrington."

"Torrington!" She stared at him, dumbfounded, for a second, before her eyes got all shiny and for a heart-stopping second, he thought she was going to cry. Over *pizza*.

"I hope you like pepperoni," he said into the silence, because he had no idea why she'd become so seemingly upset.

"Sorry." Laurie blinked and then, with a wobbly laugh, wiped her eyes before she set Max back down. "You must think I'm a complete basket case, which maybe I am. It's just... that was so nice of you."

Which was not what Joshua had expected her to say. "It... it wasn't that much trouble," he assured her. A forty-minute round trip drive, but who was counting?

"Maybe not, but... well." She grimaced, seeming embarrassed. "I guess I'm just not all that used to people doing nice things for me. Which I don't like admitting, but..." She shrugged. "Thank you."

"You're welcome." He didn't want her to feel embarrassed for not having people in her life who would do things like this for her. Heaven knew, he was the same, and he didn't have the background she did, the lack of family and support.

The reason *he* didn't have those people in his life, Joshua knew, was because after Mia had left him, he'd chosen to cut them out. But now, for the first time in three years, he felt like letting them back in... and he knew that was thanks to Laurie. "Let's dig in," he told her with a smile, "before it gets any colder!" He flipped open the lid of the box. "I think it's all right, though, but you didn't say whether you liked pepperoni or not."

"I *love* pepperoni," Laurie assured him with a grin, and Joshua found himself smiling back. All right, he really didn't feel stupid anymore. He felt as if he'd done exactly the right thing in coming over tonight... and he was very glad that he had.

"So, were you happy with the sales today?" he asked once they had large, gooey slices on their plates and were digging in.

"I haven't totaled up the amount, but judging from the merchandise I had to restock, I'd say yes." She gave a rueful little grimace. "I know every day won't be like this one, but it felt like a very good start."

"And once you get the bakery part fully going, it will be even better," Joshua replied, which had Laurie laughing.

"I know you're not convinced about the bakery part," she exclaimed, wagging a finger at him. "But you will be."

"I look forward to it."

For a second, their gazes locked, and the moment spun out in a way that made Joshua's heart give a funny little flutter. He really wanted, he realized, to kiss her. As his gaze arrowed in on her lips, he saw she had a speck of tomato sauce at the corner of her mouth. And before he could overthink it, or even think at all, he found himself leaning forward and raising his hand to wipe it away.

Laurie's breath hitched audibly, and her eyes widened as his thumb gently swiped her lower lip. Her blue-green gaze stayed trained on his and the moment, which had already felt expectant, became positively charged. Joshua felt himself lean forward a little more. Laurie did, too.

Unfortunately, it wasn't enough for them to actually kiss—they had a whole table with a large pizza on it between them. But before Joshua could consider the mechanics of the thing, Laurie jerked back and then rose from the table, spinning away as she headed for the sink.

"Drink?" she asked, her voice pitched a little high and strained. "I only have water or milk, I'm afraid."

Joshua sat back in his chair, his stomach plunging with disappointment—and dread. Had he just made things unbearably awkward between them? He really hoped not. Maybe he should have just lunged over the pizza and kissed her, messy as that might have been.

"Water's fine," he managed in a mostly normal voice. "Thanks."

They were both silent as Laurie filled two glasses at the sink and then brought them back to the table. As she sat down, Joshua saw a faint flush pinken her cheeks, but beyond that she didn't seem distressed or uncomfortable, so that was something, he supposed.

Still, he felt pretty crushingly disappointed—he really should have just gone for it. Next time, Joshua decided, he would.

"So we didn't get to finish that conversation this morning," Laurie remarked in a surprisingly steely tone. "About your store."

Okay, time for a major subject change, it seemed. "What about it?" Joshua asked warily.

She shrugged as she took a sip of water. "Well, I know it seemed like a no-go area for discussion for you, so you might just tell me to drop it, but... why don't you want to change it? I mean, you've chosen to stay in Starr's Fall and run the store when I'm assuming you could have sold up and gone back to New York. Right?" Her gaze was clear and open and all too penetrating.

Joshua took a sip of his own water, mainly to stall for time. "Yes," he admitted finally as he set his glass down. "I suppose I could have done that." Except there hadn't been much to go back for—no job, no apartment, no Mia.

"So if you chose to stay," Laurie resumed, "why not make the most of it? Make it the best it can be?"

There were a lot of complicated answers to that question, Joshua reflected, none of which he liked thinking about, much less explaining to someone else. And yet... he couldn't shake the feeling that Laurie deserved his honesty. She'd been so honest herself, after all, in so many ways.

"A few reasons, I guess," he finally said, struggling not to fidget in his seat like a little kid. "None of which reflect all that well on me, to be honest."

Laurie propped her elbows on the table, her pizza momentarily forgotten. "Let me be the judge of that," she told him with a small, crooked smile.

"All right," he agreed, finding, to his surprise, that he was actually leaning into this whole honesty thing. He was *tired* of the lonely life he'd chosen. Being grumpy and isolated had been his default setting out of stupid self-protection, but that didn't mean that he couldn't change. At least, he could try. "Well." He placed his hands flat on the table as he organized his thoughts. Where to begin? How much to say?

All of it, some treacherous little voice whispered inside him. Well, maybe not all, but most. "The bookstore wasn't always the way it is now," he began to explain. "When my dad ran it, it was a little bit like you were describing. There wasn't coffee on tap or chairs to sit in, but it was a place people came to browse, chat, that kind of thing. My dad loved it. Everyone asked him for recommendations; he was always hunting out books for people... It was absolutely his thing."

"It sounds like it was a wonderful place," Laurie replied after a moment, when he'd trailed off into silence. "But I feel like there's some kind of 'but' coming."

Joshua shrugged. "I don't know if there is or not. When my dad had a stroke and I came back... well, I closed up the store to look after him, and so people got in the habit of it not being there, I guess. And then after he'd died, I decided to take it over... There wasn't much waiting for me back in New York, and I knew it would have broken my father's heart if I'd sold it. Although, to tell you the truth, I'm not sure there would have been any buyers. But... I knew I could never be like him. I didn't have it in me. And so... I decided not to try." That was definitely an abbreviated version, but at least it was a start.

"I can understand that," Laurie said quietly. "I've done the same, at various points in my life."

"Have you?" He heard the complete skepticism in his voice. "From where I'm standing, it looks like you've done the opposite. Coming to Starr's Fall... Starting over...? That's a whole lot of trying."

"Well, I haven't lived my whole life that way," Laurie confessed with a small smile. "But I didn't mean to hijack this conversation

and start talking about me. You said there were a few reasons. That
was just one."

"Well, we can talk about you next," Joshua told her. "Only fair if
each of us has a turn in the hot seat."

"I suppose that's true," Laurie replied, although he thought he
saw a flash of alarm in her eyes, and he understood it. He might
have wanted to choose honesty, but that didn't mean it was easy...
or comfortable. "So... what was your other reason?" she asked. "Or
reasons?"

"Just that it felt easier to hide away, I guess," Joshua replied
slowly. "I wasn't in the best frame of mind, to be honest. My dad
and I... we didn't actually get along." He felt his throat thicken at
just the mention of his dad. This was something he never told
anybody, not even Aunt Maureen, although she probably had
guessed. "It's not something people really knew," he continued
stiltedly. "Because to everybody else in Starr's Fall, he was this great
guy." He grimaced. "I don't mean that he wasn't. Just that at home...
he was different. Well," he sighed, "he was different with me."

"How?" Laurie asked. Her voice was soft, full of sympathy, and
to his surprise, Joshua found the words positively rolling off his
tongue, as if he needed to explain it all, and maybe he did.

"My dad's life was the store," he stated. "That wasn't necessarily
a bad thing, because people loved him for it. But at home he was, I
don't know, distracted. Disinterested. I was this geeky music kid,
and I didn't really want to spend time in the store, although he
made me mind it sometimes. I didn't love reading."

"Not even military history?" Laurie teased gently, which made
him smile.

"*Especially* not military history. That was my dad's thing.
Anyway. We were never all that close, but when my mom died...
well." He frowned in thought. "Sometimes a tragedy like that
brings people together. Sometimes it tears them apart. In my dad's

and my case, it was the latter. We stopped talking. I was angry about missing my college application. He was angry that I wanted to leave. I was angry that he refused to talk about my mother, even to acknowledge her. He loved her a lot. She basically held us together. But when she was gone..."

Not, Joshua knew, that either of them had ever talked to each other about any of it. They'd simply co-existed, side by side and silent. It had been, he reflected, the most miserable year of his life. Lonely, grief-stricken, wanting his dad to reach out, unable to reach out himself. When he'd left for New York, he'd told himself he'd never look back and he'd *thought* he hadn't, except maybe that was exactly what he'd been doing the whole time, without even realizing it.

"And then when your dad got sick...?" Laurie prompted gently.

Joshua gave a nod of acknowledgment. "Three years ago. I came back right away. It felt... it felt like the only thing I could do, even though I admit I didn't want to. I was teaching music in the city, I had a concert coming up of my compositions—nothing major, mind you, just a small community thing, but it was something." And he'd had Mia. Should he mention her? How could he not? "And I was engaged," he confessed. "To another musician. Mia. A violinist. I felt like my whole life was in New York."

"But you left it all for your dad," Laurie remarked quietly. "That shows a strength of character, as well as loyalty. Which, as far as I'm concerned, *does* reflect well on you."

"I'm not sure about that," Joshua replied, and now he sounded gruff. "I didn't come back filled with kindness and charity. I resented being here, and I'm afraid I let my dad know it, even after he'd had a stroke. Not exactly devoted son behavior. There wasn't any touching reconciliation before he died. I wish there had been." His throat was thickening again, and he realized he was as close to tears as he'd ever been since his dad's death. "I feel like that would have made a difference."

"Oh, Joshua." There was an ache in Laurie's voice as she reached over to place her hand on top of his. Without realizing he was going to, Joshua threaded his fingers through her own, and somehow, sitting there like that, their fingers entwined, felt more intimate, more *tender*, than if they had somehow managed to kiss over the pizza box.

This was *better*.

Well, Joshua decided upon reflection, *almost*.

"And after he died?" Laurie asked gently, after a few moments had passed. Their fingers were still threaded together. "What happened then?"

Joshua gave a little shrug. "I went into hibernation, of sorts. By that point, Mia had broken up with me—by text—and my life had shrunk to my dad's palliative care and trying to keep the store afloat. My job as a music teacher had been peripatetic anyway, and they'd filled the role. I'd had to give up my apartment, and so there didn't seem to be anything left to go back for, and so I didn't." He gave a small, apologetic sort of grimace. "I also didn't want to, at that point. Maybe it was the grief... both for losing my dad and for the relationship we never had. And losing Mia, the idea of life with her... Though in retrospect, I'm not sure we would have ever worked out. But it still hurt. The truth is, I didn't want to do much of anything."

Gently, she squeezed his fingers. "That's understandable."

"And I haven't moved on from that," he concluded with a sigh. "In three years. Even if I should have."

"I'm not sure there are any *shoulds* in this situation," Laurie replied.

"Maybe not." Joshua sat back, realizing he felt exhausted. Sharing all that had taken its emotional toll, and while he didn't regret it, he still *felt* it. He thought about turning the tables on Laurie and asking her to share some of her emotional stuff, but he didn't think he had it in him, and considering what a big day she'd had, he figured she probably didn't either.

"So the question is," Laurie asked after a moment, her tone turning quiet but playful, "what now?"

"What now?" Joshua repeated. For a second, he thought she was talking about them. As a... *couple*. Their fingers were still entwined, after all, although he couldn't tell if she even noticed.

"Yes, for you. For the bookstore," she clarified and, almost as if she were making a point, she slipped her hand from his. Joshua felt the loss. "Just because it's been one way doesn't mean it has to stay like that," she added, before hesitating and then continuing, "Someone once told me that it was up to me to choose how to be. No one could choose for me, or take that choice from me, and it... it meant a lot, at the time. It still does."

Which made him want to ask her all kinds of questions, but not now. "I suppose you're right." He decided to keep it light, for both their sakes. "So, are you not-so-subtly hinting at a refurb again?"

She laughed and gave a teasingly defiant shrug. "Why not?"

Why not? Joshua considered the question, suddenly feeling a little uncharacteristically reckless. Why *not* be different, *choose* to be different? Coming here tonight had already started that process. There was no reason why he shouldn't continue it.

"All right," he told her impulsively. "Why not? I'll consider doing some kind of refurbishment... But only if you'll help me." Belatedly he realized how much he was asking of her. She'd just opened her own store *today*, for heaven's sake. "That is," he began to backtrack, "you don't have to—"

"I'd *love* to." Laurie's eyes sparkled with both humor and excitement. "When do we start?"

"Is tomorrow too soon? Unless you have to mind your own store—" Which she probably did.

"No, I'm closed on a Sunday, so it works." She gave a definitive nod, her eyes still sparkling. "Tomorrow sounds great. It's a date." Immediately, she blushed. "That is, I didn't mean like a *date*-date—"

"Well," Joshua replied, emboldened by the evening, by the possibility the future presented for the first time in *years*, "maybe I did."

14

Laurie woke up smiling. Outside, fall had arrived in a torrent, and rain was spattering against the windowpane like bullets. At some point in the night, Max had abandoned his usual place curled up by her feet to come up and snuggle under the covers against her stomach.

"Good morning," Laurie told him sleepily as her fingers found his fur. She pulled the duvet up over her shoulder and snuggled down a little deeper, content to simply drift in a pleasant haze of memory for a few more moments.

Maybe I did...

Joshua's words played through her mind, causing her smile to widen as her eyes fluttered closed. A date. Today was really going to be a date. Not that they'd discussed it any further than those three little words, but still. They held so much possibility. So much promise.

She did not, Laurie knew, have much experience with dating— a few awkward fumbles with a boy in the care home when she'd been a teenager, which she wanted only to forget, and a friendship in college with a fellow student, Tim, that she'd *thought* had been going somewhere, until he appeared with his very serious girl-friend one day. All those shared laughs over their textbooks clearly hadn't meant anything.

Laurie had been more hurt than embarrassed; Tim clearly hadn't ever considered her that way, and fortunately she had managed not to reveal her feelings to him. Beyond that, she'd had three rather dull dates with a work colleague, more just to gain the experience than hope for a relationship. Things had fizzled there before they'd even begun.

And that, she thought with a small sigh, her eyes still closed, was the sum total of her romantic experience. Pretty lamentable, all told, but she recognized it was a classic sign of her chaotic and isolated upbringing. When people disappointed you time and time again, you either withdrew emotionally or, as some girls in her home had done, ended up giving your heart—and your body—to just about anyone who asked, in a desperate bid for love.

Laurie might have been lonely over the years, but at least she hadn't had her heart broken.

Although, she realized, of all the men she'd ever had a flicker of interest for, Joshua Reilly had by far the most potential for breaking that vulnerable organ right in two.

And, she acknowledged, ever the optimist, the most potential to give her the greatest happiness she'd ever known. A life of love shared with another person. After years of living as a solitary being, it felt almost miraculous.

Right. Enough dilly-dallying. Laurie lifted Max and set him gently on the floor before throwing off her covers and rising to meet the day.

Forty-five minutes later, she was showered and dressed, having chosen a pair of denim overalls and an old t-shirt since they were going to be going through the dust-ridden store. It might be a date, but dressing up was clearly not an option.

Although it was still bucketing down, she decided to head down the street to The Rolling Pin for coffee and croissants. Since Joshua had brought dinner last night, she thought it only fair that she bring breakfast.

The Harpers' teenaged daughter Bella, whom Laurie recognized from the opening yesterday, was behind the counter as she and Max came into the bakery with a cheerful jangle of bells on the door.

"Hey!" Bella's face brightened as she flicked her long dark hair over one shoulder. "How did the rest of the opening go?"

"Really great," Laurie assured her. "Is it okay to bring Max in here?"

"Oh, yeah, sure." Bella shrugged. "My parents love dogs."

"You have a Burmese Mountain dog, if I remember?" They'd brought him yesterday when they'd all come in, and bought him a couple of rawhide chews, to boot.

"Yes, Hugo." Bella's voice was full of affection. "He's a big teddy bear. What can I get you?"

"Two coffees, please, and..." Laurie scanned the glass display case of various croissants, muffins, and scones. Everything looked absolutely scrumptious. "What do you recommend?"

"Everything's amazing," Bella stated firmly. "My dad is like, literally, *the* best baker. And they've all been freshly made this morning. But if I *had* to give a recommendation, I'd say the blueberry croissants. *So* good."

Laurie smiled at the girl's enthusiasm. Clearly The Rolling Pin was a family business. "I'll take two, please," she said, and Bella went to make the coffees.

It was extraordinary, Laurie mused, how different the cheerful bakery was from the dusty dishevelment of Reilly's Antiquarian Books. Bella was clearly happy to be behind the counter at nine o'clock on a Sunday morning, but it sounded as if Joshua hadn't been as a teenager. The bookstore didn't seem to be a love he and his father had shared. Was that because of his dad—or because of him? Did he even really *want* to be in Starr's Fall, running a bookstore?

The question caused her a tremor of trepidation. Maybe Joshua *should* return to New York, where he could pursue his love of music. Three years on, the heartbreak of his broken relationship might have healed enough to think about going back. Maybe he shouldn't be refurbishing the bookstore but selling it.

It wasn't a suggestion Laurie wanted to make.

"Here you go," Bella said, handing over two drinks in a cardboard tray and a pleasingly crisp white paper bag holding the croissants.

"Thank you." Laurie paid, and then, successfully juggling the tray, bag, and Max's leash, headed back out into the downpour. The rain was sheeting it down, and Laurie hunched over the precious coffees as she hurried down the street, Max whimpering plaintively behind her. He was not a fan of the rain. As she went, she heard the bells ringing at the big white church on the town green.

She'd never been an avid churchgoer, but she'd gone on occasion throughout the years, enjoying the sense of peace and presence she felt in the quiet of a wooden pew. Maybe she'd try Starr's Fall church. Liz Cranbury had mentioned she went, although Annie had offered a whispered aside that that was because the minister, David Rice, was fiftyish and single.

By the time Laurie got to the doorway of Reilly's Antiquarian Books, she was well on her way to being soaked, and she was immensely grateful that Joshua threw open the door the second she arrived, so she tumbled in, holding forth the tray of coffees.

"I don't think they're too wet," she told him in greeting, "even if I am." Max, disgruntled, gave an enormous shake, splattering them both with drops.

"And so am I, now," Joshua replied with a smile. "You didn't have to get me coffee, but thank you."

"And croissants." Laurie held up the bag. "It seemed only fair since you brought pizza last night. You *do* drink coffee, don't you?"

"Definitely," he assured her. "Let me take your coat so you can get dry."

Laurie didn't think she was imagining how easy things felt between them, as if those three little words Joshua had spoken last night—*maybe I did*—had unlocked something between them.

As she shrugged off her coat, Joshua put his hands on her shoulders to take it, and the warmth of his palms, even through the layers of her coat and shirt, were enough to make her tingle.

"Thank you," she murmured, and even though things still felt easy, they also felt something else.

Expectant.

"So, have you thought about what exactly it is you want to do?" she asked as Joshua hung up her coat and she took one of the coffees from the tray.

"That's what you're here for," he replied. "My creative consultant. Shall we chat through your amazing ideas while we have our coffees?"

"My amazing ideas!" Laurie shook her head, smiling. "I'm not sure they're that amazing, or even that I have that many. But sure."

Joshua emptied two armchairs of books and they settled themselves by the window, the rain streaking down it, obscuring the view of the street. As Laurie took her first sip of coffee, she gazed consideringly around the store. "It really is a good space," she mused out loud. "Nice high ceiling, and the bookshelves are wonderful." They were solid and substantial, made of mahogany, and pleasingly old-fashioned.

"But...?" Joshua prompted, laughter lurking in his voice. His brown eyes glinted over the rim of his coffee cup.

"But everything else is pretty much a disaster," Laurie stated matter-of-factly, and he let out a huff of laughter. "You need to organize the books into sections, first of all. And probably get rid of the ones that look like someone used Reilly's Antiquarian Books as a dumpster. Unless those really are valuable?" She gestured dubiously to a teetering pile of tattered, yellowed paperbacks.

"No, they're not, and that's essentially what people did," Joshua confessed. "My dad accepted everything."

"Well, that's where we should start, then," Laurie stated. She tore off a bit of her croissant and chewed it slowly, frowning in thought.

"What is it?" Joshua prompted after a few moments. "You look like you want to say something but you're not sure if you should."

Which was exactly what she was feeling. "Well..." Laurie hesitated. She didn't *want* to mention this, but she felt she had to. "I guess I just want to make sure this really is what you want," she said slowly. "I mean, you could sell up and move back to New York. Nothing's compelling you to stay here."

"I think that ship has sailed," Joshua replied after a moment. She couldn't tell anything from his tone, which had been neutral, worryingly so.

"Has it? I mean, I know your job and—and other things—aren't just there waiting for you, but you moved before. You could again." She held her breath, afraid to hear his answer, but still glad she'd said something. Well, sort of.

Joshua squinted suspiciously at her, a smile lurking about his mouth. "Hey, are you trying to get rid of me or something?"

"*No*," Laurie replied, too quickly and forcefully for her own dignity. "Not at *all*." Just in case he'd been left in doubt, which she was pretty sure he couldn't have been.

"Well, good, because I don't want to go anywhere," Joshua told her. "I realized that last night, actually. I admit, I *may* have been acting resentful about being here, because..." He paused, his face screwed up in thought. "I don't even know why. Maybe because I had a lot of unresolved issues and feelings around this town, this store, and, most of all, my dad. And I did feel disappointed about leaving the life I'd built for myself in New York. But... you can't go back, and I don't want to try. I want to go forward. Here." He let out an embarrassed laugh. "All right, that's plenty of sappy introspection, I think. How about we start organizing some books?"

Laurie smiled and nodded. She was both relieved and pleased by what he'd said, and she took it to heart in terms of her own life, as well. *You can't go back*. Was wanting to look for her mother a kind of going back? Maybe she should abandon the whole search, not that she'd even started it properly, and just focus on moving forward.

And yet how could you move forward when you weren't even sure about who you were?

Organizing the books into categories was, Laurie realized an hour later, a laborious job. They'd decided on a division of labor, which meant her job was to take books off shelves, and Joshua's was to put them into the categories they'd decided on—fiction, history, travel, and memoir. There weren't, Laurie had soon discovered, too many other types of books. As Joshua had explained, his father's specialty had been military and naval history.

As they worked, with Max curled up on one of the armchairs Joshua had cleared of its piles of books and papers, they chatted through some more ideas—having a reading area with armchairs and tables, a coffee machine, a chalkboard with recommended reads.

"You could host a book club," Laurie continued, warming to her theme, "or even start a town literary festival! That could bring more people to Starr's Fall."

"It could," Joshua agreed, sounding approving but also cautious. "I'm not sure I'd even know how to begin to organize something like that."

"I bet you could find some info online. And if there are any local authors…"

"Besides Betty Stein and her self-published *The Scintillating History of Midnight Fashion, Starr's Fall's Premier Fashion Boutique*?" Joshua quipped. "Jenna very kindly sells copies from her general store. I took twenty myself, but I'm afraid I haven't shifted any yet."

"Well, I'm sure Betty could be included in the festival," Laurie replied generously. "Along with a few *slightly* better-known names?"

"I suppose it's an idea," Joshua remarked thoughtfully. "But we have to get all this sorted out first."

"We're getting started," Laurie told him bracingly. They'd managed half an aisle so far. They only had five to go, plus all the various piles around the store. She glanced at her watch. It was already nearing ten in the morning. This was going to take all day, at a minimum. But then, she could think of worse ways to spend her Sunday…

"And what about your music?" she asked him as they continued to sort, stack, and shelve books. "Maybe you could find a way to incorporate it into the store. It doesn't have to be one or the other, you know." She stopped, waiting for him to respond, because she'd already sensed this was something of a sensitive area.

"I guess not," Joshua replied slowly, his gaze on the books.

"Although I'm not really sure books and music go together. They certainly didn't when I was growing up."

"Of course they can," Laurie exclaimed. "You could have a music section in the store, first of all. You could even sell old records and stuff—aren't they coming back into style? And have music playing in the background while people browse—maybe even one of your own compositions." For a second, she held her breath, and then dared to add, "I haven't heard anything you've composed, you know. I'd love to, sometime."

Joshua was silent for a long moment. Laurie couldn't see the expression on his face, but she worried she'd pushed too hard and offended him.

"Maybe," he said at last, and it felt like a win.

"Okay." She'd leave it at that, Laurie decided, and reached for another book.

"So you've never told me why you moved to Starr's Fall," Joshua remarked after ten minutes or so had passed in the companionable silence of sorting and stacking books. "I mean, I know you wanted to start your store—"

"And bakery," Laurie interjected, smiling, although she knew where this was going.

"And bakery," he confirmed. "But why here? Most people haven't even heard of Starr's Fall."

"True." Laurie slid a book off the shelf and glanced at its title: *A Comprehensive History of King Philip's War.* She'd never even heard of that war, never mind knowing anything about its history.

"Laurie?" Joshua prompted, and the gentleness she heard in his voice made her realize she wanted to tell him. Not just the carefully curated parts she'd mentioned to Annie or Jenna or Henrietta Starr, but *all* of it.

Gulp.

Slowly, she put the book on the growing stack of history tomes in front of her. "I picked Starr's Fall because it is where my mother was born," she stated bluntly. "My biological mother."

Joshua was silent for a moment, considering. Finally he asked, "Do you know anything about her?"

"I thought I knew her name," Laurie replied, and heard a very uncharacteristic trace of bitterness in her voice. "But someone recently told me they thought she'd probably made up her name. Which I think is probably true."

"Why?"

"Because there are no Lysanders in Starr's Fall," Laurie explained on a heavy sigh. She felt flat rather than sad; she wasn't sure which emotion was worse. "According to the lady who should know most of all, Henrietta Starr herself. And when I did an internet search on the name, nothing came up. There aren't any in the town records online, either, although I haven't braved going to the town hall to check for myself."

"Why not?" Joshua asked, his voice so gentle it almost sounded tender, and was more than Laurie could bear. She had to blink several times to clear the haze of tears that had sprung to her eyes.

"I think," she managed, grateful her voice didn't sound too clogged, "I'd rather not know than not be able to know. To *never* know. At least right now there's always possibility."

Joshua was silent for a long moment. "I can understand that," he said at last. "Inertia sometimes feels like a better choice than action, because at least then you always have choice, even if you never take it."

Which went some way to explaining his own living situation.

"Still," Laurie admitted, "it's depressing. I don't know what I expected... I *knew* it would be hard to find anything about her, and I also suspected she wouldn't still be in Starr's Fall, after all this time. And yet..." She trailed off with another sigh. How could she explain it? She'd known, head-wise, that it was most likely a wild goose chase, but heart-wise...?

That felt different.

"All right," Joshua said, his tone turning briskly practical. "What *do* you know about her, exactly?"

Laurie took a deep breath. "I know her name," she told him. "That is, her most likely fake name. Helen Lysander. I know her birthplace was Starr's Fall and that she was eighteen years old when she had me. I know she chose not to name the father, and that she gave birth in Hartford. I know she gave me up for adoption to a couple in New Jersey." She paused to draw another steadying breath. "That's all."

"Still, that's something," Joshua replied musingly, rubbing his chin. "Eighteen years old... How old are you?"

"Twenty-five."

"So she would be forty-three now, twelve years older than me."

Laurie experienced a jolt, like missing the last step in a stair; she'd never considered the possibility that Joshua might have *known* her mother. That felt... weird.

"I doubt I knew her," he said with a grimace, seeming to read her mind. "Twelve is quite a lot in teenaged years."

Laurie nodded slowly. "I suppose."

"Still..." He paused, frowning, before he glanced at Laurie with a soft yet curious look. "Laurie... what happened to your adoptive parents? The couple from New Jersey?"

She swallowed hard. This was part of her personal story that she didn't like sharing because it was just so categorically awful. She didn't even like thinking about it, or *them*, and she tried not to, yet she knew it was part of who she was, even if she didn't want it to be.

"They gave me back," she explained briefly. She stared down at her feet, willing herself not to cry. There was a reason why she never talked about this. It hurt so darned much.

"Gave you *back*?" Joshua sounded horrified, which was the usual response whenever she mentioned it, which was basically never for exactly this reason. Occasionally it had had to be trotted out—when she'd been assigned a new social worker or gone to a new foster family. But to willingly offer this information, this tattered, bleeding piece of her soul? No, thanks.

"Yes, it happens sometimes," she said, still staring at her feet. "It's called 'disruption,' when an adoption breaks down. Usually it happens within a few weeks or months of a placement, but sometimes later. Obviously it's a last resort and can be hugely traumatic for everyone." She sounded as if she was reciting an adoption leaflet, which she basically was. It felt easier—safer, too—to stick to the facts.

"And how old were you?" Joshua asked in little more than a whisper. He still sounded horrified.

"Four." *Four.* Four years her adoptive parents had lived with her, loved her, or tried to. Four years of taking care of her, of wiping her tears away and kissing her goodnight, and then...

How? How could they do such a thing? Even after all this time, the question still reverberated through her, like a resounding gong, echoing down the years, offering no answers.

Joshua was silent for so long, Laurie wondered if he'd heard her. Then, in a hoarse whisper, he began, "Four *years.* How could they..." He stopped, shaking his head.

"I know some of the facts," Laurie told him. Her voice sounded briskly practical, but inside she felt as fragile as an egg. It wouldn't take much to break her, to crack her right open. "I was a difficult toddler. I had separation issues, I was very clingy, cried a lot. Or so my social work report says. I also know they were having marital difficulties and didn't have a lot of family support. Parents on both sides were dead or absent, no siblings. They were older, too, and didn't have much experience with children. A social worker had been involved since I was two, trying to help resolve things. In the end, they got divorced, and I was like the ugly piece of furniture neither person wants to keep. So I went into foster care."

"Couldn't you have been adopted again?"

Laurie shrugged. "I had a long-term placement that could have ended in adoption, but my foster family chose not to. So then I went to another family, and by that time, I was pretty difficult. To be honest, I don't remember much of it. It's all a blur of people and places... but I acted out. I was behind in school. I stopped trying to make people love me, and then I finally ended up in the home for teenagers, which frankly was a relief. It's such a rollercoaster, getting your hopes up, feeling afraid, wondering if this family will be nice or not. If... if they'll love you, which is why you act like you don't care if they do or not." Her voice trembled. The cracks, Laurie knew, were starting to show. "By that point, I knew I'd just rather not try at all." Her lips were trembling now too, and she felt a tear pool in her eye before slipping down her cheek. She dashed it away, but not in time.

"Oh, Laurie..." Joshua's voice was gruff with emotion.

"It wasn't as bad as it sounds..." Laurie began, only to have a sound like a sob escape her, and she had to wipe her eyes again. *Help.* She was going to lose it in a way she hadn't in a long, long time. Talking to Joshua had ripped open old scars she thought had healed, faded. She'd certainly acted as if they had, yet now they felt raw, wounded, bleeding.

"I bet it was worse," Joshua replied, and then in three long strides he was at her side, and then he was pulling her into his arms.

Laurie came willingly, wrapping her arms around him as Joshua pulled her close. One hand was on her back, fingers spread wide, the other wrapped around her waist, his chin resting on top of her head.

It felt so achingly wonderful to be held. To be touched, even. She couldn't even remember the last time she'd been this close to another person, feeling them breathe against her, accepting their warmth. Laurie buried her face in the hollow of his throat as the tears continued to slip unchecked down her cheeks, and this time she didn't try to stop them.

15

"Meeting come to order!"

Annie banged what looked like an actual gavel on the table, trying to get the attention of the dozen women who had been milling about the church basement. It was a surprisingly cozy space, lined with old sofas and pictures of the productions the church theater group had put on throughout the years.

"Pastor Dave considers himself something of an *actor*," Annie had explained as Laurie had studied some photos of the church's production of *Hairspray* from a few years ago. "To be fair, he does have a very nice singing voice."

After one more bang of the gavel, the women, who had continued chatting and laughing, finally sheepishly took their seats. It was the monthly Starr's Fall Business Association meeting, and Laurie's first time attending. She was already enjoying herself; ten minutes in she'd chatted to Annie, Jenna, Lizzy Harper, and Rhonda, a wiry, tough-talking woman in her fifties who ran The Starr Light Diner. She'd been introduced to Zoe Wilkinson, a woman who looked to be in her late twenties and had a shock of bright pink hair, a nose ring, and a wide smile. Betty Stein, elderly proprietress of Midnight Fashion, had also set up some of her books on the store's illustrious history, in the hopes of making a sale.

"She does it every month," Annie had told Laurie in a whisper. "Brings *dozens*. We've all bought one, but she says they make good gifts."

"Or door stops," Laurie had suggested, and Annie let out a snort of laughter.

"We need to have a chat after this meeting," Annie had then said to her, like a warning. "I've heard all sorts of things about you and a certain Mr. Reilly."

Laurie had blushed and chosen not to reply. It had been a week since she'd told Joshua the sad story of her childhood and then cried in his arms. She'd worried the whole unfortunate episode would make them both feel unbearably awkward, once she'd pulled away, but it hadn't, at *all*. Joshua had given her a handkerchief—he was, of course, the kind of man who carried a handkerchief in his pocket—and then made them both cups of tea. They hadn't talked anymore about the past, but it felt as if something had shifted between them. Strengthened. There was an intimacy there, born of shared stories, that lent a depth to their friendship, and Laurie was glad for it.

She'd also hoped it might be the foundation for something more, but so far nothing romantic had happened. She'd continued to help Joshua clear up his store while managing her own, and she'd booked onto an online dog grooming course and finally received her certification to run the bakery side of her business. She'd had a steady stream of customers—sometimes a trickle, sometimes something approaching a flood—but enough to keep things going as she continued to explore offering new services, to create additional streams of revenue.

Life had felt busy and full and *good*, and she was so very

grateful for all of it. It had meant she hadn't had any time even to think about her biological mother, and she was grateful for that, too.

And meanwhile, she hoped something might come of their friendship. In the last week, she and Joshua had seen each other every day, admittedly so they could work on his store in the evenings, but they'd also shared cups of tea or coffee and chats late into the afternoon or evening. She'd spent more time with him, Laurie acknowledged ruefully, than she had with just about anyone else ever, although considering the solitary nature of her life so far, that wasn't as much as it sounded.

"First item on the agenda," Annie announced. "The streetlights."

This was met with a groan from just about every member of the association, accompanied by various grimaces and eyerolls.

"What's the problem with the streetlights?" Laurie ventured hesitantly.

"They don't work," Annie stated flatly. "The township is responsible for them, but they keep putting off repairing them."

"It's the light bulbs," Betty chimed in. "They keep burning out. They last about five minutes."

"You might not have noticed," Jenna put in, "because it isn't so dark at night yet. But wait until after we go back to standard time at the end of the month. You'll feel like you're stumbling around in a crypt when walking down Main Street."

"I'll write another letter to the township," Annie said on a sigh. "And how the lack of lighting affects businesses as well as safety. Is everyone willing to sign?"

A chorus of yeses and a round of nods was the cheerfully resigned response.

Annie glanced down at the agenda she'd circulated to everyone before the meeting. "Second item. Christmas."

"I'm doing my usual Christmas dinner for the month of December," Rhonda volunteered. "Nine ninety-nine for roast turkey, stuffing, mashed potatoes, and green beans, and yule log with peppermint ice cream for dessert."

"Not bad," Annie remarked with approval, and Rhonda gave her a nod.

"Bring Barb and I'll do you a two-for-one special."

"Aw, Rhonda..." Annie's eyes glistened briefly with emotion. "Thanks."

"I can decorate my windows," Betty offered. "Red and green outfits. And I wear a Santa hat when I'm in the boutique. If anyone wants one, I bought them in bulk—"

"I think we're all right, Betty, thanks," Annie interjected hurriedly. "But your windows will be spectacular, as always." She looked around the table rather beadily. "But the real question is, are we going to do something special? Something organized? The Fall Festival is the only town-wide event we have in Starr's Fall, and as you all very well know, we could certainly use another one."

"Have you not had a Christmas event before?" Laurie asked. She was surprised; based on what she'd experienced so far, the town had a great sense of community, even if its retail spaces could use some help. She would have expected them to do something over the festive period.

"We used to have a wonderful Christmas tree lighting on the village green," Betty told her mournfully. "But then the evergreen there was struck by lightning."

"Betty, that was twenty years ago," Annie reminded her briskly. "We had the tree lighting plenty of times after that. Mike from the garage just brought the tree in and set it up for us."

Laurie didn't think she was imagining the slight pinkening of Annie's cheeks at the mention of Mike.

"So does that still happen?" she asked.

"Sadly, no." Annie grimaced. "About ten years ago the tree fell over in a windstorm and *almost* brained Doug Vance—"

"Wouldn't have been a bad thing if it had," Jenna muttered under her breath, shooting Laurie a laughing look.

"He threatened a lawsuit and that was that," Annie finished.

"He's one of those city types," Betty explained kindly. "Doesn't spend much time here."

"But he still managed to be wandering around in a tornado," Jenna put in. "Idiot."

Clearly no one had a very high opinion of Mr. Vance.

"So what kind of organized event are you thinking about?" Laurie asked. She *loved* Christmas. Back in Trenton, she'd always done her best to decorate her apartment, buy a present for Max, go to the midnight carol service at the church a few blocks away. But the idea of Christmas here in Starr's Fall, maybe even spending the day with more than just Max, was wonderful. And being part of some town-wide event—whatever it was—just added to the excitement.

"We-ell..." Annie began slowly, "we've always liked the idea of doing some kind of evening event, keeping stores open late, decorating the streetlights—"

"If they work," Lizzy Harper put in with a smile.

"Maybe having someone dress up as a Santa and hand out presents to the kiddies," Annie continued.

"Mike," Jenna declared, "would be a wonderful Santa."

And now Annie was definitely blushing. She cleared her throat and tapped the gavel for good measure. "So, do we want to try a Winter Wonderland Evening or similar this year? It will take a lot of organization..."

"I say let's do it," Lizzy replied. "Why not? If we all pitch in, it shouldn't be too bad."

"I'd definitely help," Laurie chimed in. "It sounds great."

"And as long as we can get all the business owners to agree..."
Annie gave Laurie a questioning look. "A certain Mr. Reilly has
been reluctant to participate in the past."

"Has he?" Laurie wasn't surprised. "Well, I can't speak for him,
obviously, but I think he might be willing to this year." She paused,
not wanting to discuss Joshua's business with this group of avidly
curious ladies but feeling something more needed to be said. "He's
doing a bit of a revamp of his store, actually."

"So I noticed," Zoe said, a sparkle in her eyes. "When I've been
walking past. We went to school together, you know. Same year."

"Really?"

"We weren't friends, though," Zoe was quick to say. "Different
groups."

"Zoe was a rebel," Jenna explained. "Got into trouble just about
every week. And suspended twice."

"Three times, actually," Zoe replied with an unrepentant shrug
and a gleam in her green eyes.

"And what was Joshua like?" Laurie asked curiously, only to be
met with a few seconds' uncomfortable silence.

"A geek," Zoe finally said with an apologetic grimace. "Sorry."

"You don't need to apologize to *me*," Laurie replied with a startled laugh. Everyone was acting as if she had some sort of claim on
Joshua... which she definitely didn't. *Yet.* As for his geekiness, that
hardly bothered her; she could imagine it—quiet, shy, part of the
school orchestra or brass band. It made her like him more.

"Anyway," Laurie resumed, "you'll have to ask him, of course,
but I think Joshua would be up for it. We were talking about organizing a literary festival at some point... maybe in the spring."

At this information, everyone goggled silently for at least ten
seconds. Laurie gave an uncomfortable laugh. "What?"

"Joshua Reilly," Annie stated, "is interested in organizing a
literary festival?"

"Well..." Laurie let out another uncertain laugh. "Maybe." She glanced around the group, feeling a sudden protectiveness for Joshua, as well as pride. Did anyone here understand how hard it had been for him, to leave New York and all his dreams there, to come home and nurse his father? Did anyone here know him at all? She had a feeling they didn't. Joshua had chosen to be reclusive, and everybody else had let him. They'd called him the Grinch, which she understood, but still... "He's changed," she stated, and Annie sat back, arms folded, eyebrows raised.

"He must have," Annie replied thoughtfully.

* * *

Was it too much? Low lighting, mood music, a bottle of wine. Joshua's stomach flipped at the thought of Laurie taking it all in and looking... regretful. Or worse. What if they weren't on the same page when it came to their friendship? More specifically, their *relationship*. Friendship, Joshua knew, wasn't going to cut it for him anymore. At least, he didn't want it to.

Laurie had invited him to the Business Association meeting tonight, which he'd politely refused. Walking into that coven of beady-eyed women would be akin to being thrown to the lions. He did, however, invite Laurie to give him a full debrief afterwards, and as it was already eight-thirty, she should be arriving any minute.

There was a knock on the door. His stomach gave a funny little flip, and he hurried downstairs. Even in the darkness, Joshua could tell that the woman standing in front of his door was not Laurie. She was taller, and more heavy set, and he thought he knew who it was just from the set of her shoulders.

"Aunt Maureen." He tried to inject a note of enthusiasm into his voice. "It's pretty late..."

"I was passing through and I saw your light on and thought I'd say hello," his aunt replied breezily. She moved past him, forcing him to step aside as she came into the store. "Goodness, things are looking tidy in here. What's brought this on?" Cue the shrewd look, a knowing gleam in her eyes.

"Just thought it was time to give the bookstore a breath of fresh air."

His aunt's eyebrows rose. "Did you now? And this wouldn't happen to have anything to do with your nice new neighbor, would it?"

"It might," Joshua allowed, and he had the dubious pleasure of seeing his aunt's jaw actually drop. She hadn't expected him to be so forthcoming, but that was just about all she was going to get.

"Well, well, well." She nodded slowly, which gave Joshua the uneasy feeling that he'd revealed more than he'd meant to, even with just those two little words. With an approving sort of nod, his aunt started upstairs. It took Joshua a second to follow.

"Wait... where are you going?" he called in something of a yelp.

"To do your dishes, run a dust rag around," his aunt replied, as if it were obvious, which normally, it would be. "Maybe vacuum. When's the last time you've changed your sheets?"

"*Aunt Maureen.*" Joshua hastened up the stairs after her, fighting against a burgeoning irritation. "I'm thirty-one years old. I can do these things myself. Besides, it's eight-thirty at night..."

"*Oh.*" Maureen had come to a halt at the top of the stairs, taking in the scene and all it revealed—the low lighting, the sensuous sound of a saxophone winding its way from the speakers, the open bottle of red wine, two glasses at the ready. Joshua gazed at it all as if for the first time and squirmed inwardly. Outwardly, too. It really was so obvious, so *basic*.

His aunt turned to him, positively dewy-eyed, her hands clasped to her chest. "My dear boy." She had a look of mingled pride and affection on her face that resembled, Joshua thought spikily, a mother gazing at her toddler who had peed in the potty for the first time.

"Don't—" he warned, but it was too late. His aunt was in full flow.

"I'm so happy for you, Joshua. So pleased you've finally taken some steps toward living again, *properly* living—"

"Enough." He cut her off mid-flow, his tone hard. "Please. Enough. This is..." He blew out a hard breath. "This is my life, Aunt Maureen, not some... project. Please, just..."

She pressed a finger to her lips, eyes twinkling. "I won't say another word, I promise. I'm just so proud..."

Proud? That he was attempting to have a private life? Be a normal person? Joshua shook his head wearily. "If you don't mind..."

"I'm gone," she assured him, trotting back down the stairs. "I'm going right now."

She blew him a kiss, her eyes still sparkling, before hurrying out the door. Joshua stood on the bottom stair, caught between exasperation, irritation, and a weary sort of sorrow. Was this what it had come to? Was he such a lonely curmudgeon, such a grump and a Grinch, as so many in the town called him, that it was treated like some kind of event, practically a miracle, that he'd invited a woman over?

Blowing out another irritated breath, he turned on his heel and stomped back upstairs. Flicked the lights back on and turned off the music. Whisked the glasses away and corked the wine. None of it made him feel any better about anything.

He was just staring at the ruined scene when a knock sounded from downstairs, and this time he was pretty sure it wasn't his aunt.

16

The moment Joshua opened the door, Laurie knew something was wrong. His eyes sparked with annoyance and his hair was rumpled as if he'd driven a hand through it, most likely in frustration. Plus, he was back to scowling. She hadn't seen him look like this in weeks, and it alarmed her.

"Should I not have brought Max?" she asked uncertainly. "It's just I kept him at home for the Business Association meeting and I thought he'd be lonely if I left him much longer." She glanced down at her dog, his head lodged between her ankles, his tail tucked between his legs, as if he sensed Joshua's mood, which he probably did because he was continuing to glower. "Is this not a good time?"

"What? Why are you saying that?" Joshua practically barked. "It's a perfectly fine time. It's the time we agreed, isn't it?"

"Well, yes, but..." She trailed off, waiting for more because something was clearly wrong.

"Come upstairs," Joshua said abruptly, and he turned toward the stairs. Silently, scooping up Max, Laurie followed him. She'd so been looking forward to this evening—regaling Joshua with anecdotes from the meeting, slowly sipping a glass of wine, feeling the mood unspool between them into something more... or so she'd hoped.

Clearly none of that was on the cards, the way Joshua was acting.

Upstairs, he went into the kitchen and brandished a bottle of wine. "Do you want some?" he asked, and it was about the most unenthusiastic offer Laurie had ever heard.

"Only if you do," she replied a bit tartly, and he shrugged, indifferent.

Laurie shook her head slowly, still holding Max. This was so far from the way they'd been together lately that she felt completely wrong-footed, as if she'd fallen down a flight of stairs and had had the wind knocked out of her. Her default had always been to ignore it and plow on being optimistic. Choose her own responses rather than worry about someone else's. And yet... she found she didn't want to do that right now. Sometimes optimism *wasn't* the right choice. And so she took a deep breath and decided to force the issue. "Joshua... has something happened?" she asked. "Why are you so grumpy?"

"Grumpy," he repeated, on something between a snort and a sneer. "You too?"

Laurie stared at him blankly, all the more confounded. "*What?*"

"Don't feel sorry for me," he shot at her, and she almost laughed, even as she struggled not to feel hurt by his tone, his words.

"Trust me," she assured him, "I don't."

He glared at her for another moment, folding his arms and refusing to reply. Something inside Laurie snapped, unexpectedly, sharp and hard.

"You know what?" she said, lifting her chin, holding Max tightly to her chest. "Never mind. I could remind you that *you* were the one who invited me over here, who hinted that we were going to have a nice evening, and guess what? This isn't it."

Joshua looked as if he might reply, but then didn't, his lips pressed firmly together, and Laurie let out a huff of exasperation and, it had to be acknowledged, hurt. She'd really expected so much more from this evening. From *Joshua*.

"Never mind," Laurie snapped, except her voice held a ragged edge that definitely felt too revealing and semi-ruined her strong moment. Well, she didn't care. She was going. She turned on her heel and marched down the stairs, half hoping Joshua might follow her... but he didn't.

Drama queen, she thought, and she didn't know whether she was talking about him or herself. Both, maybe. They hadn't needed to get to this point, had they?

Out in the street, Laurie shivered in the cold, and Max let out a little whimper. "I *know*," Laurie told him. She had to blink back tears, annoyed with herself. She wanted to be stronger than this... but maybe she wasn't. Then she heard the door of the bookstore open.

"Laurie." Joshua's voice was full of regret.

Slowly Laurie turned. Joshua's face had collapsed into contrition, his shoulders slumped as he walked across the street toward her. "I'm so sorry, Laurie. I've been acting like a complete ass. I know I have."

"Why?" Laurie asked in a small voice. She couldn't bounce back that quickly, as much as she might want to.

Joshua shook his head as he raked a hand through his hair. "I don't even know."

"Really?" Laurie couldn't keep from sounding skeptical, even a little sneering. After all that drama, he couldn't even *say*?

"But I'll try to explain." He let out a breath, jamming his hands in the pockets of his jeans. "My aunt came over right before you did."

This did not seem like enough to put him into this sort of mood, Laurie thought, still feeling reluctant to be overly understanding. "And?" she prompted.

"I don't know. It's hard to explain. It's this *town*." He glanced around the darkened street, his expression a mixture of frustration and weariness. "It's like you can't escape what you once were, what everyone has known you as. I'm the guy everyone feels sorry for because his mom died and then his dad, and his fiancée dumped him and he's always so grumpy. And I feel like I'll never be able to shake any of that, which is why I haven't tried. I haven't even tried to try... until now."

The words had come out in a rush that Laurie did her best to absorb. It was a pretty deep conversation to be having in the middle of the street, but... she got it. Sort of. She supposed, in some ways, Joshua felt the opposite of how she did. She longed for a place where she could be understood, known and accepted. And meanwhile Joshua was resenting and running away from it and everyone, because he felt trapped. She could understand it, but it reminded her of how different their histories were. But maybe that was where they could help each other.

"Okay," she said after a moment. "I get that, especially in a place as small as Starr's Fall. But this has to do with your aunt coming over because...?"

"She just reminded me of it." He sighed again and drove a hand through his hair, messing it up further. "And it made me feel... trapped, I guess. And kind of stupid. And like everyone was just... all up in my business." He glanced up at her, managing a wry smile. "And I more or less took it out on you. I really am so sorry. Let me make it up to you."

"I think I'll let you." She smiled at him, everything in her softening, because she knew this had to have been hard for him to admit—and in the middle of Main Street! The thought made her want to laugh. "The truth is, though," she told him slowly, feeling her way through the words, "from where I'm standing, you *are* changing. At least from when I first met you, which admittedly wasn't that long ago." She smiled wryly. "But don't *not* change just because everyone will notice and remark on it. Because of course they will. This is a small town and there are probably a hundred people who could tell me stories of when you were in diapers, and still think you're about sixteen, if that."

He gave a grimacing sort of smile. "Exactly."

"But that's also the beauty of a place like this," she continued, an ache entering her voice. "A place where people *know* you... have known you for your whole life. Where they accept you, maybe too much, because like you said, it might be hard for them to accept that you can change. But that's a gift, in a way. To be that known. That understood."

"I know," Joshua replied in a low voice. "And I know you haven't had any of that, so I probably sound like even more of a selfish jerk."

"Apples and oranges," Laurie told him briskly. "And anyway, it isn't a contest, who has had the hardest childhood or whatever." That was just about the last thing she wanted. "And," she continued, "it doesn't matter what anyone thinks, anyway. Remember what I said about choosing how to be? That helped me so much. No one gets to tell you how to be, how to react, how to *live*, except yourself."

"Wise words." Joshua smiled faintly as he shook his head. "All right, enough of a pity party from me," he announced, holding out his hand. "Follow me back upstairs?"

"All right."

"And close your eyes."

Laurie stared at him. "Close my *eyes*?"

"Yes, close your eyes and I'm going to recreate how everything was before my aunt came over and I let her ruin it. My choice, not hers, but I'm changing the script now." A smile lurked about his mouth, glinted in his eyes, and made Laurie's heart turn over. "Come on. Close your eyes. Just for a few seconds, while I get it all ready."

"All right." Laurie let him lead her back upstairs, only peeking to check she didn't trip on the steps, and then guide her to the kitchen table, where she sat down, her hands over her eyes and Max in her lap as she heard Joshua start to move around the kitchen. She heard a cork being eased from a bottle, and then the low, sultry sound of jazz music from his speakers, and she started to smile.

"Okay," he said after a few more moments. "Open them."

Laurie lowered her hands from her eyes and blinked the room back into focus. The light was low, coming from just a few table lamps, and the soft sound of the music stole around her soul. Joshua was standing in front of her, holding two glasses of wine, a small, uncertain smile curving his mouth and making her ache with happiness, with gratitude.

"How's this?" he asked, and she reached for a glass, her smile spreading across her face like melted butter.

"Perfect," she told him, meaning it utterly.

* * *

Two days later, Laurie was sliding a tray of homemade dog treats into her new glass display case when Liz Cranbury came into Max's Place, Frou-frou in a carrier on her chest.

"I know," she said before Laurie had even greeted her as she gestured to the carrier. "Ridiculous, right? She's not a *baby*. But her legs are really short, and she gets so tired, poor thing."

"No judgment here," Laurie replied easily. "Would Frou-frou like a treat?"

"I'm sure she would."

Laurie took one of the sweet potato and pumpkin treats and fed it to the little dog, who gobbled it up happily.

"I love this place," Liz remarked on a happy sigh as she looked around. In the three weeks since she'd opened Max's Place, Laurie had made several improvements—adding a glass display case for her baked treats by the cash register, another armchair in the window that she'd picked up from Goodwill in Annie's truck, and a bulletin board where customers were invited to pin photos of their dogs. There were eleven photos so far. She'd also kept up a *fairly* brisk business, which had been encouraging, although running a one-woman show was pretty all consuming. Annie had suggested she hire someone part-time, but the budget didn't extend to employees just yet.

"It just feels so homey," Liz remarked.

"That's the vibe I'm going for," Laurie replied cheerfully. She was feeling more optimistic than ever today—the sun was shining, the leaves were out in full regalia of scarlet and gold, and she was closing early to go on a hike with Joshua up to Starr's Fall, the waterfall high above the town that had given it its name.

Two nights ago, they'd shared a lovely evening and the better part of a bottle of wine, after that slightly rocky start. But then the wine, the music, the mood... it had all *felt* romantic, and Laurie had wondered—and hoped—that Joshua might kiss her. And so he had —a peck on the cheek when, at eleven o'clock at night, conscious she had to work the next day, she'd finally uncurled herself from his sofa and said goodbye.

Well, that was fine, she'd told herself. She'd rather take it slowly and be sure. But she'd lain in bed, staring up at the ceiling and reliving the moment when his lips had brushed her cheek for at *least* an hour.

But today, Laurie had determined, was a brand-new day... in all sorts of ways.

"Coffee?" she asked Liz. She'd taken on board the suggestion she'd given to Joshua about having a coffee station in the bookstore and had set up a coffeemaker behind the cash register. The good townsfolk of Starr's Fall could now happily traipse from store to store, having a hot beverage at each one.

"That'd be great." Liz smiled her thanks as she strolled around the store, inspecting merchandise, and Laurie poured her a cup from the pot she almost always had brewing. "You've really made something here," Liz continued, and now Laurie heard a wistful note to her voice that gave her pause.

"What do you do for work?" she asked as she handed Liz a mug. "I'm not sure I know."

"You wouldn't, because I don't do anything," Liz replied ruefully. "I worked for a fashion magazine in the city donkey's years ago, but I gave that up when we moved out here to have kids. Two daughters... both moved away now." She gave a small, sad sigh. "I always meant to try something new, but somehow, I never did. Now, however, I'll need to." She grimaced. "Divorce is expensive."

Laurie gave her a sympathetic smile. "I'm sorry."

Liz shrugged philosophically. "It's not easy, but sometimes things end, don't they?" She pursed her lips. "Especially when a twenty-eight-year-old secretary is involved. Talk about clichéd."

Now Laurie was the one grimacing. "Ouch."

"I know, right?" Liz let out a tired laugh. "But I'm trying to see this whole thing as a chance to do something new. *Be* something new."

"I'm all for reinvention," Laurie told her. She propped her elbows on the counter. "What would you like to do?"

Liz's shoulders sagged a little. "Truthfully? I have no idea. I'd love to do something with fashion again, but I don't know what, especially in a small town like this. And I couldn't leave Starr's Fall. Greg might have got the house, but this place is still my home." Her expression firmed, her mouth flattening into a determined line. "And it always will be, as far as I'm concerned."

"Is your ex-husband still in Starr's Fall?" Laurie asked, thinking that could potentially be a little awkward.

Liz shook her head. "No, thank goodness. He sold up and moved back to New York to relive his bachelor days. Bought a loft in SoHo or something."

It seemed awfully unfair, that Liz's ex-husband got the house out of the divorce when all he'd done was sell it, and Liz wanted to stay, but as Annie had once said, life was like that sometimes.

"Well, what about helping out in Midnight Fashion?" she suggested. "That place looks like it could do with some new ideas."

Liz let out a hoot of laughter. "That's putting it very diplomatically. I don't know how Betty keeps that place open. The mannequins in the window give me the creeps."

"They are a little bit like something out of a horror movie," Laurie admitted, a smile twitching at her lips. Made of meant-to-be-life-like flesh-colored plastic, with very fake-looking hair, alarmingly red lips, and staring eyes, the mannequins alone were enough to put her off entering the store, never mind the clothes they were wearing, which had been in fashion about thirty years ago. "And Betty must be getting on in years," she continued as she sipped her own coffee. "Maybe she'd appreciate a little help."

"Maybe," Liz replied a bit doubtfully. "She's always seemed like she knows exactly how she wants to run things, but who knows? I could feel her out, I guess."

"It's an idea," Laurie said with a smiling shrug. "Or you could start your own boutique...?"

Liz made a face of mock horror. "Two fashion boutiques in Starr's Fall? Competition? I don't think so. I mean, imagine if there was another pet store in town."

"True," Laurie agreed.

"Of course," Liz assured her, "we'd all still shop at this one."

* * *

A few hours later, Laurie was closing up Max's Place and heading across the street to Reilly's Antiquarian Books—Joshua was having a new sign designed but it hadn't arrived yet—and opening the front door with a jangle of bells. The store looked *so* much better, with the books all organized on shelves. Hand-painted signs indicated various sections, and two admittedly shabby armchairs were tucked in the front window along with a selection of magazines. A bulletin board above the cash register read "Reilly's Recommended Reads"—a romance Laurie had enjoyed, and a book on music Joshua had liked. She'd teased him that he needed to read a little more in order to offer recommendations.

"Hello?" she called into the store. "Anybody home?"

"Here." Joshua came downstairs, a backpack over his shoulder. "I was just getting a few things together." He'd promised her a picnic by the waterfall, which sounded to Laurie like just about the most romantic thing ever. *Hopefully.*

"No problem," she replied easily, and he gave her a quick, sure smile before he shrugged on his jacket.

It was a ten-minute drive to the start of the hiking trail, through the town and then out on a meandering road with farms on either side that soon turned to dense forest. Joshua pulled into a small clearing that had a sign marked "Starr's Fall Walking Trail—No Littering!" and not much else.

"It takes about forty-five minutes to hike up to the waterfall," he told her. "Will Max be okay?"

"He'll be fine," she assured him. "I think I'll be the one gasping for air."

Fortunately, the trail wasn't overly steep, crisscrossing the hillside, between birches that were in glorious yellow leaf, and scarlet maples. It was a gorgeous day, the air crisp and clear without being too cold, the sun shining down on them, the sky a deep, beautiful blue. Everything, Laurie thought, was perfect.

Halfway up the hill, Joshua caught her swinging hand in his with a wry, questioning smile. In response, Laurie squeezed his hand, and he squeezed back. She found herself grinning.

Yes, this day really was turning out to be perfect. As perfect as she ever could have wished.

They didn't talk much as they walked—even though the ascent was fairly gentle, Laurie still had to catch her breath—but then they came around the final turn in the trail, and there was the waterfall, gushing from a steep cliff face frilled with coppery-toned ferns, the water foamy and white, drops sparkling in the sunlight.

"*Oh*." Laurie couldn't keep from gasping out loud. "It's beautiful."

"It is, isn't it?" Joshua agreed, his tone almost tender, and when Laurie turned to him, she saw, with a leaping sensation in her chest, that he wasn't looking at the waterfall—but at her. His eyes glinted with bits of gold as he tugged gently on her hand, until she was standing right in front of him, her heart starting to beat rather hard. "Laurie..." he said, like a question, and she answered with a nod.

Then his lips were brushing hers—once, twice—before settling on them softly, and a sigh escaped her like a held breath. *At last.*

His arms came around her, pulling her closer so she could feel the hard wall of his chest and their hips bumped, causing heat to flare deep inside her. Then he deepened the kiss, so her senses spun, and it felt as if the whole world was bursting into song, or maybe just she was.

Laurie knew she'd never felt so happy, so at *home*.

Joshua eased back, smiling a little, as he rested his forehead against hers. "Happy?" he asked softly, and Laurie, her heart so full it felt as if it were bursting, could only nod.

Yes, happy, she thought. So, so happy.

17

"Hello...? Miss Starr?"

Laurie poked her head through the front door of the Starr mansion, her arms full of grocery bags. She'd taken to stopping by to see Henrietta Starr once or twice a week, to bring some groceries as well as offer a bit of companionship. The older woman's chilly hauteur had started to thaw, if only a little, and some days she even seemed downright pleased to see Laurie.

"I'm in here," Henrietta called, sounding decidedly disgruntled. Today, perhaps, was not going to be one of those days.

Still, a bit of grumpiness could not spoil Laurie's relentlessly cheerful mood. It had been just over two weeks since her and Joshua's waterfall walk, and she found she couldn't stop smiling. She floated about Max's Place, feeling as if she were hovering about six inches off the floor. She was like Cinderella, dancing around with a broom, or Snow White, singing to Max and any other wood-land creatures who happened along—so far only a robin who had landed on the windowsill, but she was going with the general vibe. Life, for the first time ever, felt like a fairy tale.

After she and Joshua had shared that wonderful, magical kiss, the whole afternoon had unspooled in a golden thread of tenderness and possibility. They'd held hands as they'd explored the area around the waterfall, and then Joshua had spread out a blanket and unpacked the picnic he'd brought—crusty bread, sharp cheddar, some slices of ham and a few crisp apples. They'd eaten and chatted and laughed under the golden sunshine, and then afterward...

Briefly Laurie closed her eyes, a smile spreading across her face as she remembered the very pleasant *afterward*. Limbs tangled, her hands in his hair, kisses that made her feel both sleepy and wonderfully wide awake.

It had come to an end only when the sun had slid behind the trees and the breeze blowing down the mountain had turned sharp and cold. Joshua had eased away from her, his face flushed, his hair rumpled, a wry smile softening his features as he'd gazed down at her.

"Maybe we should head back."

"Maybe we shouldn't," Laurie had replied recklessly, and he'd laughed and kissed her again. But soon enough, Laurie had shivered with cold, and the shadows had lengthened, making them realize they really did need to get down the mountainside before the sun set. October on a mountainside in New England was no joke. But they'd held hands the whole way, and to Laurie it had felt as if a brand-new world had opened up in front of her, as beautiful as the valley of trees in all their shades of russet and ochre spread out below them, shimmering with possibility and promise.

Two weeks on, she still felt that way. She'd seen Joshua just about every day, whether it was him bringing coffee and croissants from The Rolling Pin before they opened their respective stores in the morning, or for a quick chat in the afternoon when business was slow. Most evenings, they'd been either at her place or his, either continuing to work on refurbishing his store—there were still a *lot* of books to go through—or watching Netflix or just chatting and drinking wine.

They'd also done a lot of lovely kissing.

So much kissing, Laurie thought as she lugged the groceries into Henrietta's kitchen. But not much more than that yet, which was fine by her, even if Joshua's kisses made her ache with longing. She still wanted to go slowly, because the whole idea of a relationship, a real one, was new to her, and even as it felt wonderful, it also felt unfamiliar and sometimes strange. A little scary. So slow was good... for now.

"What do you have all that for?" Henrietta demanded as Laurie plonked a bag of groceries onto the kitchen table.

"It's just a few staples," Laurie assured her airily. She'd been slowly and sneakily stocking Henrietta's fridge with some microwaveable meals as well as ingredients for simple things to make—butter and jam for toast, cheese and cold cuts for sandwiches. The food did seem to disappear, so hopefully Henrietta was eating it.

"I'm perfectly capable of shopping for myself, you know," Henrietta informed her tartly.

"Of course I know that," Laurie replied. "But I was at Miller's Mercantile anyway, so I thought I might pick up a few things." She'd had a brief catchup with Jenna, and asked after the mysterious Zach, whom she *still* hadn't met, nearly two months into her life in Starr's Fall, before enjoying a lovely peruse of the store's aisles of groceries and necessities, admiring the barrel of dill pickles floating in brine, the sacks of Lyman apples, the pleasing old-fashionedness of it all.

Laurie glanced at Henrietta, who was sitting stiffly at the kitchen table, a cream-colored sheet of stationery in front of her, along with an elegant fountain pen. "What are you doing?" she asked curiously.

Henrietta hesitated, and then picked up the pen and rolled it between her gnarled fingers. "I'm writing a letter," she finally stated, "to my daughter."

Laurie stopped in mid-closing of the fridge to stare at her uncertainly. From what she'd gleaned of Henrietta's life from the sparing details she'd given her, she'd never married or had children. She'd spent two years at college in New York City and the rest of her life here in this house.

Slowly Laurie closed her fridge. "Your daughter?" she repeated, a question.

Henrietta smiled faintly. "I suppose I don't really have the right to call her that. I gave her away at birth—long before your own mother did the same to you, my dear. About fifty years before, I should imagine. It was the early 1950s." She lapsed into silence, her gaze distant and a little sorrowful.

"Do you... do you want to talk about it?" Laurie asked cautiously. She realized she was not entirely surprised by Henrietta's revelation. Something about the older woman's knowledgeable demeanor, the way she'd been so certain of her facts—the details on a birth certificate, the possibility of the mother changing her name. Had she done the same, once upon a time? Based on what she'd just shared, it seemed likely.

Henrietta let out a small, tired sigh as she put down the pen. "Do I want to?" she mused. "I haven't spoken of her to anyone in all that time. She'd be seventy now. Seventy! And yet I still picture her as a baby, with the most beautiful blue eyes... Oh, I know all babies have blue eyes, I'm not that much of a spinster, but her eyes were particularly lovely." Another small sigh escaped her, a sorrowful puff of sound. "I do remember that," she finished quietly, gazing down at her hands, now clasped on the table.

Laurie drew out a chair and sat down opposite Henrietta. The older woman's face was a mass of wrinkles, wreathed in sorrow, even grief. It was both strange and moving, to glimpse the other side of the equation, Laurie realized, when she'd only experienced her own. She'd often wondered what her mother had been like, what she'd felt and thought. Had she not had parents to support her when she'd found out she was pregnant? Why had Laurie's biological father not been named? Why had she chosen the family she had to adopt Laurie? Had she ever wanted to get in touch?

There had been so many unknowns, and it had made it hard to imagine what her mother had been like, even as Laurie had ached to know, to understand. Yet here was Henrietta, who had gone through more or less the same thing, decades earlier. Could Henrietta give her, if not direct answers, then at least hints and clues, as to what her mother might have been like? What she might have felt, and why she'd made the decision that she had?

"Do you want to tell me about it?" she asked quietly.

"There's not very much to tell." Henrietta was back to being brisk. "I went to college in New York, to study literature. My parents didn't want me to go... They were very traditional. But I had so many dreams! My head was full of them. But in the start of my second year I fell in love." Her mouth twisted. "Or so I thought. The truth is, I was terribly naïve. I thought love was a feeling, something fizzy and exciting. I didn't realize it should be far more than that, something real and solid. Something you depend on, rather than hope for."

Laurie swallowed hard. She was feeling pretty fizzy about Joshua at the moment—but that didn't mean it wasn't real.

"And what happened?" she asked Henrietta after a pause when it seemed as if she wasn't going to continue.

Henrietta let out a deep sigh, her head bowed. "I became pregnant, that was what happened. A tale as old as time, and as clichéd as anything you'd read in those lurid confessional magazines, back in the day. The man involved—well." She glanced up at Laurie, her gaze as shrewd as ever. "He certainly didn't want to know. He gave me fifty dollars and asked me to 'take care of it.' By that point, I was too far along to think of any such thing, not that I know if I could have. He was married, you see. I hadn't known, or at least I hadn't let myself know." Her mouth turned down at its wrinkled corners. "The heart is deceitful above all things, my dear. Never forget that."

Laurie found she had to swallow again. Hard. Her throat ached with the effort. This was starting to feel a little personal.

"And so you gave the baby up for adoption?" she surmised.

Henrietta nodded. "I didn't even realize I was pregnant until I was nearly five months gone. What a shock it was! Like I said, I was terribly naïve." She shook her head, her expression both sad and rueful. "A friend had to tell me. She was more worldly-wise than I was, and she had an older sister."

"You... you didn't think of keeping it? Her?" Laurie asked rather timidly. "The baby, I mean?"

Henrietta's gaze widened. "Oh, my dear, I couldn't possibly have done such a thing. The shame of it, back then... and of course, I was—am—a Starr. I had a name to uphold. I didn't even tell my parents. I hid it for as long as I could, and then my friend helped me to arrange to go to a home in upstate New York, for unwed mothers. I told my parents I was summering in the Adirondacks with friends. You hear about such places, how terrible they are, but actually this one was perfectly adequate. The carers were brisk but kind. But of course everyone there was just miserable. You couldn't keep it from feeling like prison. It could have been the most pleasant place in the world, and it wouldn't have mattered to me. All I wanted was for the whole thing to be over, so I could forget it had ever happened."

Laurie blinked, unable to keep from feeling a little stung. She understood the sentiment, of course, and suspected it was how most women in Henrietta Starr's predicament had felt. And yet...

what about that poor, innocent baby, whose only problem was being born? Had it—*she*—deserved to be so forgotten? Uncomfortably, she realized she didn't know whether she was thinking about Henrietta's daughter... or herself.

"I see," she said quietly.

Henrietta looked over at her, her eyes brightening with what Laurie realized were unshed tears. "Oh, my dear, I really don't think you do," she said softly, reaching over to clasp Laurie's hand with her own gaunt one. "I thought I could go back to how I was... a young, carefree co-ed, gallivanting about town, but I couldn't. I felt changed beyond all recognition... and no one but me could see it. It was as if my heart had been removed from my body, replaced by an empty shell... and not one person saw beneath my smile. I fooled everyone, but I found no joy in it." She smiled sadly. "I ended up dropping out halfway through my third year. I would have been asked to, in any case, my grades were that dreadful. And so I came back here, to Starr's Fall... and I never left."

"Henrietta..." It was the first time Laurie had called her by her Christian name, and yet she realized she had no idea what to say. It sounded like such a long, lonely life.

"Oh, it wasn't as bad as all that," Henrietta assured her with some of her usual asperity. "I involved myself in the community. There were summers in Maine and debutante balls in the city... A few beaux, as well, although no one who turned my head, never mind broke my heart." She glanced around the kitchen in all its dated shabbiness—the wheezing fridge, the peeling linoleum, the electric light hanging from its frayed cord. "It's only in the last decade or so that I've started to let things go," Henrietta told her, although Laurie suspected that had to be a *slight* understatement. "My parents died in the early seventies, and then, maybe fifteen years ago, I slipped in the bath and stupidly broke my hip. That slowed me down a fair bit."

She gave a small smile, her eyes twinkling. "But don't paint me as some wretched Miss Havisham character because I assure you, young lady, I am not."

"All right," Laurie replied, smiling back. "I won't." She gestured to the sheet of stationery on the table. The only word Henrietta had written so far was *Dear*. "So what prompted this?"

"You did, my dear!" Henrietta told her. "In all my years, when I thought about my—my daughter, I'd assumed she was happy. I think I had to, at the start, simply to survive, and then I just *did*. And when I considered contacting her—and in truth, I never did, not seriously—it felt selfish. Why disturb her perfectly wonderful life? But after I met you, and saw how you were searching... I wondered if I wasn't being selfish, but rather scared. Afraid that maybe her life hadn't been as wonderful as I'd hoped... Or, really, of being rejected myself."

Henrietta gazed down at her hands. "But there is not so much time left anymore, and I don't know what I could possibly have left to lose. And... I realized I'd like to know. What happened to her, whether she's happy. So here I am."

"And you have her personal information?" Laurie asked. Could it be that easy for Henrietta, after so many years, when it hadn't been for her?

"Well, it did take some doing," Henrietta admitted with a touch of pride. "I had her adopted name, from the original record, and that was all. But I went to the library to use their computer, and I found her on that Face website."

"Facebook?" Laurie guessed.

"Yes, that's the one. At least, I think it's her," Henrietta amended. "The age is right, along with her maiden name... and, do you know, I think she has my father's nose, poor woman."

Laurie suppressed a laugh as she shook her head slowly. "And you were able to get her mailing address off Facebook?"

"No. I wanted to write this letter on paper, the way I know how, and then I thought I'd perhaps ask you to transcribe it electronically, if you wouldn't mind? There is some kind of way to do that, I believe? I fear it is most likely beyond my capabilities."

"Of course I will," Laurie said with alacrity. She would be happy to help Henrietta Starr find her long-lost daughter while dragging her feet about trying to locate her own mother. Oh, the irony.

"And as for you," Henrietta said, seeming to read her thoughts, "don't leave it as late as I have, although admittedly you have some years before that happens! Your mother might have changed her name, but that doesn't mean she doesn't want to be found now."

* * *

An hour later, Laurie had made Henrietta grilled cheese and tomato soup for lunch and was heading back to Max's Place to open for the afternoon, her head swirling with all sorts of thoughts.

Even if her mother wanted to be found now… how could Laurie find her? A fake name felt like a pretty comprehensive dead end.

And yet… *Helen Lysander*. It was such a unique name, a far cry from Jane Doe or something similar. Had her mother chosen it for a *reason*? Could it hold a memory, or even a clue? It was the only thing she had to go on, and yet she still wasn't sure how to begin.

Only, Laurie realized as she unlocked the door to Max's Place, Max frolicking about her ankles the minute she stepped across the threshold, that she wanted to. After weeks—and months and years —of dithering out of fear, just as Henrietta had said, Laurie was finally ready to find some answers.

Now she just had to figure out how to do that.

18

The idea of her mother's false name was still flitting around in Laurie's mind several days later, when she headed over to Joshua's after closing up Max's Place for the evening. It was nearing the end of October, and the breeze that blew down Main Street was *cold*, many of the trees lining the street now stark and leafless. The chrysanthemums that had once filled the planters with joyous colors were now mostly brown and dead-looking, but harvest wreaths on various doors and carved pumpkins leering from doorsteps helped bring a festive cheer to the scene. It wasn't yet winter, but Laurie felt as if she could taste it in the air.

The last few days had been good for business, with her home-baked dog treats proving to be a hit, along with all her other products. Someone had asked about puppy-training classes—another potential arrow to add to her quiver. She'd already started the dog grooming course online, hoping that by the time she finished it, she'd have saved up enough to buy the necessary equipment for the back room.

She'd also made some progress with turning her apartment into more of a home. Annie had driven with her to Jenna's barn, and they'd loaded up the back of the truck with some furniture that Jenna insisted she didn't want—a lovely gate-legged table, a velvet loveseat, and even an old Player piano, the kind you might see in a saloon in the Old West. Laurie had taken it all, enjoying the fact that her apartment had a little bit of Henrietta Starr's vibe to it. She'd had the piano delivered to the bookstore, much to Joshua's initial chagrin and then delight.

"A piano?" he'd exclaimed with definite skepticism. "In a bookstore?"

"A Player piano!" Laurie had replied, her excitement undimmed by the doubt she'd expected from him. "It can play itself. Customers will have such fun with it, and you can play it normally too, and wow us with your compositions."

A small, wry smile had tugged Joshua's mouth. "I love it," he'd said, and put his arm around her. "Thank you."

Now, as she came into the store, he greeted her with a quick kiss that was enough to make her heart flip over. Two and a half weeks on, and everything between them still felt new and, yes, fizzy. Laurie thought of what Henrietta had said, about love needing to be solid and real, and then pushed that unhelpful thought away. Fizzy feelings were fine at the start of a new relationship. They didn't have to be warning signs.

"Good day?" he asked as he released her.

"Yes, a good day," she told him. "And how about you?" She glanced around the store, which was looking so much better, with everything—well, almost—organized and neatly shelved.

"Business is picking up a little," Joshua told her. "I think people are curious, and so they stop by, maybe even buy something. But when that wears off…"

"Don't do yourself down," Laurie mock-scolded him. "People will keep coming back, especially with all your new stock." In addition to the used books that made up the bulk of the store, Joshua had agreed to bring in some new titles. They'd spent a couple of hours poring over possible inventory online, with Laurie wanting him to get in more fiction and Joshua feeling he needed to stay true to his customer base of military historians. They'd reached a compromise of sorts, and Joshua had ordered plenty of both, so the store would have something to offer everyone.

"I'll need to make room for it all," Joshua told her as they both looked around the crowded store. They were still sorting through stacks and stacks of old books; last night Laurie had come upon dozens of copies of various Shakespeare plays loaded into paper bags and left in a dusty corner. Joshua had told her they'd been donated from the old high school, before it had closed ten years ago.

"The new stock isn't coming for a few weeks, though, right?" Laurie replied. She ran her fingertip along the weathered spines of the Shakespeare plays—Joshua had consigned most of them to the trash, but he'd kept one copy of each "for posterity's sake," because it was Shakespeare, after all. The old high school copies made up the majority of the newly shelved "Shakespeare and Other Dramatic Works" section of the store.

"Right." He came behind her and slipped his arms around her waist, gently turning her to face him. "What's up?" he asked as he smiled down at her. "You seem a little distracted."

"Do I?" Laurie realized she was still thinking about her mother. It was like a buzzing in the back of her brain, drowning out every other noise. "I spoke to Henrietta Starr the other day," she told Joshua. It wasn't her place to reveal the achingly personal things Henrietta had shared with her, as they had, Laurie felt sure, been said in confidence. "Something she said got me thinking," she said instead. "Made me wonder... Maybe my mother's name—the alias, I mean—has some kind of significance." As she said it, she couldn't help but think how desperate it sounded. *Major* wishful thinking. "I know it might be a reach," she continued hurriedly, "but it could be something to go on, maybe, couldn't it?"

Joshua's eyes lit up as he smiled warmly down at her. "That's a really good idea," he said. "It's such an unusual name, isn't it? Helen Lysander..." He paused, considering. "It rings some sort of bell, but I can't think why or how."

"I know, I can't, either. So even if it is a clue, I'm not sure how to figure it out." She gave a small, wry laugh. "But I want to, at least. After dragging my feet for ages, afraid to find anything out, I actually want to, now. I think."

Joshua pulled her close for a hug. "That's good news, isn't it?"

Laurie rested her cheek against his shoulder, reveling in the simple pleasure of them breathing, *being* together. She didn't think she'd ever get tired of it. "Yes," she replied after a moment. "I hope so."

They headed upstairs where the spicy scent of curry wafted through the kitchen.

"Just about the only thing I can make," Joshua told her wryly as he lifted the lid off a pot and stirred its contents. "That, and spaghetti bolognaise. Very basic."

"But delicious, I'm sure."

"Let's hope so." Joshua replaced the lid and then turned to her with a practical smile. "So, what do you want to do?" he asked. "About your mom?"

Her mom. The words sounded so strange, and yet for most people they were as familiar as an old shirt, as normal as waking up and stretching in the morning. She thought of Henrietta writing to her daughter after all these years. If Laurie was able to track down her biological mother, would she have the right—the invitation—to say she had a *mom*?

"I don't know. Maybe try another internet search? Type in Helen Lysander without the Starr's Fall and see what comes up?"

There were a lot of rabbit holes she could disappear down, Laurie suspected, if she went down the Google route, which was part of the reason why she'd avoided it so far. The other reason was that she'd simply been too scared.

"Well then, let's do it." Joshua slid out his phone and waggled it in front of her. "If you want to?"

Laurie hesitated. She'd thought she was ready to find some answers, and she was, but… it was still scary.

"All right," she said, and was about to reach for the phone when Joshua, a strange look coming over his face, suddenly withdrew it. "What…?" she asked uncertainly as he shook his head slowly.

"I just had an idea…" Swiftly he turned and headed back down to the bookstore.

Surprised and more than a little apprehensive, Laurie followed him. "Joshua… what are you doing?" she asked. "What idea?"

He was standing in front of the shelf of Shakespeare's plays they'd organized last night, running his fingers along the cracked and battered spines just as Laurie had done a few moments ago. "Ah, here it is." He took out a slender volume while Laurie looked on, utterly baffled.

"Shakespeare…?"

"*A Midsummer Night's Dream.*" He flipped to the front of the book and showed her the cast list. "Look, two of the main characters, Helena and Lysander." He screwed up his face in thought. "I read the play in tenth grade, but I can't remember much of it. Helena loves one of the guys—Demetrius, I think—but then Lysander falls in love with her when he gets a sleeping potion. Or love potion or something. But do you think… do you think your mother might have been thinking of the play when she called herself that? Helen Lysander? It feels like too much of a coincidence, otherwise. I mean, both names…"

Slowly, haltingly, Laurie took the book from him and flipped through it, the names Helena and Lysander jumping out at her on almost every page. *Could it be...?* "She might have," she allowed cautiously. "Maybe she just liked the play?" A sense of the futility of the whole thing crashed down on her, making her shoulders sag. "But it doesn't really get me anywhere, does it?" she told Joshua. "Maybe she read the play in high school, like you did? But then probably so did every teenager in Starr's Fall."

"But maybe it meant something more to her," Joshua persisted. "Couldn't it have? Something more than the average student forced to read Shakespeare?"

"It could have... but I don't see how that helps me, really." Although it did give her a glimpse into what her mother might have been like. Laurie could almost picture her—quiet, thoughtful, dreamy. Or was that just more wishful thinking? "I'm not sure there's any real way to figure out who she is," she finished sadly. "But if you don't mind, I'll take this with me. I might read the play, just..." She smiled a bit shamefacedly. "Just to feel closer to her."

"I think that's a good idea," Joshua told her, his tone turning tender. He drew her close and Laurie let herself rest in his arms, her cheek against his shoulder. In that moment, part of her didn't *want* to find her mother. Didn't want to open herself up to the possibility of disappointment, maybe even of pain. Surely she'd had enough of both in her life already.

And yet... with Joshua's arms around her, she felt as if she could do almost anything. Why not this?

* * *

"You realize," Joshua told Laurie several days later, as he slipped his coat on, "the gossip will be rampant and unabashed."

Laurie looked at him seriously. "Does that bother you?"

Joshua considered the question. Did it? They were going over, at Annie's invitation, to her farmhouse to carve pumpkins for Halloween, which was in just two days' time. Annie would be there, along with her mother Barb, and Jenna Miller and her brother Zach. Knowing Annie, she would have corralled a few others as well, and everyone would be speculating about him and Laurie. Making sly comments, giving sideways glances and smirks. It was the Starr's Fall way, which was why he'd avoided such events for the last three years.

But now, Joshua knew, he felt different. Well, sort of. He wasn't looking forward to all the gossip, but he wasn't actively dreading it, either. At least not as much as he used to.

"It doesn't *bother* me," he said at last. "But I don't relish it, either."

"Does anyone?" Her eyes sparkling, Laurie stood on her tiptoes to kiss him. Joshua caught his arms about her waist and pulled her closer. They'd been dating—although neither of them had clarified it as such—for three weeks, and it had been the happiest few weeks Joshua had experienced in a long time, maybe ever. Mia, he'd come to realize, had never made him feel as light inside as Laurie did. Laurie made him smile just to think of her; Mia, a fellow musician, had been too intense and serious for that, and he'd never felt like he'd been enough for her, a dispiriting sense of diminishment that he'd never experienced with Laurie.

"We should head over," Laurie murmured against his lips. "Or we'll be late."

"I don't mind being a little late."

"Well, I do." Laurie pushed playfully away from him. "Barb gets tired pretty easily and I want to make sure to say hello to her."

Joshua had heard that Annie's mother had Parkinson's, and her health was starting to fail. It saddened him, because he knew what it felt like to lose a parent in increments, and he'd always liked Barb. She'd never had a bad word to say about anybody, including him, which, considering how grumpy he'd been these last few years, was saying something.

"All right, we'd better get going," he said with some reluctance, and they headed downstairs to his car. Laurie had brought Max, and he sat on her lap as they drove to Annie's farmhouse on the outskirts of town, chatting about inconsequential things.

They hadn't talked about Laurie's mother and how to find her since Joshua had made the *Midsummer Night's Dream* connection. But he had the sense that it had become something of a no-go area for Laurie, which he supposed he could understand. She'd told him she'd read the play, but she hadn't said anything else about it, and her tone had been a bit repressive, especially for her, and not inviting questions.

Joshua knew all too well how difficult and emotional it could be even to *think* about such things, never mind talk about them with someone else. He hoped that by giving Laurie a little space and time, she might open up eventually... and maybe even take those next steps to find her biological mother.

As they climbed out of Joshua's car in front of Annie's farmhouse, he breathed in the cold air, sharp with a touch of frost. The sky was a deep indigo and scattered with stars, a huge harvest moon, glowing yellow, rising above the dark fringe of evergreens beyond the farmhouse. It was almost Halloween, and it felt it. Autumn was already on the wane. Smiling at Laurie in the darkness, Joshua reached for her hand, threading his fingers through hers.

She gave him a startled look and then a shy smile, and he knew what she was thinking. Walking into Annie's house holding hands was, in Starr's Fall, akin to sending out save-the-date notices. Well, so be it. He was ready and willing to stake his claim.

They walked hand in hand up the steps to the back door, Max trotting behind them, and sure enough, as Annie threw it open, her narrowed gaze immediately zeroed in on their twined fingers. Gently Joshua squeezed Laurie's hand, a reassurance.

"Come in, come in," Annie greeted them, throwing the door open even wider. "We've got pumpkins at the ready, along with apple cider. If you want something stronger, though, all you have to do is ask." Her gaze was still fixed on their joined hands. "Joshua." She snapped it up to his face and gave him a wide smile. "*So* great to see you."

"And you, Annie." His tone was wry, letting her know he could guess exactly what she was thinking, and Annie laughed aloud and kissed his cheek.

"Good for you," she whispered in his ear. "And I have to say, good for Laurie."

Once upon a time, comments like that would have made him prickle in self-defensiveness, flare in irritation, but now he just smiled and headed inside.

Jenna and her brother Zach were already there, sipping apple cider and chatting with Annie's mother Barb, who was, Joshua saw with some alarm, looking particularly frail, although she beamed as they came into the room. Max tucked his head between Laurie's ankles as he always did.

"Joshua! Laurie!" Jenna hugged them both, and Zach gave them a wave and a quick smile. He'd been in the same class as Joshua in high school, and thirteen years after graduation he still looked like he belonged in a boy band—floppy blond hair, a quick, cheeky smile, and glinting blue eyes. In high school, Zach had been something of the school heartthrob—and he'd known it. He hadn't been arrogant, Joshua acknowledged, just annoyingly certain. The two of them hadn't been friends.

Still, that was a long time ago, and as far as he knew, Zach was a pretty good guy, even if his dating life was the talk of the town. Joshua stretched out a hand, and Zach shook it firmly.

"I can't believe I'm finally getting to meet you," Laurie told Zach. "I keep hearing about you and your many dates."

Zach rolled his eyes good-naturedly, although Joshua got the sense that he did not particularly appreciate the town's relentless gossip mill. Well, who did?

"Reports of my love life have been greatly exaggerated," he quipped, and Laurie laughed before going to greet Barb with a hug.

Soon enough Annie was organizing them all with pumpkins and wicked-looking carving knives, making jokes about Michael Myers and offering a prize—a gallon of Lyman apple cider, naturally—to the most artistically carved pumpkin. The banter and chat flew, and Joshua even found himself contributing; it felt like exercising a muscle he'd forgotten about, causing a pleasurable ache, a noticeable stretch.

He really had become the most unpleasant hermit, he acknowledged as he carefully carved out two triangle eyes in his pumpkin. Never doing anything or going anywhere, and why? To protect himself? It hadn't worked. He'd been more or less miserable... until he'd met Laurie.

She'd changed him, he acknowledged, gazing at her across the table. She was intent on her pumpkin, her face screwed up in concentration, her tongue poking out with effort as she attempted to carve a decorative swirl. Just looking at her, Joshua's heart swelled with—what? More than affection, and nothing as basic as desire, although admittedly there was that, too, for sure. Kissing Laurie—and stopping there—had been the most exquisite agony.

But the allegedly dreaded L-word? They'd only known each other for a few months, dated for a few weeks. Surely it was too soon...

Then Laurie glanced up and caught his gaze, giving him a teasingly quizzical smile, her eyes sparkling with humor and happiness, and Joshua knew, with a thud of certainty that was the emotional equivalent to falling flat on his face—yes, the L-word. That was exactly what he was feeling right then. And it terrified and excited him in just about equal measure.

"So who is auditioning for the latest Starr's Fall production?" Jenna asked as she scooped seeds out of her pumpkin, depositing them in the bowl Annie had provided, set in the middle of the table. "Zach, you're a budding thespian, aren't you?"

"Ha ha," Zach replied dryly. Clearly he wasn't.

"What's the show this year?" Joshua asked. The town's theater group, led by Reverend Rice, the able and enthusiastic minister of the Congregational church, put on a play or musical every year. The town possessed a handful of devoted actors—mainly keen teenagers and enthusiastic but less-than-capable elderly participants—who clubbed together to put on a show that was always, against all expectations, surprisingly good. When his mother had been alive, Joshua had gone to see it every year. He didn't think he'd been since she'd died.

"*Romeo and Juliet*," Annie announced with a cackle. "And guess who wants to be Juliet?"

"Not Eloise," Jenna replied with a groan, before explaining to Laurie, "she's been in every show since about 1970, and she's eighty if she's a day."

"Eighty-two," Barb put in, her voice thin and wavery but her smile as bright as ever. "But she's got lots of verve."

"That she does," Annie agreed. Joshua saw her give her mother a tender look of affection that almost made a lump come to his throat. He thought he knew exactly how Annie felt.

"Come on, Zach," Jenna teased, nudging her brother's shoulder. "You could be Romeo to Eloise's Juliet, couldn't you? She's one woman in Starr's Fall that you haven't dated. Yet."

"Actually, I think I took her to dinner once," Zach replied with a decided lack of humor. Joshua was definitely getting the sense that

Jenna's younger brother did not enjoy all the ribbing, good-natured as it was. He certainly understood getting a little fed up with the same joke being repeated over and over. He'd lost count how many times he'd been called the Grinch over the last three years.

"Does the drama group do a play every year?" Laurie asked. Joshua thought she meant to sound casual but there was a needling note of urgency to her voice that he recognized, even if no one else seemed to.

"Yes, no matter what," Annie replied firmly. "Rain or shine. During the pandemic, they cobbled it together on Zoom, I don't actually know how."

"But it's not always Shakespeare, is it?" Laurie continued, and with a jolt, Joshua realized where she was going with this.

"Oh, no," Annie assured her. "I don't think the good people of Starr's Fall are literary enough for that! They alternate between musicals and plays, and the Reverend tries to do something by Shakespeare every five years or so. I think that's about all we can take, to be honest."

"So... have they ever done *A Midsummer's Night Dream*?" Laurie asked, and Annie gave her a curious look.

"I can't remember..." She glanced at Jenna and Zach. "Can you?"

Zach shrugged while Jenna frowned in thought. Laurie looked as if she were holding her breath. Could her mother have been in the Starr's Fall production? Was that why she'd chosen the name Helen Lysander? It made, Joshua thought, a certain sort of sense.

"They did, years ago," Barb piped up. "Right when Reverend Rice first came to Starr's Fall. Don't you remember, Annie? The little Bryson girl was Puck. She amazed everyone. I don't think she was more than twelve at the time."

"Oh, right..." Annie let out a rueful laugh. "Goodness, that had to have been at least twenty-five years ago, Mom. Maybe more." She put an arm around her mother's shoulders. "What a good memory you have," she said softly, and Barb beamed.

Joshua met Laurie's gaze over the table of half-carved pumpkins. Her face had gone pale, her eyes wide and dark with knowledge. Twenty-five years ago would have been just about the right sort of timing for her biological mother to have been involved in the production.

19

"It might not mean anything," Laurie said for the third time. Or was it the fourth? She kept repeating it, half warning, half mantra, because she was so afraid to hope.

"But it *might*," Joshua answered, which was how he'd replied all the times before. They were driving back from Annie's, speeding through the darkness with their carved pumpkins in the trunk, Max on Laurie's lap. She'd buried her hands in his fur for warmth. Although the night was frosty, this cold came from inside. Realizing that there might actually be a way to find out who her biological mother was terrified and excited her in almost equal measure, with terror winning out slightly.

"Even if we find out that *A Midsummer Night's Dream* was put on right around that time," Laurie continued, feeling the contrary yet urgent need to poke holes in just about everything, "she might not have been in it. And even if she was in it, we might not find out who she was."

Joshua was silent, probably because she'd said all this before, more than once. "Sorry," Laurie murmured. She knew she was close to babbling.

Joshua reached over to squeeze her hand. "It's okay to be scared about this," he said quietly, and Laurie found she had to blink hard.

"I don't even know what I'm scared of," she confessed. "Running into another dead end or *not* running into a dead end. Knowing, or not being able to know. I guess this is why I've dithered and dragged my feet for so long. I've kept myself from hoping because —because hoping *hurts*."

"But not hoping is worse," Joshua told her, sounding like he was speaking from experience. "But if you decide you do want to find out if you can, the first step is talking to Reverend Rice. You could stop by the church tomorrow. I'm sure he keeps memorabilia from all the productions. It's kind of his thing."

"Memorabilia…" A memory was sparking on the edge of her mind, but she couldn't think what it was.

"Cast lists and programs and so on," Joshua continued. "Or you could go to the newspaper archives. There's no town paper anymore, but the archives are all online. They always did a write-up of the show, along with a photo, as I remember."

"A photo!" The word came out in a near-screech that had Joshua jamming on the brakes.

"*What*—"

"Sorry," Laurie said breathlessly. Her mind and heart were both racing with realization. "I just had a thought. The church basement. We had our Business Association meeting there a few weeks ago, and there were photos from past productions on the walls. Lots of them." She could picture them, framed in a line, with the title and date of the production underneath. Could her mother be in one of those wrinkled, aged photos? Had her smiling face been staring right at Laurie from underneath the dusty glass while Annie had been going on about streetlights and Christmas fairs?

"You know, you're right," Joshua told her, his eyes lighting up as he turned to look at her. "I remember seeing them when my mother used to take me to the church's pancake breakfast. I think that's the only time I've been in its basement, to be honest, but we could check...?"

As if on cue, the white spire of the church loomed up in front of them as they approached the village green. Even though it was after nine at night, the lights were on.

"The weekly AA meeting," Joshua explained. "Everyone pretends they don't know who goes."

"Do you think..." Laurie swallowed. Did she really want to do this now? *And yet, now or never...* "Do you think we could go in and see? Now?"

Joshua hesitated, considering, as he looked at the clock on his dashboard. "I think as long as they've gone already. Reverend Rice will be locking up. We could ask him." He swung into a parking space alongside the green as he gave her an encouraging smile. "Can't hurt, right?"

Actually, Laurie thought, *it could*. Getting her hopes up only to be dashed if they ran into another dead end... And yet, wasn't *not* knowing—if she could know—worse than knowing nothing?

And, in any case, what about the best-case alternative? Finally finding out who her mother really was... though that was the scariest possibility of all.

Silently they got out of the car and walked across the darkened green. Joshua slipped his hand into Laurie's as she hunched further into her coat. The wind blowing down from the hills outside town was practically arctic.

The reverend was just locking the doors as Joshua had said he would be as they came up to the church.

"Reverend Rice," Joshua called. "It's Joshua Reilly—"

"Why, hello, Joshua." Reverend Rice smiled at him in easy friendliness. He was a tall, lanky man with a shock of gray hair and blue eyes twinkling kindly under bushy eyebrows, and Laurie liked the look of him immediately. "Can I help you?"

"I know it's late and you were just locking up, but my friend Laurie here—I'm not sure you've met yet—was hoping to take a quick look at some of the photos downstairs of your past productions."

Laurie smiled hopefully at him, only to see his face crease in obvious bafflement. It was, she realized, a weird request at this time of night.

"I'm sorry," she said in a rush. "I wouldn't normally think of disturbing you at this sort of time, but... it's kind of important. I think..." She swallowed hard. "I think I might know someone in one of the photos. Maybe."

Reverend Rice still looked confused, although he seemed good-natured about it, and with a little shrug, he unlocked the door. "I'm happy for you to have a look." He ushered them into the darkened narthex, switching on the lights as he went. "Are you looking for a production or person in particular? I might be able to help, since I've been in all of them." He gave them both a humorous look.

"*A Midsummer Night's Dream*, about twenty-five years ago," Laurie blurted. Her hand was clammy in Joshua's, and she felt faint with nerves.

The reverend's eyes lit up. "Oh, yes, that was only my second production. One of my favorites. I'm sure there's a photo of it downstairs." He led them to the basement, which had the faint smell of coffee and sweat in the air, as, Laurie suspected, many church basements had. The reverend walked along the wall of pictures until he came to the second to last, tucked near the corner. "Here it is. *A Midsummer Night's Dream*. Lovely production. Lots of high-schoolers involved, which was so encouraging."

Slowly Laurie slipped her hand from Joshua's as she went to stand in front of the cast picture, faded now from age, the photograph wrinkled beneath its frame. It showed a smiling group of teenagers and retirees, all in their costumes. Was one of those fresh-faced teens her mother? It seemed impossible. Surely this was just a ridiculously wild goose chase, the most pathetic wishful thinking...

Then she saw her, in the back row, tall and slender, with a proud, almost fierce look on her face. The kind of expression Laurie was pretty sure she'd never had on her own face, and yet... the teenager had light brown hair with the same weird kink in the middle that Laurie had. The same spattering of freckles across the nose. The same *chin*.

Suddenly she felt overwhelmed, as if something heavy had crashed right down on top of her. She was breathless; she was near tears. Joshua came to stand beside her. He didn't speak, but she knew the moment when he saw the girl. *Her mother*. She wasn't sure how she knew that he knew—he didn't gasp, or even tense. But something shifted in the air between them, and then he silently took hold of her hand again and squeezed her fingers. Briefly Laurie closed her eyes.

"Do you have a cast list?" Joshua asked the Reverend. His voice sounded normal; Laurie knew hers wouldn't have.

"I keep all the programs upstairs in my office," Reverend Rice replied. "It might take me some time to find it... if you stop by tomorrow, I could have it for you by then?"

"That would be great," Joshua said. He was still holding her hand.

Laurie pointed, with a finger that thankfully didn't tremble, to the woman in the back row. "Could you tell me, please, which character that is? The girl in the blue dress?"

The Reverend peered closer, squinting a little. "Ah," he said. "That was our Helena."

* * *

Late the next morning, Laurie flipped the sign to closed on Max's Place and headed back down Main Street toward the church. Last night Joshua had asked if she wanted him to go with her to get the cast list, and she'd said no, to both their surprises. He'd looked a little hurt, and she tried to explain, but hadn't quite been able to, that this felt like a personal and private thing, something she wanted to absorb and understand on her own before she shared it with anyone else, even Joshua. Having been so private himself, she hoped he understood that.

Now almost November, the weather had turned to winter, or close enough, with a chilly breeze funneling down the street. The last of the leaves clung to the trees like tattered rags, flashes of scarlet and gold underneath a steel-gray sky. Laurie hunched her shoulders, burrowing her hands deep into the pockets of her winter coat. She felt rattled and jumpy, and yet also resolved. Finally, after weeks of thinking she'd never be able to, she was going to discover the name of her mother. What it might mean, and what she would do now, she didn't know, but it would be something.

The doors to the church were unlocked and Laurie slipped inside, grateful for the warmth. She'd barely had a chance to look around, breathing in the scent of dusty hymnals and candle wax, before Reverend Rice popped his head out of his office on the side of the narthex.

"Hello again," he greeted her with an easy smile. "It's Laurie, yes?"

"Yes."

"I found the program for *A Midsummer Night's Dream*. Looks a bit dated now." His tone turned rueful. "I became much more adept with graphic design as I went along. Come in, and I'll get it for you."

He ushered her into his office, which was no more than a desk and a couple of filing cabinets and a window overlooking the hills that rolled out from town. Starr's Fall was up there somewhere, Laurie thought, recalling that magical day by the waterfall, when Joshua had kissed her for the first time. The memory grounded her now, when everything felt so uncertain, the very ground underneath her shaken by what she was about to find out.

Her mother... She was going to find out who her mother was.

"Here you go." Reverend Rice handed her the program, no more than a single sheet of paper folded in half, with the name of the play written on the front in a flowery font. "I told you it was pretty basic," he said with a little laugh.

"That's all right." Laurie's voice came out in little more than a whisper and she had to clear her throat. "Thank you." She was itching to open the program and scan the cast list, but she didn't want to do it with the Reverend, kind as he was, looking on.

"It seems as if this person may be rather important to you," he remarked gently. Laurie could only stare at him, speechless. "If you ever want to chat about it, I'm always here," he continued. "And it would be remiss of me not to invite you to our Sunday services. Ten a.m., come as you are. Everyone's welcome."

"Thank you," Laurie said, and she managed to find a smile. "I'll try to come sometime."

Back outside, she barely noticed the cold wind as she headed back up Main Street, the program carefully folded into her pocket. She hadn't opened it yet; she wanted a quiet moment, a private space for such a momentous and nerve-racking occasion. She'd just passed The Starr Light—with Rhonda waving from the lunch counter—when she realized she didn't actually want to do this alone... and she knew exactly who she wanted to do it with.

Abruptly, Laurie turned and headed back to the street, causing Rhonda to frown at her in question, and then turned left onto Winter Street, walking past the stately houses before coming to one of the more dilapidated ones on the street.

"Hello...?" she called as she opened the door.

"I wasn't expecting you today," Henrietta replied from the living room, "but I'm glad you're here. I've finally written my letter, and I want you to send it to her on that Face site."

"Facebook," Laurie replied with a slightly wobbly laugh. She was still feeling a bit shaky inside, and suspected she would for a while. She came into the living room, where Henrietta was seated in an armchair, a book in her lap and a pair of reading glasses perched on her nose. Laurie had lent her one of her romance novels, which Henrietta had sniffed at before reading avidly. It looked like she was halfway through another one already.

"Why have you got such a long face?" Henrietta demanded, and Laurie let out another, even wobblier laugh.

"Have I? I'm just feeling nervous, I guess." She perched on the edge of the loveseat opposite Henrietta. "I think I know my mother's name. At least, I *will* know it."

"Oh?" Henrietta's eyes narrowed. "How's that?"

Carefully Laurie took the program out of her pocket and smoothed the slightly crumpled paper. "With this. Helen Lysander —I think she took her false name from *A Midsummer Night's Dream*. There was a production years ago—"

"I saw that," Henrietta interjected with a sniff. "It was dreadful. The poor Reverend does what he can, but Eloise Whiting needs someone to tell her that she can't act."

"Oh, well, I don't know anything about that," Laurie replied, even as she recalled that Annie had mentioned someone named Eloise was hoping to play Juliet in this year's play. "But my mother played Helena. At least, I'm pretty sure she did. There was a photo of the cast, and she looked a lot like me. And it would make sense, wouldn't it? Her taking the name."

"It would." They were both silent and then Henrietta clucked her tongue. "Well? What's her name then, child?"

Laurie smiled shamefacedly. "I don't know yet. I haven't looked." She braced herself for one of Henrietta's acerbic barks, but instead the older lady's face softened into lines of sadness.

"Oh, my dear," she said gently. "Are you so scared to find out?"

"I don't know what I'm scared of," Laurie said, just as she had to Joshua. "It just feels like taking a leap into the unknown. It might mean nothing. I still might not be able to find her. But... once I know, I know."

"But," Henrietta pointed out, and now she was sounding more like her usual self, "you thought you knew when her name was Helen Lysander. Knowing her name then didn't change anything, did it?"

"No..." Laurie acknowledged slowly. "But this feels different somehow. Bigger."

"You've come this far," Henrietta pointed out. "It would be a shame to lose your nerve at the very last hurdle."

"You're right." She was being silly, Laurie thought suddenly. And such a drama queen! At the end of the day, it was just a name, and there was no reason not to know it. It didn't actually change anything. Quickly, before she could overthink it any more than she already had, she opened the program and scanned the typed cast light.

Next to Helena was the name Rose Callington.

For a few seconds, Laurie forgot to breathe. *Rose Callington.* It sounded like a name out of one of her romance novels. She felt, bizarrely yet surely, as if she knew her already, could hear her voice, her laugh. It was as if they'd just been introduced, and all by a name.

I'm being fanciful, Laurie thought, and then immediately thought, *No, I'm not.* She hadn't expected it and couldn't have explained, but she had a bone-deep certainty that she *knew* this woman. She didn't normally put much stock in serendipity or destiny or things like that, but right now she felt as if she had some deep soul memory of this person, this name. *Rose Callington.* Had her mother held her in her arms, if ever so briefly, and looked down at her tiny, scrunched-up face, caught in the complicated snare of motherly love? Had Laurie looked back and *seen* her?

She thought of Henrietta talking about her daughter's eyes. *She had lovely blue eyes, I remember that.* Did Rose Callington remember Laurie's eyes? And did Laurie somehow remember her mother? She'd been carried in her body for nine months, after all. Rose must have gazed down at her face at least once.

Her optimism came roaring to the forefront, reminding her that the glass wasn't just half-full, it was overflowing. *Rose Callington.* Rose Callington was her mother.

"Well?" Henrietta asked, sounding exasperated.

Laurie blinked her into focus, a smile spreading across her face. "Her name is Rose Callington," she said, "and I'm going to find her."

20

Laurie walked around in a daze for the rest of the day, repeating her mother's name over and over again in her mind, and sometimes out loud, in a whisper that felt somehow sacred. *Rose Callington. Rose Callington. Rose Callington.* She felt too full of thoughts and feelings, a tangled, complicated mixture of hope and fear, joy and sorrow, to open Max's Place up again, chatting with customers and ringing up sales, and so instead she clipped on Max's leash and took him for a walk—away from Main Street, and everyone she knew, all the hellos and how are yous she would inevitably face and usually loved. Right now, she wasn't ready to face anyone, not even Joshua.

He'd texted her, asking if she'd discovered her mother's name, and she hadn't replied yet. It wasn't like her, to leave him—or anyone, really—hanging, but this felt like too precious a secret to share, at least not yet. She wanted to keep it to herself for a little while longer, to figure out how she felt.

Because mingled in the wonder of knowing who her mother was was a grief deeper than Laurie had ever let herself feel before. Of course, she'd struggled with sadness before. No foster kid trudged through the system without feeling sad, or angry, or bereft, or bitter, and most often all four, at one time or another. But she'd chosen not to let herself wallow in those emotions, had been as positive and upbeat as she knew how, because it had felt stronger.

Now the grief had slipped in by a back door, crept under her skin and into her soul and stayed there, because when she'd been confronted with her mother's name, she'd suddenly become a *person* in a way she never truly had been before.

Before today, her biological mother had been more of a concept than a reality. In the language of foster kids, "bio moms" were spoken of a bit derisively, because no one wanted to betray the hope and hurt they invariably felt in regard to that relationship, or really, the lack of it. Laurie had simply tried not to think about her too much at all, and focus on the future—but of course, her mother had always been there in the back of her mind, hadn't she? It was why she'd moved to Starr's Fall, a decision that she'd half-convinced herself was nothing more than a fortuitous opportunity. *It looks like a nice place to live*, she'd told herself, all the while knowing that, if she managed to screw up the courage, she'd look for her mother.

And now she'd found her, and somehow, already, it felt as if it changed everything. Suddenly, Laurie felt the weight of grief for all she'd lost, as well as the hope for a future she was just starting to let herself dream about. Together, it was a whole lot of emotion to deal with, and she didn't know how else to deal with it all except by putting one foot in front of another and letting her mind unpick the tangles.

Laurie walked for several hours, all the way out of town and into the hills, wandering down hiking trails, mindless of the cold that nipped at her nose and cheeks. The wooded hills of northern Connecticut stretched out in front of her, dark evergreen interspersed with leafless maples or birches, bisected by the occasional glittering surface of a pond or small lake, but Laurie barely saw any of it. In her mind's eye she was with her mother, chatting and laughing and catching up on twenty-five years of missed memories.

For most of her life she'd never let herself think like this, not even remotely, but now she wanted to. Needed to, because why not be optimistic? Wasn't that what she did, who she was? Who she'd chosen to be?

Well, darn it all, she was going to be as optimistic as she could about this. Which was why, on a picnic bench in the middle of the woods, with Max curled up by her feet, she sat down, took out her phone, and loaded Facebook. Typed in Rose Callington and held her breath, although she realized she wasn't scared, not anymore. Now, amazingly, she felt sure.

There were only two Rose Callingtons on all of Facebook, and one was a teenager in San Diego who liked skateboarding and chai lattes. The other one was a forty-three-year-old woman who lived in Greenwich, had a private profile, and whose married name was Farrow.

This time, Laurie didn't dither at all. That sense of certainty pervaded her whole being, radiated outward. She typed a simple message.

Hello, my name is Laurie Ellis, and I believe you are my biological mother. I hope this doesn't come as a shock, but I now live in Starr's Fall and would love to connect with you. I run a pet store called Max's Place and I've met so many people here, people who I think you might know still, as it seems as if everyone has lived here forever! I hope you'll be in touch. Laurie.

She pressed send without even reading it through twice. Maybe she was being foolhardy or even naïve, but it just *felt* right. When she got back home, Laurie decided, she'd also type out Henrietta's letter to her daughter. Why shouldn't there be joy to be found there, as well? Why not simply jump and *believe*?

It was getting dark by the time Laurie made it back to Max's Place, with Max being decidedly grumpy at having been led uphill and down all afternoon. He had to be hungry, and she was starving, not having eaten all day.

As she unlocked the door, she glanced across at Reilly's Books —the new sign advertising both old and new books had come— and saw the light upstairs was on. She should check in with Joshua, tell him all she'd discovered, but rehashing the day felt utterly exhausting, and Laurie was still working through how she felt about it all. She'd text him, she decided, and then talk to him tomorrow.

She fed Max and heated up some soup in the microwave for herself, texting Joshua while it warmed.

> Sorry I've been a bit AWOL today. Just figuring things out. Talk tomorrow.

And then she turned her phone off, although she couldn't have even said why, only that she felt as if she was in this bubble of secret knowledge and hope, and she absolutely did not want to do anything that would pop its translucent fragility.

After she'd had her soup, Laurie took out her laptop and Henrietta's letter and began to type it out onto the account Henrietta had found—Sophia Wexler, a seventy-year-old with a humorous glint in her eye and a pointed chin like Henrietta's, and apparently her father's slightly beaky nose. She was married, had four children and seven grandchildren, and lived in upstate New York. All in all, from her Facebook profile, it looked as if she'd had a good life, and Laurie was glad both for her and Henrietta.

The letter Henrietta had written was, Laurie thought, exactly like her.

Dear Sophia, I imagine this missive will take you somewhat by surprise, especially after all these years. You must be seventy now, as I am ninety-one, and so neither of us is in our youth, or even our middle age. But it is the passing of years and the awareness of one's mortality, along with a young friend I have made, that has made me reach out after all this time. I am your biological mother, you see, although I don't particularly like that phrase. I gave birth to you, but I never mothered you, as you very well know, I am sure, and so I have not earned the right to say such a thing, but there it is, I know no other way to say it. I won't go into the details of your conception or birth, only that it was the 1950s and you can imagine what the traditions and expectations of a young woman were. I send this simply to let you know who I am, that I am still here—if only just—and if you wish to reach out to me, then please reply to this message, through the young friend I mentioned previously, as at my age I do not possess either the time or inclination to use a computer. With my sincere regards, Henrietta

Laurie let out a gusty breath and pressed send... just as another message pinged into her inbox. It was from Rose Callington Farrow, and it was a mere one sentence long.

Dear Laurie, shall we meet?

* * *

Just two days later, Laurie was walking up Madison Avenue in New York City, her heart thudding against her ribs. She'd arranged to meet her biological mother in the city—at Rose's suggestion—and was now looking for the trendy little French bistro she'd directed her to.

Laurie had barely slept since she'd received that first reply. She'd responded immediately, and in return Rose had immediately suggested this bistro, and the complete and utter swiftness of the thing had made Laurie just about wild with hope. She'd lain awake imagining their reunion, their reconciliation, all the ways they'd get to know each other. She pictured them laughing over cocktails, having heart-to-hearts over lattes, shopping on Fifth Avenue with expensive-looking bags with handles of gold cord. It was like something out a romcom, but why not? *Why not*, at last, for her, when she'd never had anything like this before?

The next morning, she'd turned her phone back on to see, somewhat to her surprise, that Joshua hadn't texted her back. It gave Laurie a second's pause as well as a frisson of unease, but then she decided that he'd taken her at her word and would wait for her to be in touch. And really, all her emotional energy and focus needed to be on her mother right now. Joshua, she knew, would understand that. She'd fill him in on everything when she got back and have so much fun doing it.

Still, when the whole day passed without him coming over as he usually did, or sending her a silly GIF, she began to wonder. Was he annoyed that she had shut him out a little? She considered heading over to apologize, but something made her stop. She was meeting her mother *tomorrow*. If she and Joshua had to have some sort of serious discussion over a missed text or two... well, she simply didn't have it in her right now.

So here she was, walking down Madison Avenue, without having even told Joshua she was going to New York City. She hadn't told anyone, not even Annie or Henrietta, although she had asked Henrietta to watch Max for the day. The older lady had a shrewd glint in her eye as she'd accepted, and Laurie wondered if she somehow had guessed.

In any case, she promised herself, she'd catch up with Joshua tonight. She'd have so many exciting things to tell him.

Francine's loomed up in front of her, an expensive-looking café with a red awning and gold lettering on the plate glass window. Inside, a waiter in a pressed white shirt and smart black pants came up to her as soon as she'd set a foot through the door.

"May I help you, madame?"

"I'm looking for..." She had to take a breath. "Rose Callington. Rose Callington Farrow."

"She is waiting for you in the back of the restaurant. Please follow me," the waiter replied smoothly, and Laurie's heart began to beat so hard she felt as if she might pass out. This was happening. This was really happening.

She followed the waiter as he wound his way through little tables covered in heavy damask, to a discreet table tucked in the back corner. As Laurie came forward, a woman rose from her seat. Her mother.

It was jolting, to see her face to face. She looked so much like Laurie, just older. Lines around her eyes and mouth. The same light-colored hair, brushing her shoulders. Except, Laurie realized as they both simply stared at each other, Rose Callington *didn't* look like her. Not anymore. Her hair wasn't actually Laurie's light brown color, but expensively highlighted and cut, and her clothes looked equally expensive—a gray silk blouse and belted darker gray trousers, with a cashmere sweater thrown over her shoulders. She wasn't smiling.

"Hello," Laurie said after a moment, in little more than a croak. She hadn't been expecting a hug—well, not really—but at least a smile, maybe even a teary-eyed one? Rose Callington just looked tired... and oddly resolute.

"You look so much like me," she remarked, and she didn't

sound very pleased about that fact. She nodded to the chair opposite. "Sit down."

Laurie sat, tucking her hands between her knees as Rose gazed at her critically, without speaking. "I'm so glad to meet you," Laurie finally ventured. "I never thought you'd respond so quickly—"

"Well, there's a reason for that," Rose interjected, her tone abrupt. A waiter came forward and she ordered a black coffee, then glanced wordlessly at Laurie.

"Um, just water," Laurie murmured. She thought they'd be having lunch—her mother suggesting *let's have all three courses!*— but somehow that didn't seem likely now. Her stomach, which had been fizzing with nerves and excitement moments earlier, was now cramping with anxiety. Something about this whole situation definitely did not feel right. It wasn't anything close to what she'd imagined.

"I arranged this meeting to tell you that I can never see you again," Rose stated without preamble, or much emotion. "I'm sorry if you were hoping for some kind of touching reunion, but that's simply not possible."

Laurie swallowed dryly. She felt sick, and her head felt weirdly light. "Can I ask why?" she finally asked, her voice little more than a whisper.

"No, you can't," Rose replied shortly. "My life is private, and frankly, none of your business. I'm sorry if that sounds harsh, but that's simply how it is, and I want to be clear. It's kinder in the long run."

For a second, Laurie could only stare at her. In all her excited imaginings, she had never envisioned something as cold-hearted and cruel as this. She'd let herself get completely carried away over the last few days, she realized numbly. The whole life she'd built for herself in Starr's Fall, Max's Place, her new friends, lovely Joshua... all of it had faded away to practically nothing, in light of the hope—the deep-seated and yet terribly naïve *belief*—that she was going to be reunited with her mother. That her mother was going to love her. She would have a family at last.

That was all that had mattered, and now it seemed it wasn't going to happen. It *never* had been going to happen. She'd been so *stupid*, so utterly, utterly stupid and optimistic... about the most important thing of all.

"You had me travel all the way to New York to tell me this?" Laurie finally asked in a papery voice. She sounded dazed rather than angry; she was too shocked even to know how she felt.

"I wanted it to be some place where no one knew either of us," Rose replied. "And I thought it was better face to face. The last thing I need is you posting a message of mine online, the whole thing going viral." Her mouth tightened, her eyes flashing.

Laurie jerked back. "I would *never*—"

"Oh, wouldn't you?" Rose replied coolly. "You seemed so very determined to inform me how everyone in Starr's Fall knew me still. Have you been bandying my name about?" This was said in such a savage voice that Laurie reeled back again, her breath escaping her in a rush, as if she'd been punched.

"*No...*"

"I don't know whether to believe you or not," Rose replied. "But let me tell you, I will deny anything and everything if you get any ideas in that regard." She fell silent as the waiter came with their coffee and water.

"I just wanted to know you," Laurie whispered after he'd left. "To *get* to know you. I don't have any other... agenda."

For a millisecond, or maybe not even, her mother's face softened. Then she straightened her shoulders, took a sip of coffee, and put down her cup again. "Well, that's not going to happen," she stated flatly.

"Can I ask... why not?" Laurie asked. She heard a tremor in her voice and realized how close to tears she was. She couldn't believe how cold her mother was being. She might have been prepared for ambivalence, complicated feelings, but this...? It was, she realized, absolutely devastating.

"No, you cannot, as I said before," Rose replied, and now she sounded impatient. She reached down and took an envelope out of her expensive leather handbag and passed it across to Laurie. "Here. This is all you're ever going to get, believe me."

With nerveless fingers, feeling as if she were almost having an out-of-body experience, Laurie opened the envelope. It was full of hundred-dollar bills, dozens. She sealed it again, feeling sick as she slid it back across the table.

"No, thank you."

Rose's mouth tilted upward in something almost like a smile, although her eyes remained flinty as she took the envelope back and tucked it back in her purse. "You have principles, do you?"

"You wouldn't know, would you?" Laurie fired back. The dazed shock she'd felt was being replaced by something hard and angry, but she knew that was no more than a thin veneer of emotion—underneath was a dark swirl of pulsing pain she couldn't bear even to think about. How could this be happening? After all her dreams, all her stupid, stupid optimism...

To her surprise, her mother—could she even *ever* call her that? —reached over and touched her hand briefly, her fingers barely brushing her own. "I'm sorry," she said quietly, and for the first time since they'd met, she sounded it.

But before Laurie could respond or even process the remark, Rose Callington had risen from her seat and walked swiftly away from the table and out of the restaurant, leaving Laurie alone, reeling, and, she discovered a few minutes later, with the bill.

21

"Where's Laurie?"

Joshua glanced up from the stock form he was filling out to see Annie Lyman standing in the doorway of his bookstore, hands on her hips, her curly salt-and-pepper hair wild about her face, and her expression alarmingly fierce.

"I don't know," he replied shortly. He hadn't seen Laurie for three days. *Three days...* It felt like an endless amount of time, empty hour upon empty hour of him wondering where she was, what she was thinking, and why she hadn't responded to his texts, although to be fair he hadn't sent many. Okay, *one*, because he didn't want to seem needy the way he had with Mia... But this wasn't about him. At least it wasn't meant to be. But he was still determined not to attempt to breathe life into a relationship that someone else had already decided was dead. Not again. Not ever.

He remembered the way he'd texted and called Mia, desperate to keep their relationship going even when he should have known it was over. Her responses—the endless silences as well as the audible sighs—had made him feel about two inches tall. He had no intention of going through that again... Not with Laurie, who mattered even more to him.

And yet *Laurie*... There had been nothing from her since she'd promised to talk soon, and so surely the ball was in her court. Joshua didn't want to pester her, but more than that, he didn't want to *feel* like he was pestering her.

Joshua knew he was in a doom spiral of dark thoughts, and he wasn't sure how to get out of it. Laurie had more or less cut off contact with him after he'd offered to go with her to the church to find out her mother's name. He'd understood her wanting to go alone—*mostly*—but that still didn't make sense of the radio silence of the next few days. Had she found something out about her mother? Was she upset, hurting?

Joshua had no idea, and his initial sympathy and understanding had, after days of absolutely nothing from her, started to wear thin. He knew all too well what it was like to be cut off, shut out. If Laurie was choosing not to include him in whatever she was going through, then fine, he wouldn't be included. But he wasn't going to stand around begging for scraps... even if emotionally, that was still where he was. He just didn't want to be.

"What do you mean, you don't know?" Annie demanded. "You guys have been in each other's pockets for the last month. What's happened?" She took a step toward him that seemed a little menacing. She was clearly worried about Laurie, and she looked poised to blame Joshua. "If you've messed her around, Joshua Reilly..." Annie added, raising one fist almost as if she was about to deck him.

"If *I* have?" Joshua replied, both stung and irritated by the assumption. "You're talking to the wrong person, Annie."

She lowered her fist, frowning. "What is *that* supposed to mean?"

He shrugged, not willing to elaborate. He didn't know what was going on with Laurie, and he certainly didn't want to accuse her of anything, but... *three days*. Three days was a really long time.

"Joshua." Annie had dropped the anger and accusation, and now she sounded worried. "What if something's wrong? Do you know if she's okay?"

"I've seen her moving around in her apartment upstairs," Joshua replied. "So she hasn't had an accident or something." Not that he was being some kind of creepy stalker and standing by his window, looking across the street at her place. Not much, anyway.

"But it's not like her to disappear like this," Annie said, frowning. "And Max's Place has been closed since Tuesday."

"I know."

"Well, aren't you *worried*?" Annie demanded in exasperation. "Or are you just nursing your hurt feelings?"

Ouch. "I'm worried," Joshua replied evenly, "but I can't force her to reach out to me, Annie. She seems to want space, so I'm giving it to her."

"Just because someone withdraws doesn't mean they want space," Annie replied quietly. Her gaze, when Joshua looked up at her, was like a laser. "You of all people should know that."

Joshua couldn't keep from wincing. How had Annie Lyman of all people drawn that assumption, unfortunately correct? He might have acted like a grumpy Grinch who didn't want anyone to bother him, but that hadn't meant he'd *liked* it. That he hadn't been lonely. It had taken Laurie for him to realize just how much.

He let out a heavy sigh and shook his head. "I don't know what I can do."

"Have you gone over to her place?"

"I knocked on the door just earlier. There was no answer." Which had also stung. He'd *seen* her moving around upstairs, albeit briefly. He knew she was there, just as she must know he was the one knocking on her door, basically begging to be let in.

"That's it?" Annie demanded. "Come on, Joshua."

"*What?*" Anger spiked his voice. "What more can I do?" He placed his hands flat on the counter as he stared levelly at her. "Look, I know what it feels like to be on the receiving end of nothing, okay? When someone wants out of a relationship, the kindest thing to do for them as well as *yourself* is let them out of it. If Laurie wants to be in touch, the ball is in her court, but I am not going over there and begging her to keep loving me. I'm not a puppy asking to be kicked." He broke off, breathing hard, appalled by all he'd admitted, especially when Annie gazed at him in a mixture of pity and understanding.

"Oh, man," she said quietly. "You've got it bad."

Joshua slammed the order book shut. "Yes, I do," he growled, feeling stupidly reckless but somehow needing to admit it. "So what?"

"You've got it bad," Annie continued, her voice hardening, "but your hurt feelings still matter more. This isn't about you, Joshua. Sometimes you've got to look past your pain." He didn't speak, his jaw clenched so tight it ached as she continued in a softer voice, "Look, you might not know that I know, but I realized you and your dad didn't get along, that your mom was the glue that held you guys together. Patrick Reilly was a great guy when it came to books, but not so much with other stuff."

"Annie..." Her name was a warning, and she held up her hand.

"I get it. Family stuff is hard, and it can be consuming, but it doesn't have to define you. I feel the same way about my own dad —great farmer, gruff father. You know? It's not everything, but it's something."

Joshua just shook his head. He didn't know what to do with all she was saying, even as he realized he agreed with her.

"I thought we were talking about Laurie," he finally said, even though he hadn't wanted to talk about Laurie.

"We are. Because she has all that too, but in reverse. No family. No father who was difficult or mother who died. *No one.*" She frowned, menacing again. "I'm assuming you know all that."

"Yes," Joshua replied briefly. He was starting to get a creeping, and then consuming, sense of guilt, coming over him like a fog, stealing coldly inside. All Laurie had done was leave him hanging for a few days, and he'd responded like some angsty teenager, throwing a minor temper tantrum and deciding, huffily, that he'd give her space.

What was *wrong* with him?

The trouble was, he realized, that stupid text—*talk later*—had opened up a wound he'd thought had scarred over. *Healed*, for heaven's sake, and so it should have. But, he realized, it hadn't been just about Mia blanking him, and the way that relationship had limped to an inglorious end, but also his mother dying, his father shutting him when out they'd both been aching with grief. The silences he hadn't been brave enough to breach. He'd reverted to form, hadn't changed, when all along he'd been accusing the townspeople of Starr's Fall of not letting him.

But it had all been him. And just as Laurie had said, *he* was the one who got to choose how to be. Nobody else—not his dad, not Mia, nor any well-meaning but fundamentally irritating resident of this wonderful and frustrating small town.

Just him. And he was going to choose now.

"I'll go talk to her," he told Annie, and she nodded, unsmiling but approving.

"Good boy," she said.

* * *

The knocking wouldn't stop. Laurie was lying on her bed, Max on her stomach as she stared at the ceiling. She'd been this way for some time. Several minutes ago—she didn't think it was longer than that—someone had started knocking on the door of Max's Place. There had been a few such instances before, in the twenty-four hours or so she'd been lying here on her bed, but Laurie had ignored them. People had eventually gone away. Admittedly, a few more enterprising souls had shouted through the letterbox, and someone—either Annie or Jenna, Laurie thought—had thrown pebbles at her window, a spattering against the glass that had reminded her of someone spitting.

But eventually they'd all gone away. Eventually, Laurie thought, *everyone* went away.

She couldn't recall much of the last day and a half, since she'd returned from New York in a fog of numbness, taking the bus from the city to Torrington Plaza and then an Uber to Starr's Fall. She must have collected Max from Henrietta, although she couldn't remember much about going there, just as she couldn't recall coming back, or feeding Max, but she knew she had, and then she'd come up and lain on this bed and stared up at the ceiling, trying to empty her mind of everything. She'd only got up occasionally to feed Max or let him out again, although she hadn't done that for several hours.

And now someone was knocking on the door, and they wouldn't go away, when all Laurie wanted was for people to go away forever, because loving them hurt too much. Joshua had been *wrong*, she thought with a sudden burst of savagery. Not hoping was far better than hoping; staying safe was better than letting yourself love.

Letting people hurt way, way too much, and optimism was for sadomasochistic fools. At least now she knew.

"Laurie!" The voice calling through the letterbox was echoey and insistent and she recognized it as Joshua's. "Laurie, *please*. I know you're up there. Come down. Let me talk to you."

Laurie rolled onto her side, settling Max next to her, and tucked her knees up to her chest. She closed her eyes and willed Joshua to stop trying. He didn't used to try with anyone, she thought wearily. He needed to revert to form.

She must have fallen into a doze, because she woke up suddenly, startling awake, only to find Joshua standing at the foot of her bed. Laurie let out a little shriek that faded into a wobbly sigh.

"How... how did you get in?"

"Mike from the garage let me in. He's a locksmith as well as a mechanic, a true jack of all trades."

"That's illegal—" she protested feebly.

"He was worried about you. A *lot* of people are worried about you, Laurie." Joshua took a step closer to her, his kindly face wreathed in concern and making Laurie ache. She didn't want him to be nice to her. She didn't think she could stand it. "What happened?"

"Go away, Joshua." She curled her knees up toward her chest.

"No." His voice was firm. "I gave you three days, which was obviously too much. I thought you needed space, but—"

"I *do*."

"No." He sounded even firmer. "Not this time. Remember how you said you get to choose how you respond?"

"That was stupid," she whispered, her eyes closed. She felt like a bag of broken pieces; everything in her simply hurt too much.

"No, it wasn't," Joshua replied, his tone gentle yet still firm. "And I'm choosing for you, right now. I'm going to make you a cup of tea and maybe some toast and let Max out because I don't know when you last did, and you can take a shower or wash your face or whatever you need to make you feel more human, and then you'll come downstairs, and we'll talk. Properly."

Reluctantly Laurie cracked open an eye. "This doesn't sound like you."

He gave her a small, crooked smile. "People can change, remember?" and then he walked out of the room, whistling for Max, who, traitor that he was, jumped off the bed and trotted after him. Laurie lay there for a few minutes, listening to the strangely comforting sounds of Joshua moving around downstairs—filling up Max's bowl, boiling the kettle. Finally she dragged herself up to sitting, blinking the room into focus. Goodness, she felt awful, which wasn't surprising considering she hadn't eaten anything in hours, hadn't showered or brushed her teeth or even gone to the bathroom.

Taking a deep breath, Laurie raked a hand through her hair and then stumbled to the bathroom.

Twenty minutes later she was showered, dressed, and more or less presentable. She came downstairs slowly, knowing she needed to have a conversation with Joshua yet still unable to summon the emotional energy for it, or anything.

As she came into the kitchen, he slipped two slices of bread into the toaster. "You look better."

"I think that's a low bar." She tried to smile but couldn't. She sat at the table, resting her chin in her hand. "Thank you."

He glanced at her, studying her for a moment, before turning back to the toaster. "You're welcome. I'm just sorry I didn't come over sooner. I was nursing some hurt feelings for what I perceived as you blanking me, but if I'd any emotional astuteness at all, I would have realized something must have happened with your biological mother. Something big." He turned to face her, and she saw nothing in his eyes but compassion. "That is what this is about, isn't it?"

Laurie stared down at the table, unable to respond. The toast popped up, and Joshua spent a few minutes getting it ready while

Laurie simply stared at the table and tried not to blink. He came over to put a plate of toast just the way she liked it—lots of butter and a little jam—in front of her, along with a cup of sweet, milky tea.

"Thank you," she whispered, and then a big, fat tear plopped right onto the middle of a piece of toast.

"Oh, Laurie." Joshua's voice was rough as he knelt in front of her and put his arms around her. "Can you tell me what happened? You don't have to. I just... I just want to be here for you."

Be here for her. It was exactly what her mother had said she *couldn't* do. Ever. Whatever just about everyone, for all her life, hadn't been able or interested to do. And here was Joshua Reilly, a lovely, *lovely* man, wanting to be the person she texted in the middle of the night, or ugly cried in front of, and she was as good as pushing him away because, she realized, she didn't actually know how to be with someone like that in her life.

But she wanted to try.

Slowly, achingly, Laurie put her arms around him. Buried her face in his shoulder as a shudder went through her. "It was awful," she whispered, and then, finally, she let herself cry.

The story came out in pieces, as Laurie ate four pieces of toast and drank two cups of tea because she'd realized she was ravenous, and Joshua simply listened, occasionally murmuring something or making a face, and amazingly, somehow the whole thing became almost *funny*, even as it remained unbearably sad.

"I'd built it up so much in my mind," Laurie finished, "that I was picturing us dancing down Fifth Avenue together before I'd even met her. I always liked to think I was optimistic, but I'd strayed into the realm of full-blown fantasy without even realizing it. I was living out some kind of Disney musical in my mind." She shook her head as Joshua reached for her hand, threading his fingers loosely through hers.

"It's understandable," he said. "I've been thinking I might ask John Grisham to front the Starr's Fall Literary Festival. Dreams are good things."

She let out a soft huff of laughter and he put his hand on the back of her head as he leaned in for a kiss, brushing his lips softly against hers. "I love you," he said, so simply that for a second Laurie thought she'd misheard. She *must* have misheard...

"I love you," he said again wryly, as if he'd read her thoughts, which he probably had.

Laurie felt her eyes fill with tears. "Don't make me cry again," she warned, sniffing.

"Crying's okay. I just wanted you to know. I don't know what is going through your biological mother's mind, or what happened in her life to make her act that way, but I love you. I want to be here for you. Now and... for a long time." He smiled crookedly. "I'd say forever, but I know we've only been dating a little while and I don't want to freak you out."

"Oh, Joshua." Laurie stared at him in wonder as a tear slipped down her cheek, but it was a happy one. "I love you, too. I could tell you I didn't know what love was until I met you, and that would be absolutely true, but it sounds kind of sappy, so maybe I'll just leave it at that. I love you."

Joshua pulled her to him, and she came willingly, joyfully. Yes, hope could hurt. *Life* could hurt because no one got through it unscathed, unscarred. But the scars were signs of survival, badges of grace. They made you stronger, but more importantly, they made you more grateful.

And right then Laurie knew there was nowhere she'd rather be.

At long last, after so many years of searching, she'd finally found her home... with this lovely, lovely man.

A sudden, insistent knocking from downstairs had them pulling apart.

"I think," Joshua said, "there are quite a few other people who have been worried about you."

"I'll go down," Laurie replied. Yes, she'd found her home, not just with Joshua, but here in Starr's Fall, with a community that had welcomed and accepted her, more than she could have ever hoped or imagined. Smiling, Laurie headed downstairs.

EPILOGUE
SIX WEEKS LATER

"Turkey and cranberry-flavored dog treats? Really?"

Joshua glanced at the tray of freshly baked treats Laurie was loading into a plastic container to take to Jenna's. It was Thanksgiving, and she'd invited over a dozen people to celebrate with her and Zach.

"Dogs deserve a Thanksgiving meal, too," Laurie replied primly, and Joshua grinned.

"Well I know it."

In the two months since Laurie had opened Max's Place, it had gone from strength to strength. She was about to complete her dog grooming course and had set up a grooming station in the back room. She'd also, in collaboration with the Connecticut Humane Society, started an "Introduction to Pet Owning" workshop for people who were considering adopting a dog or cat. Just a week ago, Joshua had adopted Pepper, a rescue cat that looked part Persian, part red tabby, and had the most imperiously disdainful expression Laurie had ever seen. Max wasn't yet convinced by the new addition.

She had other plans in the works too—a pet therapy afternoon once a week, where people brought their dogs and cats, and other people were able to spend time with them. Henrietta had even said she *might* think about attending. Laurie also wanted to expand her range of goods to include items for small pets; Rhonda from The Starr Light had a hamster and was looking for toys and bedding.

Other things had happened too, both good and bad, hard and hopeful. Annie was looking into a care assistant to help her with Barb, and Henrietta had not yet had a reply from her daughter. Laurie, as she'd expected, had never heard from her mother again, and while that had hurt, it hadn't hurt as much as it once might have.

Liz Cranbury was now the sales assistant at Midnight Fashion, and Bella Harper was playing Juliet in the church's production; Eloise had agreed to play the more appropriately aged part of the nurse. A Winter Wonderland Evening was planned for the middle of December, along with a Christmas tree lighting and visit from Santa; Doug Vance had lodged his complaint with the township, which had been summarily dismissed.

Life in Starr's Fall, Laurie had reflected, had its fair share of troubles and sorrows, but it was also *good*. It was wonderful.

Now Laurie loaded Joshua up with several containers of dog treats as she reached for the two pumpkin pies she'd baked the day before. She could hardly wait to head over to Jenna's to celebrate with all her friends. Jenna had promised a table positively groaning with food, including a twenty-pound turkey with all the trimmings.

Outside, the day was crisp, clear, and eye-wateringly cold. The whole world glittered with frost, the lamp posts—the township had finally fixed the streetlights—outlined in sparkling white.

Laurie was just locking up, balancing the pies in one arm while Joshua kept hold of the treats and Max, when she saw a beat-up station wagon pull up in front of the shuttered store three doors down.

"Who do you think is coming into town on Thanksgiving morning?" she asked Joshua. "Everything's closed."

He shrugged, and then they both watched an unfamiliar woman in her forties, her dark hair, with a single silver streak through the center, pulled back into a ponytail. She came out of the car slowly, as if her body ached, wrapping her duffel coat more closely around her. After another few seconds, a teenaged boy, maybe fourteen or so, slouched out of the passenger seat. His hair was shaggy, his bangs sliding into his eyes, his bony shoulders hunched. They both, Laurie thought, looked as if they'd been battered down by life.

The woman headed towards the empty store, pulling out a key. Laurie's heart lifted.

"Hello," she called, and the woman startled. "Are you new here? Are you moving in?"

The woman glanced between her and Joshua, who smiled and waved. The boy didn't make eye contact.

"Yes," she said after a second's pause. "We're moving in." She nodded toward the shuttered storefront. "We're... we're hoping to start a boardgame café here, actually."

"A boardgame café!" Laurie was delighted. "That's amazing."

The woman smiled faintly, deepening the creases around her dark blue eyes. "Well, I hope so."

"I'm Laurie Ellis, and this is Joshua Reilly," Laurie said, and Joshua murmured his hello. "I run the pet store Max's Place, and he has the bookstore across the street."

"Oh." The woman looked startled, and also a little moved, by the generous welcome. "It's very nice to meet you. I'm Maggie Parker, and this is my son Ben." She put a hand on his shoulder, as if anchoring him in place, and he gave a nod and a mumbled hello, his gaze still on the ground.

"Nice to meet you, too." Laurie had a desire to welcome this woman even more; she looked so tired and sad, and yet with hope already kindling in her eyes. That, Laurie thought, was the magic of this town, of its residents. They welcomed you in; they held you close. "I'm so glad you're here," Laurie told the woman impulsively. "Welcome to Starr's Fall."

ACKNOWLEDGMENTS

It's been so fun to create the world of Starr's Fall, inspired by the five years I spent living in West Hartford, Connecticut. I absolutely loved revisiting New England with all of its quirky, small-town charm. I must thank, first of all, my lovely editor Isobel Akenhead for being willing to work with me on something totally new! It's been wonderful, and I am so grateful she took another chance on my writing. I'd also like to thank everyone on the Boldwood team who have been so welcoming—this is my first book with Boldwood, and I have felt so warmly included in the Boldwood family. I'd also like to thank my own family, who helped me access some Connecticut memories—we last lived there in 2008, so some things have certainly changed, although this corner of New England remains wonderfully charming! Lastly, thanks to my readers who are so supportive and encouraging. I hope you enjoy this new series, and I look forward to sharing more stories set in Starr's Fall with you.

ABOUT THE AUTHOR

Kate Hewitt is a million copy bestselling author of historical, contemporary and romantic fiction. An American ex-pat, she lives in a small market town in Wales with her husband and five young(ish) children, along with their two Golden Retrievers.

Sign up to Kate Hewitt's newsletter to read the first chapter of her upcoming novel and a free short story.

Visit Kate's website: www.kate-hewitt.com

Follow Kate on social media here:

facebook.com/KateHewittAuthor

x.com/author_kate

instagram.com/katehewitt1

bookbub.com/authors/kate-hewitt

LOVE NOTES

LOVE IN EVERY CHAPTER

WHERE ALL YOUR ROMANCE
DREAMS COME TRUE!

THE HOME OF BESTSELLING
ROMANCE AND WOMEN'S
FICTION

 WARNING:
MAY CONTAIN SPICE

SIGN UP TO OUR
NEWSLETTER

https://bit.ly/Lovenotesnews

Boldwood

Boldwood Books is an award-winning fiction publishing company seeking out the best stories from around the world.

Find out more at www.boldwoodbooks.com

Join our reader community for brilliant books, competitions and offers!

Follow us
@BoldwoodBooks
@TheBoldBookClub

Sign up to our weekly
deals newsletter

https://bit.ly/BoldwoodBNewsletter

Printed in Great Britain
by Amazon

47460652R00145